Best wishes to

Rosemary Courtney
from

Frederick Manfred
2-4-1976

THE MANLY-HEARTED WOMAN

Books by Frederick Manfred

THE GOLDEN BOWL, 1944

BOY ALMIGHTY, 1945

THIS IS THE YEAR, 1947

THE CHOKECHERRY TREE, 1948

THE PRIMITIVE, 1949

THE BROTHER, 1950

THE GIANT, 1951

LORD GRIZZLY, 1954

MORNING RED, 1956

RIDERS OF JUDGMENT, 1957

CONQUERING HORSE, 1959

ARROW OF LOVE, stories, 1961

WANDERLUST, trilogy, 1962*

SCARLET PLUME, 1964

THE SECRET PLACE, 1965**

WINTER COUNT, poems, 1966

KING OF SPADES, 1966

APPLES OF PARADISE, stories, 1968

EDEN PRAIRIE, 1968

CONVERSATIONS, 1974***

MILK OF WOLVES, 1975

THE MANLY-HEARTED WOMAN, 1975

*A new revised version of a trilogy that was originally published in three separate volumes, *The Primitive, The Brother, The Giant.* Mr. Manfred wrote under the pen name of Feike Feikema from 1944 through 1951.

**Originally published in hardback as *The Man Who Looked like the Prince of Wales;* reprinted in paperback as *The Secret Place.*

***Moderated by John R. Milton.

THE MANLY-HEARTED WOMAN

by Frederick Manfred

CROWN PUBLISHERS, INC., NEW YORK

Printed in the United States of America

Published simultaneously in Canada by General Publishing Company Limited

Designed by Ruth Smerechniak

Library of Congress Cataloging in Publication Data

Manfred, Frederick Feikema, 1912–
    The manly-hearted woman.

        I. Title.
PZ3.M313705Map   [PS3525.A52233]   813'.5'4   75-25887
ISBN 0-517-52374-4

FOR MY FRIENDS
William Everett Lemons, Jr.
and Max Roger Westbrook

GLOSSARY

BLUE MOUNDS • *a large outcropping of Sioux quartzite in southwestern Minnesota*

HELPER • *guardian spirit*

HORNS of the CAMP • *the opening or the gate to an encampment*

MAMA • *woman's breasts*

RIVER of the DOUBLE BEND • *Big Sioux River*

RIVER of the RED ROCK • *Big Rock River, a tributary of the Big Sioux River*

TALKING WATER • *present-day Lake Benton in Minnesota*

TAMNI • *womb*

WAKANTANKA • *The Great Spirit*

WINTER COUNT • *an Indian calendar made of pictographs painted on a buffalo hide; instead of saying, as the white man does, "two summers ago," the Indian said, "two winters ago"*

YUWIPI • *little mischievous spirits from the other world*

FLAT WARCLUB

A RUNNER WAS SEEN COMING THROUGH THE HOLE-IN-THE-HILLS. He was coming very fast. He was carrying a war pipe.

The lookout of the bluff above the lake quickly gave a warning to the encampment below, several different signals with his arms. Some little boys near the horns of the camp, the gate to the encampment, saw the signals and ran to tell the camp crier, Heard From Afar. The old crier quickly got to his feet and hurried to an open place to see better. He signaled to the lookout to repeat the message. The lookout did so.

Heard From Afar immediately went crying through the circle of tepees. "Listen! There is a man coming with a message from our sister band The Nation Of The Blue Mounds. He is carrying the war pipe!" Heard From Afar cried the message in four directions in a clear bugling voice. He had the sound of a wise horse.

Braves appeared in the door of their tepees. After listening to the message, they reached back into the tepee for their capes and then proceeded over to the council tepee in the center of the camp. They walked with silent gravity. Little boys watched their elders go in awe. Women next appeared in the doors of the tepees. They watched their men go with a hand to their mouths wondering what was to come next. Several of the young lads ran to bring in the horses from the ravine behind the camp to have them ready in case they were needed.

The runner beat across a wide slough. At times he disappeared in the depths of green cut-grass. He leaned forward as he ran. He held the war pipe ahead of him in a sacred manner.

The dogs heard the beating of his feet through the ground and began to bark. They ran in streams toward the edge of the slough. Their pink mouths worked like the pincers of angry crabs.

The women hurried out and began to roar after their dogs, trying to call them off. "Blackmouth, get back here. You, Hairy-face, here! Wolf, you mocker, you wouldn't snap at a mosquito if it weren't for your braver friends, get back here! Get!"

The little boys ran out through the horns of the camp to stop the dogs and wrestle them to the ground. They yelled and barked like dogs themselves.

One of the young lads getting up the horses recognized the runner and called back to the camp. "It is Lightfoot who comes hurrying."

Heard From Afar picked up the cry. "It is Lightfoot who comes running. Let his uncle High Stomach make ready for him."

Lightfoot came puffing in through the horns of the camp. His body shone with sweat. He gleamed all over like a red horse just emerging from a long swim. Quickly his black eyes swept the big circle of tepees, instantly saw his uncle High Stomach standing in the door of his tepee. His aunt Makes Cross had just gone out to the drying racks to gether up the fresh jerky. She was one of those who lived constantly in fear of enemy raids. She turned, arms half-filled with strips of stiff meat. Lightfoot ran straight for his uncle's tepee.

The dogs and the little boys coming after followed Lightfoot, roaring and barking. Behind them followed the mothers roaring and shouting at both to get back.

High Stomach held the doorflap to his tepee to one side. His eyes glittered at the war pipe in his nephew's hand, full of respect. Carefully shielding the war pipe, Lightfoot ducked down and disappeared within. High Stomach ducked inside behind him and closed the flap after them.

The dogs, and then the little boys, fell silent. The dogs retreated to the shady spot behind their own tepees. The little boys held their ground a dozen feet away. The little boys stood with eyes as big as coneflowers waiting to see what would happen next.

The wind began to rise. It ruffled the smokeflaps of the tepees. It made the water along the sandy beach talk in the manner of a laughing idiot. The short grass on the far hills smoothed out like well-combed hair, while the trees in the clefts of the hills began to undulate like the manes of running horses.

Off to the southeast, an easy walk away, lay the horns to the killing shunt. Several days before the beaters of the camp had held a buffalo drive. Some hundred had been driven into the shunt and then down along a narrow causeway onto an island in the middle of Lake Talking Water. The grass along the causeway had been so flattened by thudding hoofs that the wind hardly caught at the dead tips. The grass on the island also lay flattened. There were many places on the island where the grass was black with the blood of slaughtering. Clouds of flies swarmed over the black patches of blood, sometimes so thick they resembled little green frogs.

The doorflap to High Stomach's tepee swung to one side, and High Stomach and Lightfoot, both dressed in capes, stepped out. Lightfoot held the war pipe before him in the sacred manner. They headed immediately for the big council tepee in the center of the camp. The little boys stared after them.

High Stomach had twice the bulk of Lightfoot, huge in the shoulder and chest, with long stringy legs and quick feet. He wore his hair in a single fat black braid down his back. His eyes were set close together like a handsome skunk's and his jowls were huge and wide.

Lightfoot was slim. He stepped along like a true runner, lightly on his toes. The calves of his legs rippled with muscle and were almost as thick as his thighs. His face was as solemn as a block of brown quartzite.

High Stomach held the door to the council tepee to one side, and Lightfoot, pointing the war pipe ahead of him, stooped inside. High Stomach followed him.

A slender high-shouldered brave came stepping along the sandy beach of the lake. Above him arched the long branches of a row of cottonwoods. The hanging branches reached a dozen paces out over the water, their leaves washing in the waves. As the brave walked along, shadow and sunlight alternately darkened and lightened his rusty skin. The brave brushed past a sand willow, leaped over a single red boulder, and turned up the path toward the camp.

The brave was deep in thought as he walked. Something had happened.

Early that morning he had gone down to his secret place to groom and ornament his hair. The place was under the farthest cottonwood limbs where the water usually was quiet. He wore his black hair bobbed, like the short tail of a horse. An iridescent clamshell, ingeniously caught in his hair over his right ear, gleamed like a revolving moon. His buckskin shirt was neatly buffed, giving it a velvet surface. His leather moccasins glinted with quillwork.

He carried a strange warclub. It was as flat as a paddle. He had shaped it out of the limb of an oak, spending hours honing it down with his quartzite knife. He believed his warclub had magic power. When the right time came, no brave or warrior on earth would be able to withstand him. No one knew, not even his mother Cornmilk, that he'd secreted his helper in the handle of his flat warclub. He had dug out the center of a knot just where he held his thumb and had cleverly inserted his helper into the hole.

His helper was a tiny black stone that had dropped out of the clouds at his feet one day. For a little while the stone had sizzled in the soaked earth. When it had cooled off he dug it up. He knew right away that the little black stone was wakan and that the thunderbirds had sent it down to him to be his helper. The little black stone was as large as a buffalo bean and it was pitted with shiny holes. The holes were little mouths, oracles, and each had a special voice for him. When in doubt about something he always stepped off to one side and consulted his helper.

That morning his helper had told him to join the next war party.

His helper had never before told him to join a war party or a hunting party. The leading braves and most of the little boys considered him a worthless fellow. After every great hunt, even after the last buffalo kill on their slaughter island, the chief of the hunting party had to distribute food to his mother so that the two of them might eat.

The little black stone from the sky had also given him his secret name that morning. He was told that, when in doubt about something, he was to think of himself as Stone From The Clouds, and not as Flat Warclub. The name Flat Warclub, his helper said, was all right for the jeering little boys and the irascible old warriors to use, but the gods were going to use his new name.

He was an only child. His father Driving Hawk had died in a raid on the Omaha when Flat Warclub was only a boy. His mother had tried living with several men so that Flat Warclub might have a father, but after a while the new husband would break a stick at her and declare himself divorced. The new husbands complained to their friends that while she might be known as That Woman As Soft As Cornmilk, she actually had a vagina that was equipped with sharp teeth. They'd been afraid of her.

Flat Warclub was about halfway up the path, when a little boy darted out to meet him. It was Skinned Knees. He was the only one in camp who liked Flat Warclub. "Listen, older friend. A man has come up from our sister tribe on the Blue Mounds. He carried a war pipe." Skinned Knees gestured vividly, showing a nimble man carrying a pipe. "He went first to the tepee of High Stomach and then to the council lodge of the village."

"Ae. Lightfoot. What did he want?"

"They are holding a war council at this very moment."

"Ae." Flat Warclub stood a moment dandling his warclub, running his hand up and down it. "Then I must go with them."

Skinned Knees began to smile. "Then at last you will become a famous warrior?"

"Yes. My helper has just told me something."

"Then you will go to the war council?"

"Yes. Thank you for telling me."

Flat Warclub went directly to the council lodge. Quietly he lifted the doorflap and stepped inside.

It took a moment for his eyes to adjust to the gloom under the slanting leather walls. Thin wisps of smoke curled off a small twig fire in the center of the lodge. The smoke was almost dispersed by the time it breathed out through the smokehole into the blue air above. When he finally made out the figures seated in a circle around the fire, some forty of them, Flat Warclub took a seat near the door. It was the seat of least honor.

Lightfoot sat in the place of honor. Before him on a flat red stone rested the war pipe he'd brought. The stem faced Legbone, an honored chief. It was within reach of his hand. Every pair of black eyes in the lodge were on the war pipe.

Meanwhile the council pipe was being passed around the circle, from the left around to the right. Each brave and each warrior took a slow leisurely suck and then, reverently, exhaled a puff of smoke skywards. Each puff wafted up toward the smokehole where it mingled with the wisps of smoke rising from the council fire. The tobacco smoke had a bluish cast and the twig smoke had a yellow-ish tint.

The breathing of all the braves in the council lodge was even and slow.

Flat Warclub waited.

When the council pipe was passed on to Lightfoot, he looked at it a moment, almost crossing his eyes as he fixed them on the red pipestone bowl, then, with a little jerk, that came from deep within him, accepted it and mouthed the wooden pipestem and took a deep puff and slowly exhaled it upward toward the sky. He passed it on to High Stomach to his left.

Every brave sitting in the circle, except Flat Warclub, had at least one eagle feather caught in his long black hair. It meant that every man there had counted at least one coup on the enemy. Flat Warclub had only a shiny clamshell caught in his hair.

The council pipe came around to First Standing sitting next to Flat Warclub. First Standing usually led their hunting parties. First Standing hesitated and looked across at Legbone.

Legbone considered to himself a moment. Legbone was a huge bull of a man with the soft expression of a kind friend. In time of trouble the whole band deferred to him because, when aroused, he was a great madman of a fighter. When but a boy, he'd found the thighbone of a giant buffalo. The thighbone in times past had turned to stone and was very heavy. Yet in battle Legbone wielded the stone thighbone as though it were but a willow switch. He really didn't like it that the band usually chose him to be chief of their war parties. He preferred the peace of his wife's tepee. He was blessed with a wife who loved him very much and who had borne him four sons.

First Standing made a lifting wondering motion with the council pipe.

Legbone nodded.

First Standing handed the council pipe to Flat Warclub.

Flat Warclub was suddenly glad. They'd accepted him in their council. Apparently they'd liked it that he had seated himself in the humble place. For the moment they were overlooking his being a good-for-nothing. Flat Warclub pointed the council pipe at the four cardinal directions, then at the mother earth, then at the father sky, and then took a solemn suck on the pipe and blew it in the direction of the smokehole. It happened that as the puff of smoke left his mouth it formed into a perfect smoke ring.

All eyes followed the rising smoke ring.

"Ae," cried First Standing.

Flat Warclub was startled himself. He had not tried to blow a smoke ring. It was an omen.

Flat Warclub handed the pipe back to Lightfoot. A pipe was never passed over the doorway.

The pipe moved all the way around the circle until it came to the man sitting across the doorway from Flat Warclub; then it worked its way back to Legbone.

Legbone placed it on the flat red stone beside the war pipe in front of the crackling twig fire.

Silence.

Suddenly Lightfoot reached forth and grabbed up the war pipe and turning, thrust it at Legbone. "Will you accept the pipe!"

Legbone leaned back as though in horror, knowing full well all that it meant. There would be killing, and the weeping of wives, and the crying of little children.

Again Lightfoot thrust the war pipe at Legbone. "Famed war chief of The People of Talking Water, will you accept the pipe?"

Legbone shuddered some more and closed his sad black eyes.

"The Omaha," Lightfoot continued, "they who went against the stream, have come a second time to use our buffalo jump. When they came the first time before the snows, we welcomed them and showed them how to use the jump. We even gave them our best buffalo man, Brokenleg, he who hobbles like the buffalo, to put on the disguise of an old buffalo and lead the buffalo to the slaughter. They made much meat and left in peace. But now that the snows are gone, and the puccoons have blossomed, the Omaha have come again, this time with their own buffalo man to lure the buffalo over the jump. They came without asking. When we sent a runner to protest, they loosed their arrows at him. They almost killed our runner. This is not a good thing. The first time they came as our guests. As we all know, the Dakota are known for their magnanimity. The second time they came as our enemy. We cannot let them believe that the Blue Mounds are now their hunting grounds. They must be chastised." Lightfoot thrust the war pipe at Legbone again, this time until its sharp red nose almost touched Legbone's high arched nose. "Do you accept the pipe?"

Legbone appeared to swell up. His black eyes crossed a little as they fixed on the point of the red pipe.

"I am waiting for what my father has to say."

At last Legbone spoke. "The Omaha are known to mock the

enemy as they fight. They are very clever. It will take a miracle to
defeat them.''

"Also they are very many," Lightfoot said. "That is why we have
come to our sister band for help."

"What has happened to their own hunting ground?"

"Their old jump on The River Of The Double Bend has collapsed. They say they are too many for their new little drop on The
Stream Of The Split Rock. They needed a better place to hunt."

"You cannot share your buffalo jump?"

"Yes. But the Omaha, they say they will not share it."

Legbone's thick lips worked. "Have you thought of removing
still farther toward the setting sun?"

"Our Dakota brothers the Tetons say they will not welcome us."

"Ah. Then you must fight off the Omaha."

" We must punish them. We must teach them to stay along The
River Of The Double Bend. We must have revenge or they will
destroy us."

"There is a question we must ask."

"Ask, my father."

"Why did you come running? Where are your horses?"

"Most of our horses were stolen by the Pawnee last fall. It happened while our people were busy butchering after a buffalo kill.
They killed our best horseman by a ruse and then chased off the
little boys helping him. Before we could mount the horses we had
with us at the jump, they were far away, disappearing down the
Kanaranzi. Thus the only horses we have left are all needed to help
defend our village."

"Did you not send a raiding party after them to retrieve your
horses?"

"What? And let the Omaha learn of it and come kill our women
and children?"

"Our sister band has fallen on evil days."

"We must punish them," Lightfoot repeated. "We must teach
the Omaha to stay in their own village along The River Of The
Double Bend."

"Yes, it must be done."

Again for the fourth time Lightfoot thrust the war pipe at Legbone. The leather thongs attached to the pipestem swished back
and forth. "Will you accept the pipe?"

Legbone rocked mightily where he sat. "Waugh! I accept the
pipe." He took it and turned it about. "Who will accept the pipe
with me?" It could be seen that Legbone was at last greatly

aroused. His black eyes rolled about like bitter cherries. "Who will help our sister band of the Blue Mounds?"

Waughs exploded all around the circle. Every man rocked agitatedly where he sat. What the Omaha were doing was an evil thing. The Yankton Dakotas had to have the revenge.

"It is good to hear all my brothers speak their hearts," Legbone cried. "It means that we shall find the justice." He leaned forward and with bare finger and thumb picked a little red coal out of the twig fire and placed it in the bowl of the pipe. Instantly a very thin wisping thread of smoke spiraled out of the packed tobacco. Legbone gave the stem a deep suck, until his cheeks fell in as if he were suddenly toothless; and then another deep suck; and then another; and on the fourth suck, the little red ember seared down into the tobacco and a cloud of smoke shot out of his mouth.

"Ahh. Hochh."

Legbone then took a quiet ceremonial puff and passed the pipe on to the man on his left.

Once again, when the pipe came to First Standing, First Standing hesitated before passing it on to Flat Warclub. He glanced at Legbone. Whoever smoked the pipe could be chosen for the revenge party.

Legbone nodded.

Flat Warclub accepted the pipe.

Flat Warclub was ready.

His helper had also told him that his father Driving Hawk needed Flat Warclub in The Other Life and had asked Wakantanka to send him on. Wakantanka had promised that Flat Warclub would be sent on and that this should happen at the moment when Flat Warclub would give his people his most precious possession. Flat Warclub knew what that meant.

At first Flat Warclub had been stunned by the message. Why should he be chosen to give such an ultimate gift when everyone knew he was only a pleasant fellow and not much good for anything? All he'd ever done that was of any importance was to find a considerable bed of clams along The River Of The Red Rock between their lake and the Blue Mounds.

It was true that when he went to his high hill to have his vision he'd been told to go look for clams. But he'd thought that ridiculous. The whole village had even laughed at the idea when he'd returned and told about his vision. The worst was that not a single maiden would look at him after that. The vision he'd had was the kind that might have come to a maiden had she been permitted to seek instruction from the gods in lonely vigil on a high hill.

It was all very sad. Flat Warclub was amorous by nature and would dearly love to have had a wife. He often dreamt of the time when he should run after a maiden and catch her and become a father upon her as she lay in the grass. His dreams were constantly filled with willing maidens, but when he awoke and attempted to catch a live maiden by the sleeve as she went down to the lake to get water for her mother she only darted from his grasp and laughed at him over her shoulder.

Flat Warclub also dreamt a lot about river clams. He sometimes saw them by the handfuls in his dreams. They were always connected with maidens. It went back to the time when he'd seen his mother Cornmilk bathing in the women's place along the beach. It had struck him strange that his mother did not have a little warclub between her thighs as his father Driving Hawk had, but instead had a thing like a river clam.

The time he'd found that bed of clams had been connected with his mother. He was washing his feet in The River Of The Red Rock when he spotted a gleaming clam in the sand. He pulled it up to have a better look at it. He knew it was a shameful thing to be thinking it reminded him of his mother. Yet at the same time he couldn't resist playing with the clam, and once, idly, ran his finger into the soft mouth of the clam. At that moment the clam, angered, snapped shut, and caught his finger. Flat Warclub, in great pain, leaped high in the air. When he came down he was halfway across the stream and he'd landed in a huge collection of clams. When he finally got his finger back by breaking the shell of the clam with a rock, he knew that his vision, much as he'd despised it, had come true. He had found much good food for his band. Accordingly, his finger stinging, he ran to tell his mother and the other women of the band. Later on he was to wonder if biting like a river clam was what his mother's other husbands had meant when they spoke of her as having vagina teeth.

Wakantanka surely knew what was best for him and his people. Thus he would have to go and join his father in The Other Life. It was also a justice that they should get revenge against the very people who had killed his father in the first place.

With a wrench Flat Warclub broke out of his reverie.

Looking about, he discovered that the forty warriors in the council lodge had already settled on a leader for the revenge party. It was to be Legbone. And Legbone was asking for volunteers.

First Standing was the first to get to his feet. He was followed by Middle Son and Red Ant. Several other braves unfolded their legs as if they meant to stand up too.

Flat Warclub jumped to his feet. "Waugh. Let me be counted among those who go to help our sister band."

Silence.

Legbone slowly raised his sad black eyes. "Some may be killed."

"It has already been told me."

"Why did you come to this council?"

"My helper told me to take my flat warclub"—Flat Warclub swung his weapon about and gestured fiercely with it—"and join my brothers."

Legbone looked down at his folded knees. He waited for others to comment.

An older man, Bitten Nose, lifted his head. He had once had the point of his nose bitten off in a savage fight. He usually held his head at an angle away from people so they would be less apt to notice his mutilated nose. He snarled up at Flat Warclub. "Once our revenge party leaves on the south road there will be no time to finger the mouths of river clams."

"I will seek clams by the river all right," Flat Warclub said, "but they will not be the kind you are thinking of."

"And that crazy club of yours," Bitten Nose sneered, "what can you kill with that? Perhaps a beetle?" Bitten Nose lifted up his head even more. The serrated marks of the toothbite across the cartilage at the end of his nose could be seen quite clearly.

Flat Warclub straightened in anger. "Does Bitten Nose care to test my club with the top of his head? I tell you, my warclub is a good thing. My helper told me to use it. I cannot go against my helper."

Bitten Nose fell silent.

There were no other sneering remarks.

Seeing that, Legbone looked up again, asking for more volunteers.

Twenty were chosen. They were all, with the exception of Legbone, young men. The rest of the men would stay behind to protect the village.

Flat Warclub hurried to his mother's tepee. He ran stooping into her lodge. "Mother, it has been decided. We go to help our sister band of the Blue Mounds. And I have been chosen to join the revenge party."

"Eii."

"Do not weep, Mother. Remember that you bear the name of a great-grandmother who was named after a famous event. Thus you must show forbearance." Everyone knew about the naming of Great-grandmother Cornmilk. A single mother buffalo had appeared across the slough from where the band had pitched their leather tents. Someone had noted that the mother buffalo's bag of milk was so full that as she walked along drops of milk fell to earth. Almost as they fell the drops of milk sprouted up as full-grown corn. It was then that they knew the mother buffalo was wakan. She had specially given them a new plant to live by. They were saved. They had both the meat of the buffalo and the ears of fresh corn to eat. About that same time a little girl was born to the band. The camp medicine man, wanting to mark the coming of corn, declared that the name of the new baby should be Cornmilk.

"Eii. You will not come back alive."

Flat Warclub could smell his mother's breath and it disgusted him. Whenever she got excited her breath turned sour. Of course it always went away again after she'd quieted down.

Flat Warclub dug out his father's famous war shield. His father had made the shield out of the triangular front of a buffalo bull's head. Flat Warclub next gathered up several strips of jerky and thrust them in his traveling kit. Then, without further word, he left.

◄ 2 ►

FLAT WARCLUB

THEY WERE TWENTY-ONE MEN AS THEY TROTTED THEIR HORSES around the east shore of Talking Water and then headed up a slow rise of land. Except for Lightfoot, each man had two horses, the horse he rode and the horse he led. The horse led was a favorite war pony.

Legbone took the lead. He was the biggest and heaviest man yet rode his horse the most lightly. His riding motion anticipated the gait of his trotting horse. His mien was compact. He rode with one brown shoulder leading. His head swung slowly from side to side and his piercing black glances darted everywhere.

Lightfoot on a borrowed horse rode immediately back of Legbone. The rest of the men were strung out behind in scattered fashion.

The war ponies trotting along behind carried each man's war gear: a full quiver of arrows, a battle bow, a favorite shield. Animal-tail pennants dangled from the shields and undulated in rhythm with the flourishing tails of the horses.

Flat Warclub was last in line. The horse he rode, Old Gray, was poor and skinny. She was a mare and belonged to his mother. His mother had inherited her from his father Driving Hawk. The horse Flat Warclub led, Many Spots, was a gelding. Flat Warclub had raised him to be his war pony. Many Spots was a beauty. He had sharply defined patches of red and white over his back. His black mane and tail gave off glinting lights as he ran along.

Flat Warclub was quite aware that Red Ant and Middle Son had not wanted him to be part of the revenge party. The two braves glowered at him as they rode along and kept urging everybody to hurry hurry, as though hoping Flat Warclub's old horse would not be able to keep up.

Flat Warclub smiled to himself. He knew his mother's old gray mare. She had great stamina. His father Driving Hawk had used the old gray mare often as his buffalo pony, and at the time she had outperformed all other buffalo ponies in the band. Furthermore, it was easier to tag after a bunch than lead it.

Flat Warclub smiled for another reason. He was happy. A plan had slowly evolved in his mind as to what he should do before his fatal day. And the more he thought about it the more he looked forward to the next several days.

Legbone led them straight for a distant height of land. The way up was smooth. Grass underfoot gradually became short. It was curly and the horses tried to stop and crop it. The horses knew what grasses made the best grazing. Soon every man was jerking up his horse's head to keep it from eating.

When they reached the top of the hogback, Legbone pulled up and held up a hand. All the other horses stopped, too, and instantly began snapping off the curly grass. The grass had a gray green sheen. It was so delicious the horses made loud crunching noises as they munched away.

The men could see a very long ways. The cloudless sky was a great vault of blue slanting down to all sides. The hogback they stood on curved ahead to the south and slowly sloped up toward a slightly higher ridge. Every one knew that at the very top of the higher ridge lay the effigy of a man chasing a buffalo.

Legbone finished his survey. "It is strange. There is not a four-legged or a two-legged in sight."

Lightfoot nodded. "There were not many buffalo this spring. All the antelope have run off to the south."

"It is strange that we do not even see the rabbit that takes long jumps."

"Our medicine man Half Sun says it is a sign. The four-leggeds are telling us that it will be a bad summer. There has not been enough rain."

First Standing said, "My horse is thirsty."

Legbone said, "A spring is just ahead. It is where The River Of The Red Rock begins."

They rode on.

Presently Legbone reined his horse to the left and they all started down a steep slope. Legbone trotted straight for a huge pink-mottled boulder.

Old Gray smelled the water and began to run like a young horse. She too ran unerringly straight for the pink rock. Flat Warclub had to rein her in to keep her in place at the end of the line.

Water spilled out from under the pink rock in a braiding stream. It was of the size of a horse's tail. It glanced down the slope in zigzag fashion. Near the bottom two other little streams, not quite as large, poured magically out of springs and joined the stream. Just below them lay a glinting pool of sky-clean water.

All twenty-one men headed for the pool. In a moment forty-one horses were sipping away. Their black tails flourished slowly as they drank the sweet water. They hardly noted the flies.

When the horses had finished and began nipping at each other, half the men led them down the hill a ways, four horses to a man, while the other half got down on their knees and had themselves a drink. They drank from the stream just where it poured into the little blue pond. Later the second half of the men had their drink.

Flat Warclub didn't drink like the rest. Where the others either lapped at the water like dogs or drank from a cupped hand, Flat Warclub removed a moccasin from his foot, dipped it full of water, and drank from it. He thought it more dignified to drink from a vessel of some sort.

Red Ant had a sneer for him. Red Ant, though slender, could sometimes be a violent man. "Don't your feet stink?"

"My helper tells me what to do."

"Too bad there aren't any empty clamshells about for you to drink from."

"I hear him."

Red Ant cast wondering eyes at the clamshell gleaming in Flat Warclub's hair. "Some have noted that you are hard of hearing on one side."

Flat Warclub laughed at him. Since what was fated was going to happen, why should he be afraid of him. Further, he was not going to let slip that his helper lay hidden in a knot in his flat warclub. He dandled his club to let Red Ant know he wasn't going to tolerate any more sneering remarks.

Red Ant looked at him curiously, one eye on the flat surface of his club. "The Omaha brave will thank you for cracking his head lice."

"My helper has told me seven will fall by this weapon. They are already dead. They eat in vain."

Red Ant fell silent but the sneer lingered on his curled lips.

Legbone dug into his parfleche and pulled out a strip of dried jerky. With his stone knife he hacked off a corner and began chewing on it. He motioned for the others to do the same. Soon everyone was sitting on the grass and gravely chewing his morsel of jerky. The horses tugged to the limit of their lead ropes and cropped hungrily at the rich grass.

Finished eating, Legbone mounted his horse, took up the lead rope to his war pony, and with a hunching of his huge shoulders motioned for the band to move on. All leaped on their riding horses and swung in behind him.

They followed the stream straight south. Very shortly the stream became a lively trickling run. Where the valley widened, it cut through a slough of deep rushes; where the valley narrowed, it cut through falling banks of gravel.

Legbone held to a course just below the crest of the hills. In clear country, silhouettes could be seen pricking along for a great distance. At the same time the course was high enough to pick out any movement ahead or below.

The sun was directly overhead when they stopped to water their horses again. They'd arrived just east of the ridge where there lay the effigy of a man chasing a buffalo. Again horse and man stopped to chew a little.

The looming ridge was high. The wind blew briskly across it. The wind flattened out the grass so that the ridge resembled a sleek mammoth.

Middle Son threw a wondering look at the summit. "Would that I might see the sacred effigy. Is there time?"

Legbone shook his head. "This is a revenge party. Today we do not seek the buffalo."

Flat Warclub had never seen the effigy either. "Legbone, it is fated that I shall soon die. I wish to see it before I go to join my father Driving Hawk."

"We cannot wait for you."

Flat Warclub said, "I can easily catch up. You will follow The River Of The Red Rock to the village of our sister band."

Legbone threw up a shoulder and said no more.

Red Ant and Middle Son smiled at each other. Let Flat Warclub go on a side trip up the ridge. He would be left far behind; and thus, discouraged, might perhaps return home. They'd be rid of him.

Flat Warclub swung onto his old gray and, grabbing the lead rope of Many Spots, set off up the slope. Both horses resisted leaving the band. They kept shying off and Flat Warclub had to fight them to go on. When the other horses neighed after them, both his horses became even more reluctant to climb the ridge. Flat Warclub finally had to whip the old gray with his quirt, and then both horses, swaying their heads from side to side, gave in and headed up the slope.

As they rose, the jingling sound of the shells on the bridles of the horses of the main party faded away behind him. Old Gray sidled up a slowly stiffening hill. Once more the grass changed underfoot, slowly becoming short grass, and then the prized gray green buffalo grass. Flat Warclub kept looking to all sides. The earth gradually tipped down and away. Soon the men on the horses below resembled fleas astride red ants.

Near the summit two huge jackrabbits jumped out of a tuft of grass. They ran across his path.

"Ae. Lovers. It is a good omen. The rabbit is never sated."

He watched the jackrabbits zigzagging down the slope in smooth, even, bounding motions. They were beautiful to see. At the top of each leap their paired ears stuck straight up like two eagle feathers.

At last Old Gray eased onto a four-sided plateau of waving grass. Old Gray sighed, and groaned, and gave her hide a rippling shudder.

Flat Warclub kept a sharp eye out for white stones underfoot. Buffalo had cropped short most of the grass. There were dried buffalo droppings everywhere.

He saw the white stones. Reverently he circled the horses around them until he could clearly distinguish two outlines in the grass. Verily, a stone man was chasing a stone buffalo. The stone

man was twice the size of Legbone and the stone buffalo was twice
the size of any buffalo bull he'd ever seen. Verily, the two-leggeds
and the four-leggeds of those days had been of wakan size.

He slipped off his horse, flat warclub in hand. He stood a moment imagining what those old times might have been like. He
could see the two creatures alive again, the big bull running for its
life and the big man after it with a spear. The man would get the
bull of course. That was how it came about that men had survived
until that very day.

He placed his warclub on the ground. He reached into his gear
and dug out a pouch of tobacco. He took a pinch of the brown
tobacco, returned the pouch, and then, kneeling first beside the
stone man and then the stone buffalo, scattered grains of the
tobacco over them. "This is done in honor of a great deed done
in great times. It is also done so that what has been fated for me
shall happen as my helper tells me it will happen."

At that moment his helper spoke to him from where it lay hidden
in the knot of his flat warclub. "Stone From The Clouds, listen.
There is as yet no danger. But if you do not hurry, you will not be
able to catch up with Legbone and the revenge party. Hurry."

Flat Warclub was startled that his helper should address him by
his secret name.

"Hurry. I do not want you to miss entering the village of The
Nation Of The Blue Mounds with the rest of your friends."

"Thank you, my guardian spirit. We will leave immediately."

Flat Warclub cast a look down at the river. Ae. Truly. His bunch
had disappeared around a bend.

Quickly he grabbed up his warclub and climbed Old Gray. He
headed the old horse down the slope.

Old Gray caught on instantly. They were going to rejoin the
other horses in the war party. She began to gallop. Many Spots
caught on, too, and began to run a little ahead of Old Gray, as far
as the lead rope would allow.

They picked up the trail along the stream, hoofprints where the
ground was soggy. Both Old Gray and Many Spots could smell
their comrades ahead somewhere.

Soon a beaver dam appeared, with water backed up into a considerable pond. Muskrat domes dotted the edges of the pond. A
pair of wood ducks paddled along the far shore. The wind was just
strong enough to make occasional smiling ripples.

Many Spots smelled something new on a knoll on the right. He pulled on the lead rope, trying to make Flat Warclub and Old Gray come his way.

"Hii. What is it that you smell, merry one?"

Flat Warclub studied the grass on the little knoll. Some pink showed through the grass. "Ae. Wild clover. But we do not have time, my friend. My helper has told us to hurry and catch our party."

Many Spots yearned for the pink clover. A sly smile appeared on his black lips. His big daisy eyes appeared to wink at Old Gray.

"Ae," Flat Warclub said then with a laugh, "have a few bites, you scamps. But you will have to answer to my helper if things go wrong."

He let them crop for the length of time it took two meadowlarks to call out seven challenges each.

"Come." Flat Warclub made them break off their greedy cropping. "The battle with the Omaha awaits us." He urged them into a gallop.

There was no wind along the banks of the little river. The sun was hot. The old gray began to sweat between Flat Warclub's legs and presently foam sudsed up between man and horse.

They came upon a wide slough behind another beaver dam. The deep grass and the tossing cattails smelled like fresh tobacco. Several beaver were slowly nosing along the far side of the pond, each with a willow stick in its mouth.

Flat Warclub caught up with Legbone and the others just as they came within sight of the tip of the Blue Mounds. They took up the tail position of the party.

Both Red Ant and Middle Son were disappointed. It became more and more obvious that they were ashamed to show up with Flat Warclub in the village of their sister band.

Flat Warclub smiled to himself. His helper had told him what was going to happen and he was content to wait until the time came.

The revenge party followed The River Of The Red Rock straight south. The river ran over red pebbles. The land on their right began to lift like a slanted drag behind a horse. Great bones of red rock showed through green grass. Not a tree, not a bush, grew on the flat uplift of land. Far at its end the uplift broke off, forming a sharp bluish cliff. The rock in the cliff was red and pink, but the distant haze made it appear to be blue. Some of the highest rocks were covered with green lichen.

All eyes were on the looming blue rim. It was a sacred place. Along the east base of the long red cliff lay heaps of white buffalo bones. Sometimes the heaps lay so thick they appeared to be snow-drifts strangely blown across deep green grass.

Flat Warclub noted some earthen mounds on the bluffs across the river. The mounds resembled the breasts of young virgins. He had seen such mounds in the land near their home on Talking Water. High Stomach had explained them once by saying they'd been heaped up by a tribe of Old Ones, a people long ago disap-peared and dead. High Stomach said the bones of the Old Ones lay under the mounds.

A lookout on a high pink rock spotted them. The lookout sig-naled back to his camp. In a moment he waved his shirt for Leg-bone to come on.

They rode to where a stream came down from the west. The stream cut through a swooping draw in the long red cliff. Legbone waggled his head once, fur-wrapped braids flopping over his shoulders, and then led them up the stony draw. They followed a path on the right side.

Presently they came to where a spring broke out of the red rock earth and trickled noisily down toward the little stream. Across the spring grew a thick clump of wild plums.

Legbone again held up his hand and pulled up his horse.

Everyone pulled up behind him. The horses smelled the fresh springwater and reached out long necks for it.

"Here we are still hidden from our sister band, The Nation Of The Blue Mounds. Let us refresh ourselves and get ourselves ready for the honored parade into camp."

The horses were watered and put out to grass. The men washed their sweat-grimy legs as well as their clouts. They put on their war dress, and painted a single black war stripe around their right eye, and dressed up their battle ponies with feathers and pennants. Lightfoot, the host, did not dress up for the parade.

Flat Warclub again preferred to be off by himself a little. His helper told him to get ready for the parade some dozen feet higher up the trickling spring. Flat Warclub fastened a handful of feathers in the mane and forelock of Many Spots, red, yellow, blue, as well as tying two squirrel tail pennants to the very end of his black tail. Flat Warclub washed himself thoroughly in the cold springwater. He got out his best shirt and slipped it on over his head. He loved the shirt. It was one his mother had spent much time on. She'd dressed the leather with a rough-edged stone and had smoked it lightly over a slow fire. The front of it was decorated with intricate quillwork depicting a battle in which his father had counted coup four times. It had long delicate fringes. It still smelled of his mother's tepee back home. He next put on a pair of fancy buckskin leggings, also beautifully decorated by his mother. He slipped on a new pair of moccasins. He combed out the tangles in his long tresses, using for a comb the rasp surface of an old buffalo tongue. He refastened the clamshell over his right ear. Last he tied the tail of a red squirrel to the handle of his flat warclub. He was ready.

Legbone gave the signal, and every man ran for his horses, this time hopping onto his war-horse and leading his riding horse. Legbone gave another signal and all headed in a brisk trot toward the camp ahead. Lightfoot rode immediately behind Legbone.

The wind of their going played with the decoration feathers in their hair and with the squirrel tail pennants in the tails of their horses. They made a noble-looking force.

"Hi-yi!" Flat Warclub cried. No enemy could withstand them, especially now that it was fated seven should die under his flat warclub.

"Eii!" the young braves cried in response.

They rode toward a huge long rock exactly resembling a giant flesher. As they curved around the rock, they came upon five maidens carrying pots of fresh water on their heads. The maidens had just come up from the stream below.

The young braves cried even louder, "Hi-yi! Eii!"

The maidens smiled wide white teeth at the handsome men. They trilled a welcome for them.

Flat Warclub noticed that the maiden last in line didn't quite smile like the others. Her eyes had a troubled look about them. Also she stood a little apart from the others. The first four appeared to be virgins but the fifth one had the look of one who didn't quite know what she was.

Flat Warclub liked the looks of the troubled one. He himself was always last in line. He felt sympathy for her. He also liked it that she had light brown skin.

"It is fated that I shall soon talk to her," Flat Warclub whispered to himself. "Perhaps I can get her to smile like the others. Ae, my helper will tell me how it shall be done."

The war party curved around a slight rise, and directly ahead lay the village of their sister band. Some fifty tepees were carefully set in a circle on the other side of the little stream. It was where the little stream curved out of the north under a low wall of red rock.

The red wall was a bit higher than the tips of the tepee poles and gave the village shelter from the northwest winds.

The dogs heard them coming and came from behind every tepee and rushed at .hem, barking furiously. Behind the dogs, coming through the horns of the camp, poured a stream of little children, dozens of them, all crying in joy to see that their saviors had arrived.

"Oo-koo-koo! Oo-koo-hoo! Now there shall be a great victory over the Omaha. We will chase them far to the south. They will not dare to use our buffalo jump again. Wana hiyelo!"

Legbone and his braves rode with their shields held high. Their black eyes flashed from left to right. Their shell decorations threw off little tongues of blue fire. The war ponies caught the spirit of the parade and becked their heads up and down and flourished their long black tails.

The older of the little children called off the names of the visiting heroes. Legbone. Red Ant. First Standing. Middle Son. As each name was called off, the little children lupped up ringing cheers and stomped the victory dance in the grass. They had a special cheer for Lightfoot. "See! Our runner returns safely. In him we place our trust in time of trouble."

Four bronze drummers emerged from the council tepee carrying a wide leather drum. The drummers were young and powerfully built. They struck up a slow abrupt beat. The beat was so strong that after a moment it made the horses walk in step. The four braves themselves shook upon each beat as though from palsy. Ahead of them walked the camp crier Wide Mouth, calling out, "Our brothers have heard our cry! They have come to save us!"

An old man and two youths were seated cross-legged on the grass on the rise to the east. Hearing the commotion below they got to their feet to see what was happening. They had delicate instruments in their hands. It was the arrowsmith and his pupils. In a moment they put aside their bone tools and came hurrying across the slope to join the clamor down in the camp. The five maidens carrying their jars of water also came hurrying under-through the oaks along the rocks.

Four times Legbone led his war party around the inner circle of the camp.

Flat Warclub noted that few if any in the camp looked at him. All had eyes for First Standing and Red Ant and the other braves up front. The only one who took a good look at Flat Warclub was the troubled maiden.

"Seven days from now," Flat Warclub promised himself as he patted the withers of his horse Many Spots, "there shall be much weeping when they bring my body back to camp. Then our sister band will remember, too late, the decorated shirt my mother made for me and, alas, my brave pony Many Spots."

Legbone pulled up in front of the council lodge in the center of the camp. The drummers gave their wide drum one last deep beat, Whomb! and then, abruptly, there was sudden and utter silence.

The various members of the visiting war party were quietly invited to stay as guests at certain designated tepees.

Flat Warclub was not invited to stay with anyone. After all the other ponies had been led away, he still sat on Many Spots holding the lead rope to his old gray.

Flat Warclub, however, sat smiling. It had been so fated.

Presently several children began to peek at Flat Warclub from the doorflaps of their tepees, wondering what he was doing sitting alone on his horse near the council lodge.

Old Gray, ever hungry, reached down looking for something to eat. But the grass was trampled too flat to crop. Many Spots nosed down too, but finally decided the scruffed-over vegetation was not for him.

Finally an odd-looking brave at the end of the camp, the place usually reserved for the most humble or the last couple to be married, came out of his tepee and with a hand over his brow stood staring at Flat Warclub.

The staring of the strange brave was so intense that Flat Warclub at last had to turn around for a closer look. Flat Warclub wondered if perhaps the staring brave had been the one elected to put him up but for some reason had been reluctant to do so.

Flat Warclub's helper whispered from where it lay nestled in the knot of his flat warclub. "Do not fear. A sleeping robe will be soon given to you. Also there will be buffalo soup. Wait. Be patient."

"I am waiting. But in the meantime does not camp etiquette require that someone should come and offer to put up my horses?"

"Patience. It will be given to you."

"My mother Cornmilk will consider it a mortal insult if they do not come and get my horses."

"Wait."

Flat Warclub nodded. He settled back at ease. He smiled in the manner of his father Driving Hawk. His father had been known to smile in such a winning manner that he could finally make even a turtle smile.

The strange brave continued to stare from the end tepee. Slowly his eyes began to blaze like a pair of black rubstones.

Flat Warclub waited. He let his eyes wander over the line of tepees in the camp circle. Every tepee was painted with both clan markings and personal insignia. The doorflaps of all tepees faced east to catch the morning sun. Across and up the stream a ways stood a half-dozen separation huts. On the flat above the red wall stood several sweat lodges.

The strange brave shuddered. Then, with a jerk, and with an odd swinging motion of his hips, he walked straight to Flat Warclub. He stopped directly in front of Many Spots and looked up at Flat Warclub. "My wife is a good cook. Will you come and stay with us?"

Flat Warclub started. What was this? A husband bragging about his wife's cooking? That was not done in the camp of The People Of Talking Water. The husband and the wife always spoke as if the food they offered was the worst in the world, even though they knew it probably was the very best. Flat Warclub stared down at the strange brave.

"Step down," the strange brave said, "and I will take your horses to a place where the grass is very good."

Again Flat Warclub thought it strange that someone should brag about food, even food for horses. It was permissible to boast about counting coup on the enemy or about a successful horse-stealing raid, but never about food.

"Come."

Flat Warclub's smile faded a little. Slowly he slid down off his horse and handed over the reins of his two horses. He agreed to the arrangement only because his horses did need good grass and he himself needed a sleeping robe.

"This way." The odd-walking brave led them to the end tepee. "We are the lowliest in this camp. Though not for long."

What an odd voice the brave had. It was gruff and low, at the same time that it was womanish. It was as though the brave's voice had not been quite able to fulfill itself. It had hardened before it had a chance to mature. As they stepped along, Flat Warclub decided to get along as best he could with the strange one. "You will not be sorry. In seven days my helper says my warclub will bring much honor to your village."

"Wait here." The strange brave looked across the little stream and called to some boys holding the horse herd. "There are some more horses to get. Hurry."

Flat Warclub was again surprised by the voice. It was almost angry. It was not the kind of voice one used to call young boys. After a while they would not obey. He and the strange brave were standing near the entrance of the end tepee and he could hear someone rustling around inside as if the someone too thought the strange brave had spoken too harshly.

After a moment, somewhat sullenly, two boys came to get Flat Warclub's horses.

The strange brave made an abrupt motion with his right hand, first extending it and then sweeping it toward his face, meaning, "Come, enter," and stepped inside the tepee.

Flat Warclub, a bit uneasy, followed him.

For a moment it was dark inside the tepee. As his eyes adjusted, Flat Warclub was surprised to discover that it was the troubled maiden sitting on the left in the woman's place. Ah, it meant that she was the brave's wife. She sat in the manner of all Dakota women, both legs tucked to one side. It was also the manner of the old Mound Builder women. Looking sharply, Flat Warclub made out there were no children. A little twig fire burned in the center hearth. Food parfleches were neatly set along the south wall. Leather shirts and dresses hung from a braided leather rope strung around inside the tepee framework. Two willow rod backrests sat on the grass floor on the other side of the little fire, opposite the door of the tepee. There was a good smell in the tepee, of sweet leather and sage leaves.

The strange-walking brave closed his right hand in front of his right shoulder and then moved it downward a couple of inches. "Come, sit beside me." He pointed to the guest backrest. "A lazyback is a good thing after a long day's ride." The brave settled on the fartherest lazyback and lay back with a langorous sigh.

Flat Warclub set aside his bow and quiver and also with an elaborate sigh settled himself on the guest lazyback. He placed his flat warclub across his lap.

The strange brave reached back for a leather pouch and got out a small red gossip pipe. He filled it slowly with scented tobacco. He lighted up with a small red ember taken from the twig fire. He puffed meditatively a moment, to get the fire in the pipe going well, and then offered the pipe to the four directions, then to the earth and sky, and last to himself where he sat in that place, and finally took a puff. Then he passed it on to Flat Warclub.

Flat Warclub also presented the pipe to the seven directions. He puffed gently. Again, just as he'd done at the council meeting in his own village, he accidentally blew a perfect smoke ring. It rose widening and wreathing toward the smokehole.

"Houw!" the strange brave exclaimed.

The troubled maiden took one look and clapped a hand to her mouth, looked down, closed her eyes, and shook her head from side to side.

"Ah," Flat Warclub whispered, "it is my helper doing this. He is telling me something again."

"Houw."

"We shall be victorious over the Omaha."

The strange brave nodded. "It can be seen to be true."

Flat Warclub handed back the pipe. As he did so he noticed how slender the brave's fingers were, tapered at the ends almost like a woman's.

The strange brave said, "It is a good thing to have you in our lodge. Perhaps now is the time to tell you in whose lodge you are staying. We, this woman and I, live as man and wife. My wife's name is Prettyhead, for reasons that you can see. And my name is Manly Heart, because here, in this place, I am known as a manly-hearted woman."

Flat Warclub stiffened. "Eii."

Manly Heart also stiffened. The she-husband did not like the tone of surprise in Flat Warclub's voice. "You have not heard of such husbands?"

Flat Warclub remembered. Yes, there had been a rumor that their sister band living at the Blue Mounds had in their midst what was known as a manly-hearted woman. Hiyelo. It had been his luck to land in her tepee. No wonder he saw no children. No wonder Prettyhead had a troubled look. "Yes. My father once spoke of such a one living with the Crows. She was a great hunter of the buffalo, he said."

Manly Heart was mollified by the reply. She took several puffs on her gossip pipe and then set it to one side. "Well, Prettyhead, twice now since our guest entered our lodge have I heard his belly rumble. Is not the soup ready?"

The soup was not even on the fire, Flat Warclub saw. It was Manly Heart's way of urging the good wife to get busy with her chores.

Face brightening over a chore she understood, Prettyhead half-filled a big earthen pot with water and set it close to the fire. She dug out some roots from a parfleche, as well as some herbs, and uncovered a large piece of buffalo beef from which she cut three chunks of meat each the size of a man's hand, and then, flourishing her braids out of the way, tossed the meat into the earthen pot, the water splashing up.

Flat Warclub became aware that his helper wanted to say something. Flat Warclub inclined his ear, imperceptibly so as not to call his host's attention to it.

"Listen. Abide with these folk," his helper said. "It is a good lodge. Wakantanka placed these people here in this camp so that you might have a place to sleep. They will make a better home for you than anyone else in the village. You have much in common. You are special, and they see this. I have spoken. Yelo."

Flat Warclub nodded inside his head. "I have heard you. Yes."

◄ 3 ►

MANLY HEART

MANLY HEART LIKED THE STYLISH YOUNG MAN. ONE GOOD LOOK at him and she knew he was fated to do something remarkable. She herself knew what it meant to become someone remarkable.

As a little girl she was already different from her friends. At the age of five her mother Clean Woman had difficulty getting her to quit playing with her brother Stalk. When Clean Woman urged her to stay in the tepee and help her with the household duties, so that she might learn how to become a good wife as well as a good mother, Manly Heart would have none of it. She ran outside instead and looked for Stalk to play with.

Stalk, who was a year older, soon began to avoid her. Their father Spear Carrier told him that it was not a good thing for a boy of six or more to be playing with his sister. At six it was time for the boy to learn how to become a good husband as well as a good provider.

When Manly Heart finally realized that neither her brother nor any of the other boys her age would play with her, she bowed her head for the time being and, sullen lipped, attended her mother and helped her with tepee work.

But while she worked with her mother, Manly Heart watched with envy as her brother joined the other boys in games of hunting and fighting and riding. It galled her that her brother should be taught to be bold in the pursuit of game and of the enemy, while she had to learn to sew and smoke meat. She saw her brother Stalk grow away from her as grown-up men taught him how to go about hunting and fighting with a cool manly air. Manly Heart was sure that she could do as well in the manly arts.

She begged her uncle Happy One to teach her how to shoot the arrow, how to mount a horse on the run, how to achieve a vision. Happy One did not know what to do. Since she was his only niece he found it hard to deny her. He had always favored her, and abashedly, almost in a shamed way, did show her how to shoot the arrow and how to mount a horse. Though he refused to tell her how to achieve a vision. Only men had visions.

At the age of twelve she finally found one boy who would play with her. When they were alone together she often led in sex play. It was taboo for a girl to suggest they look at each other's naked bodies and the boy was at first shocked by her behavior. But he told no one and presently began to look forward to those times when they could be alone. It was then that Manly Heart began to understand a little why her brother should be called Stalk. His name had a double meaning.

Soon all the young boys began to speak of her in derision. They said they would make sure that when she became a fully grown maiden she would never be given the chance to help carry the sundance pole. Only virgins were permitted to cut and get the sapling cottonwood for that great occasion. How could she be considered a virgin so long as she persisted in playing with the lout Hollow Horn? Hollow Horn like to brag to his friends that he could make milkweed juice a dozen times a day. For shame. And the young boys made the sign of ultimate disgust, first pointing the right hand downwards over the heart with fingers tight together, and then holding out both forefingers and letting them fall inward toward the belly.

Manly Heart endured their sneers until the day she learned that play with Hollow Horn might lead to babies. She was horrified. For her to have a baby before marriage would be the final shame.

Abruptly she began to shun him. Hollow Horn didn't like being rebuffed and for some time thereafter told foul stories about her.

When she turned fourteen, her father and mother decided it was time she got married. It would help settle her into her true role as woman. It happened that a very old chief known as He Is Empty wanted a sit-beside wife for his last days. He no longer was interested in the joys of the flesh. Instead he had taken an intense liking to gossip. He loved young people and thought it would be instructive and pleasant to talk with a young woman.

Again Manly Heart was horrified. Marry that old dried-up parfleche? When she was avid to play with her brother Stalk if it could only be permitted? Never.

But the old chief He Is Empty employed a nephew of his to bring two ponies to the door of her father's tepee, and when that did not prove to be enough, brought two more ponies, as well as all of the fine earthenware of his deceased wife.

The beautiful earthenware settled it. Clean Woman had for years coveted the black-orange-brown pots. She instructed Manly Heart to get married to old He Is Empty. She said that the old man would not live long and then Manly Heart would be a wealthy widow and could have her choice of any of the young men still available. Sullen-faced, Manly Heart finally agreed. She could see that her name, because of her playing around with Hollow Horn, was not a good one and that she would have trouble finding a good man.

Life with He Is Empty turned out to be much more lively than she expected. At first she did serve only as his sit-beside wife, handy for gossip and raillery, as well as for making him special manly perfumes which he liked very much. And then about two months after they were married, as they slept together one night warm and cozy in a buffalo sleeping robe, he woke up with a considerable stalk in bed. Hiyelo. Before it could become limp, he mounted her. Despite all the bad that had been said about her, it actually was the first time for her. She was both delighted and shocked, delighted that it was so pleasurable and shocked that old men could still do such things.

From that point on He Is Empty gradually awakened more and more as a man. At first he took pleasure with her once every two weeks, then once every week, and finally twice every week. Also he appeared to grow younger, both as to the skin around the eyes as well as to the vigor of his strolls about camp. It turned out that the whole encampment was pleased with the marriage. The marriage had erased the chance that they might have raised a bad girl in their midst. Also it had restored what had once been a wise man to his rightful place in the council.

About three years after they were married, when she was seventeen winters old, in The Moon Of The Flowering Puccoons, old He Is Empty took pleasure with his young wife twice during the night and once again in the morning. He was exultant. For a little while he resembled a very young man. He sat glowing by the little stick fire in their hearth while sipping at a bowl of soup. He bragged that, after the past night, he was sure to become a father. Not even the best stallion in the village, Plum Eyes, had ever mounted as many mares in the space of one day. He finished his soup and held his bowl out for more. "Wife," he said, "it is a good day to die and you have given me much pleasure. I desire more soup."

Smiling, for she had come to love the old man in her way, she picked up the buffalo horn spoon and refilled his bowl.

He sniffed with pleasure at the rising steam from the soup. He relaxed against his lazyback. "Wife," he said, "I look upon you with much pleasure. It warms my heart to see how firmly you twist your hair into two long braids. It delights me to see how neatly you keep your doeskin dress. And I am well pleased with thee also for taking the daily bath and anointing your skin with the perfume of the wild rose. Would that I could take you with me into the next world."

"It would make me glad to go with you," she said.

"It is good to be a man again."

"It is good to see you so happy."

"No longer are you my sit-beside wife. You are now my lie-beside wife."

She put the spoon to one side. She smiled down at her lap.

Then, as he reached out a hand to touch her to let her know that she pleased him beyond all saying, he pitched toward her, and fell dead out of his lazyback.

Manly Heart missed her old man husband very much. She scarified her legs and breasts in mourning. Weeping she helped her brother Stalk and her father Spear Carrier put up a scaffold upon which to place her old husband's body. Her husband had no kin, thus every evening when the sun went down she found herself weeping alone at the foot of his scaffold. Finally, when the wind and sun, and the gobblehead vultures, had consumed his skin and flesh, so that there was nothing left but dried bones, she and her father and her brother buried the old bones at the edge of one of the burial mounds across the river.

After a decent interval, she had many suitors.

At first she rejected them all. She wasn't sure she wanted to get married again. Her old husband He Is Empty had been very gentle with her. She knew that some husbands beat their wives. She had heard the wives yelling in pain inside their tepees. To those wives the beatings came as a great shock since parents never chastised their children.

She often took walks alone. She did so despite the warning of their camp crier Wide Mouth. Wide Mouth told her it was dangerous for anyone to be wandering alone along The River Of The Red Rock. Pumas had lately been seen. And of course there were the Omaha.

She found a little pond near the big river. She studied her reflection in the water where it reached out from the red rock she sat on. After all that had happened to her she was not one to be vain. She could see that she was not as comely as many of the other maidens in camp. She had good large breasts and they at least could be said to be womanly. But she had the bold eyes of a man as well as the strong chin. Her black hair was coarse and did not grow as fast as a woman's. And lately she knew she had several times caught herself walking like a man, a slow rolling gait, open-legged. Yankton women tended to walk with a close tight walk with their knees brushing each other.

She stared a long time at her image floating on the still water. There were a few wrinkles at the corners of her eyes. There was even a wrinkle on her high forehead.

"Ae, I am not a Yankton beauty. Thus he who next marries me will do so for my old husband's horses."

Her black eyes looked back at her with milky despondency. Her life was not worth keeping. It was better to throw it away.

On the way back to camp she decided to hold a giveaway. It was a custom among the Yanktons for the bereaved to give away all their possessions, both their own as well as those of the deceased, after the bones had been buried. She had been slow to hold such a giveaway because she was not sure she truly believed the custom was a good one. She decided she would do it to put to the test how much her own people liked her and if now they had truly come to respect her.

She wept in the customary manner as she carried all her goods and possessions out of her tepee and set them on the grass in the middle of the camp. She wailed loudly as she dismantled her tepee and laid out the lodgepoles and the buffalo hide covering. Everyone in the camp watched in silence. A few of the older women gathered near. Nothing was said.

When she had finished placing everything she owned in the middle of the camp, she settled down on the grass and covered her head with a foxskin shawl. And waited.

After a decent interval of silence, medicine man Person In The Moon emerged from his lodge and approached her. He surveyed the dismantlement of what had once been the home of He Is Empty. He had not approved of the marriage between He Is Empty and Manly Heart but at the time had said nothing. Person In The Moon was a very slender man, almost as if he'd been made out of willow withes rather than out of oak branches, and he had odd purple shadows under his eyes. Also both his lower eyelids sagged a little so that one could see a fat yellow tear trembling in them. Not everyone liked him. When he was a little boy he had dreamt of The Person In The Moon and after that everyone knew of course that he would never marry a woman. He was one of those who couldn't stand to have a woman touch him. Many of his kind, when they appeared in a band, sought out another man to live with, usually a young boy. But Person In The Moon did not care much for men either. He liked only his old mother Wise Crow and lived with her. Soon visions and prophecies began to come to him and the village accepted him as their shaman.

The whole camp waited for what Person In The Moon might have to say.

At last he clasped his hands in front of his stomach, with the back of his left hand down. "Peace, woman. We do not wish for your possessions. You have suffered enough. You have shown the proper respect for the deceased husband. If the others in this camp care to listen to what I have to say, they will hear what my helper has told me. Listen. I say this to you. Keep the household goods and the tepee and the horses. I have said." Person In The Moon turned slowly and in an hieratic manner returned to his lodge. His old mother Wise Crow, standing beside his lodge, held the leather doorflap open for him and then both disappeared inside.

After a moment Clean Woman appeared at Manly Heart's side and helped her daughter to her feet. Together the two women set up the tepee again and carried all the goods inside.

About two months later, Manly Heart married a widower named Red Daybreak. He'd come around visiting her with his lover talk

and letting her know that he was a good provider and a bold brave
in war. She knew he was all these things but she was also aware that
there had been something dark about his first marriage. And it
wasn't either that he'd beat his first wife, because in a leather
village such things were always heard.

She found out what the darks with him were the fourth night of
their marriage. The first three nights he slept beside her as a sister
might. Even the fourth night began in felicity. They crept into their
sleeping robe, and chatted, and laughed a little about the strange
antics of a pet dog, Four Eyes, he'd brought to their marriage, and
then, turning their heads away from each other, fell asleep. Of a
sudden at dawn she'd felt clutching fingers at her throat; and then
the next thing she knew he was upon her trying to thrust his stalk
into her. She fought him. She was very strong and almost managed
to free herself from the gripping hand on her throat, but in the
loose-limbed way she writhed and wrestled she at last happened
to open her thighs and he was into her. Sweat had also helped him.
To her considerable surprise she discovered that it was somewhat
pleasurable. And then, when he had finished, he let go of her
throat and began to sob upon her breasts.

It was strange behavior. It was so strange in fact that she didn't
tell anyone, not even her mother. Who would believe it? But she
was sure of one thing. The same thing had no doubt happened to
his first wife. And on one of those nights, in one of his more violent
fits of passion, he had accidentally choked his wife to death.

Manly Heart considered what to do. She knew she was much
stronger than his first wife. She could fight him off.

She considered divorcing him. But that way lay shame. No one
had shunned her for marrying the very old man He Is Empty, but
if she declared she was divorcing Red Daybreak because of the
strange way he took pleasure with her the whole camp would laugh
at her.

She lay awake most of the next night getting ready for his attack
at dawn. Somewhat to her disappointment, he didn't bother her.
He slept like a lazy dog beside her.

The second night she was so sleepy she couldn't stay awake.
Thus it happened that he was at her throat and then at her thighs
before she knew it. Once more her powerful muscular body saved
her.

It disturbed her that the deadly wrestle with Red Daybreak was
also pleasurable. It wasn't quite the pleasure her mother Clean

Woman said a woman should expect from a husband, a crazy kind of fainting away as though a vision were about to come upon one, but still it was enough to cause the corner of one's mouth to smile in a twisted way.

The next day she caught him looking at her with grudging respect. It was the kind of look one brave would give another after a show of prowess. Deep back in his black eyes a recognition was growing that she was a match for him. Her sturdy squarish body was proving to be as powerful as his.

As time went on he attacked her less and less often. Where her first husband, ancient He Is Empty, began slowly with her and then gradually worked himself up to mounting her more and more, her second husband, dark Red Daybreak, began wildly with her and then gradually fell off to less and less.

Manly Heart was greatly puzzled by the behavior of the two men. Several times she found herself a lonely red rock to sit on to ponder on the ways of men. Now that she had married twice she began to understand that many of her women acquaintances in the village were living strange private lives with their husbands.

Six months after they were married Red Daybreak no longer touched her. While he was friendly during the day when around her and would talk with her about the various events of the day at supper, at night he was a stranger to her. Once it got dark he would not talk to her. It was as though he in turn was afraid she would attack him.

She became ever more lonesome. She took to humming, and then to singing, to herself as she worked around the tepee.

The singing made him angry, especially when she did not sing the words clearly. He accused her of singing love songs meant for another man.

She couldn't resist tormenting him a little. "Perhaps."

"A woman who sings to herself surely is singing to a secret love."

"Perhaps."

"Are you singing a song for some other man?"

"Are there not wife-stealers in our camp?"

"Who?"

"Eii. Perhaps I am only singing to the ghost of He Is Empty."

"Houw. He was but a shell."

"I am only sorry that we did not have children."

"With him?"

"Even with him."

He fell silent. He was so crestfallen that even his single war feather appeared to hang limp.

She got sick of having him around. He wasn't much of a man. She thought she preferred him more during those days when he had tried to strangle her.

When one day the Soldier Society got up a hunting party, she asked if she could go along. She said that both she and her husband Red Daybreak had good hunting horses and that if he could go she could go because she could ride and shoot as well as he.

Her husband was ashamed of her and looked the other way.

Turning Horse, who had been selected to lead the hunting party, had seen her run and shoot. He'd several times had target practice with her and had been beaten by her. He respected her prowess and was known to say that it was too bad she wasn't born a man. Also he was inclined to be gentle with the strange ones in camp. He had once pointed out Crazy Leg, the bachelor, as one who spoke better medicine than Person In The Moon.

"You know that my old husband He Is Empty prided himself on his horses," Manly heart said. "It was because of the four beauties he brought to my father's tepee that my father said I should marry him."

"I know this."

"Thus I too have a good hunting horse," Manly Heart said. "Besides the horse my new husband rides."

"Houw."

"Do you not want the best hunters to go with you?"

"Get your horse and get your bow. Hiyelo. We shall try it this once." Turning Horse glared around at the half-dozen hunters sitting on their horses ready to go. "Let there be no lewd remarks." Then he turned a baleful eye on Red Daybreak. "Nor will I hear any backbiting from you. Unless you wish to stay home and breed dogs."

Red Daybreak sat angry on his red horse, glaring down at its black mane. He was proud of his male dog Four Eyes. He'd found Four Eyes lost by the river one day and had recognized it instantly as one of those of an ancient breed. It was said that the Old Ones had the breed when they came across a pond that was as endless as the sky. Four Eyes was black over its back and over the top of its head, and tan below. It had two tan spots just above its eyes, giving it the appearance of four eyes. It was a small dog but it could carry good-sized loads strapped onto its back without tiring. It tended to stay home more than the mongrel dogs did. Finally the flesh of that breed was said to taste better than the flesh of other dogs. All the women of the camp knew this and they were eager to have their bitches bred by Four Eyes.

Manly Heart watched her husband with contempt. Ae, that was all he was good for now, to peddle dog seed. Himself he had none. It came to her that that was why she had not had a child by him. Not once that she could remember had their been any sign after his attacks that he had discharged seed as a buffalo bull might upon a buffalo cow. While curiously enough, with old He Is Empty, toward the end of his life, there had been some little sign after each time they'd taken pleasure that he might just possibly become a father.

Red Daybreak was no good.

"Have you got your horse and your bow?" Turning Horse asked kindly.

"I will get them," Manly Heart said.

Manly Heart ran swiftly to her tepee. She took off her woman's clothes. She dug through an old parfleche where she had stored mementos of her first husband. There was a breechclout she'd made for He Is Empty which he'd never worn. She'd decorated the front of it with porcupine quills in the shape of an arrow. Smiling, she slipped it on and found that it fit her perfectly. She next got out his favorite hunting shirt and slipped it on. It too fit perfectly. She selected He Is Empty's favorite bow and a quiver of arrows. She picked up a bridle and then went out and got up on her old husband's hunting pony White Hooves.

When she came riding up to the hunting party, her new husband Red Daybreak took one look at her clothes and again looked the other way in shame.

The other braves did the same. Only Turning Horse looked upon her gravely and asked if she was ready.

"My horse and my bow yearn to find the buffalo."

There were no buffalo near or on the Blue Mounds plateau, and they had to hunt for stragglers along the sloughs of The River Of The Red Rock. They finally found a small herd grazing near a beaver dam an hour from camp. The ground was very soggy and the buffalo had trouble getting started. It took but a moment to turn the leaders, several swift cows, back in on the herd. The herd milled around and around. As they did so, Manly Heart and Turning Horse and Red Daybreak and all the other braves rode in and out of the flying mud and shot them down. Not one buffalo escaped. When they counted the slain animals afterwards, they discovered they'd downed ten young calves, eleven cows, and five bulls.

When the hunting party stopped to catch its breath, they discovered that Manly Heart like the others had shed her hunting shirt upon making their run at the buffalo. The sun glistened on her round sweaty breasts as it did on their own brown chests. After one quick glance all the braves avoided looking her way again.

Red Daybreak threw her a desperate look asking her to go get her shirt.

Manly Heart had shot down three cows, one bull, and two calves and thought she deserved better from her husband. What had a naked bosom to do with anything when she was as great a hunter as anyone in the party? Especially when she was sure her husband had only downed one buffalo, a little red calf?

She plunged in with the rest of the men when they butchered up the carcasses, carefully cutting away the hide, slicing off the precious hump meat, cutting off the quarters. She covered herself with blood from head to foot. Like the others she helped herself to a chunk of raw liver, dipped it in bile, and ate it with relish. The raw liver of a young cow could sometimes taste as sweet as bumblebee honey. It was always a special ritual treat on the spot for the successful hunter. She helped the men hang the meat on the packhorses. Because there was plenty of meat they took only the choice parts.

They washed up in the river. Like the men, she removed her clout and swam naked with them. That time all save Red Daybreak took her for granted. She was a good hunter.

When they arrived at the thick clump of wild plums just east of the camp, Turning Horse decided the hunt had been successful enough for them to make a triumphant entry in through the horns of the camp. Already the little children had spotted them coming and were dancing for joy along the Blue Mounds stream. Turning Horse made the sign to dismount, placing the first and second fingers of his right hand astride his left hand and then lowering the two fingers and pointing at the ground. Every one leaped happily to earth and began to paint himself.

Manly Heart had taken the precaution of carrying her old husband's decoration kit with her. She knew they would have a successful hunt. She began to paint her face to show how many buffalo she had killed.

Again her new husband tried to dissuade her with covert gestures, telling her she shouldn't act like a man.

Manly Heart burned. Her limp mouse of a husband, who could be a man only when cruel, had gall to be telling her how to behave. With a quick short motion she gestured defiance at him, placing her thumb between the first and second finger of the same hand and pushing it sharply at him.

Turning Horse saw the gesture and had to choke back laughter. He was enjoying the way Manly Heart was carrying on. She'd earned the right that day.

Red Daybreak heard the choked laughter and hid his face from the others. He went off by himself a ways to paint his face.

Manly Heart couldn't help but taunt him. "Be sure to use vermilion for the red calf."

Red Daybreak once more had to hide his face.

Finally they were all ready. Turning Horse mounted his horse, grabbing the lead rope to his packhorse. The other Soldier Society members followed him. In a moment they formed a parade line with Turning Horse in the lead. Manly Heart was given the right to ride third in line behind Raincrow for all the buffalo she had killed. Red Daybreak brought up the rear.

Slung chunks of raw meat gleamed on the packhorses. Blood dripped on the grass as they rocked along. The buffalo hides, neatly turned inside out, showed patches of purplish fleece fat.

The little children were given permission to run out and meet them. They came crying like happy yuwipi. They dipped like swallows around and through the parading hunters. From the face paint markings they could tell who the great hunters were. They cried out the names of Turning Horse and Raincrow. They cried out the name of Manly Heart.

"Oo-koo-hoo! The hump meat will taste very good."

Manly Heart rode smiling and looking straight ahead.

"Wana hiyelo! The blood! The blood!"

The women of the camp stood watching with a hand over the eyes. They smiled white at all the food. Not one had a dark look for the way Manly Heart was behaving. It was good in their eyes that she had helped to bring in the meat.

The people of the Blue Mounds sat up all night cooking and eating.

But Red Daybreak sat by his hearth, a downcast brave. He ate listlessly of the broiled flesh buffalo hump.

Manly Heart did not trust the limp manner. She knew he could be a beast. She suspected he was probably thinking of divorcing her. Should a man be unhappy with his wife, he could give her away at the next dance. Any woman given away to the young men at a dance had to give up her tepee and her possessions and go back to her mother. She knew Red Daybreak was capable of being very mean.

When they went to bed, Manly Heart gruffly ordered Red Daybreak to lie beside her in her sleeping robe.

Shocked, Red Daybreak gazed at her with ringed white eyes.

She asked, "After such a great killing, are you not like other men, wanting to take pleasure all night?"

He said nothing. Though he did slide into her sleeping robe beside her. He was afraid not to. He groaned with a kind of whimpering sound.

It was almost dark. She could just make out his abject eyes. "If you wish, you may pull at the wings of where I have been punctured by the gods."

He jerked away from her dumbfounded. He slid out of the sleeping robe and sat apart by himself. "Ae. But surely you would not ask me to do such a thing."

"I have been told it is a custom among the Mandan. The men delight in pleasing their wives and the women cry with joy when their wings are pulled."

He sat as stiff as a piece of red rock.

"I demand it of you."

"Now it is you who are being cruel. Suppose I told the men this at our next council meeting?"

"They would laugh you out through the horns of the camp."

"It is still a cruel thing."

"You have never given me pleasure. And now I demand it."

He sat like a red rock for a long moment.

She made a gesture with her right hand, raising her first and second fingers so that her nose slid between them. "Come, it will be very fragrant for you."

Finally, craven, like a beaten dog come to a bowl of food, he tugged at her wings a little.

She let him touch her twice, and then, in vast contempt, belched disgust and hurled him from her. "Get away. You are no good."

Fury flashed in his eyes for a second, and he showed his teeth. "But it was what you asked me to do?"

"You are no husband."

Several nights later, Raincrow, the brother of Red Daybreak, invited them over for a treat. Raincrow and his soft wife Wren had been awakened one morning to discover a young mud turtle trudging through their leather lodge. They considered it a gift from the gods in answer to a prayer. The evening before Raincrow had expressed the wish that, oh, wouldn't it be a fine thing if they could only have some turtle soup again.

With some reluctance, Manly Heart agreed to come.

As they sat around Raincrow's hearth, sipping noisily of the turtle soup, Red Daybreak after a while managed a sickly smile. The two brothers, though different from each other as flower from weed, loved each other. Red Daybreak had several times said that if his brother Raincrow should ever die in battle he would be from that moment on related to nobody, so much he depended on his brother.

When they'd finished the meal, the men relaxed against a lazy-back and the women sat at ease with both knees tucked to one side. Raincrow was a josher and he loved to tease his sister-in-law Manly Heart. He gave his wife Wren a hilarious and exaggerated account of how Manly Heart went at the killing of the buffalo. He said that, wherever Manly Heart rode with her horse White Hooves, blood spouted like cloudbursts upon the ground. Later, he said, when they went to butchering the fallen buffalo, she went at the cutting so savagely, slicing off a hump here and a quarter there, he was afraid she'd finally hack off one of her breasts.

Manly Heart roared with laughter. She thought Raincrow's raillery very funny. Back in her thoughts she had several times decided that Raincrow was perhaps a vigorous husband. His joking confirmed it.

Wren laughed heartily too, in a lesser way.

Red Daybreak looked upon his wife's hilarity with his brother with stoical indifference.

Raincrow ogled her with a wise eye. "My wife Wren boasts that you can make moccasins faster than any woman in our village, and set up tepees faster, and make clothes faster. Tell me, after seeing your bravery in our last hunt and your prowess with your bow, tell me, what is there you cannot do?"

Manly Heart turned serious. "There is one thing I cannot do."

Raincrow raised his brows questioningly. Raincrow had very dark skin. There were times when his cheeks had the color of an overripe gooseberry.

"I wish I might learn the song that men sing."

"Why should you want to sing in the manner of men?"

Manly Heart gave him an appealing look. "But some women do."

"Well,"Raincrow said, "I suppose that is true. My little wife Wren says there are times when she does."

Manly Heart scowled around at her husband Red Daybreak. "My husband is no good. And I live for nothing. I am not happy with my life and I have several times thought of throwing it away to the vultures."

Raincrow's face blackened over. He did not like to hear bad things about his brother. At the same time he did not like to hear either that his favorite sister-in-law was not happy. He raised himself from his lazyback and picked up a little twig and began to break it into tiny pieces. He threw the pieces one by one into the hearth fire. He pushed out his thick lower lip in torn thought. Finally he said, "You can already do so many things very well. Why must you have everything?"

"The next husband I marry," Manly Heart said stoutly, "shall be a real sport. One who has had an elk vision and so has gotten great power over women through his elk love medicine."

"Ha," Raincrow snorted. "Such a one you will not like either. He will be spending all his time combing his hair, and culling his lice, and perfuming himself, and will have little time for the hunt."

"Does my brother-in-law want me to marry one of those who puts on the dress of a woman and who does embroidery work?"

"Do not speak ill of my brother. We played together in my mother's sleeping robe."

"My new husband is no good. He cannot even peel a wild onion."

Raincrow at last leaped up enraged. He pulled off his leather shirt and dropped his breechclout. He stood totally naked before them. His phallus hung in a little curl. It smiled at them with the tiny smile of a baby mouse. He grabbed up his phallus and his testicles full in his hand and swore by them. "By the power of my seed I declare that my brother is a great man. Houw. You must be one of those women who have a namni with teeth in it, that he does not care to take pleasure with you." He gave his phallus and testicles a final shake. "I have said." With that he sat down.

Manly Heart was enraged in turn. She jumped to her feet too and pulled off her leather skirt. She stood completely naked before them. She grabbed herself under the thigh. "Your brother has nibbled me. Ask him if has found teeth in my wings."

Wren was so ashamed of all she saw and heard that she picked up a sleeping robe and buried herself in it.

Raincrow stood with his mouth open. He stared so hard his eyes appeared to retreat under his brows. Then he dropped to the ground and lay back on his backrest. He was suddenly exhausted. Manly Heart was too much for him.

Red Daybreak was so ashamed of his wife that he got to his feet and sought to cover her nakedness with her skirt. "Come. Let us go home."

"Why should we go home? What will we do when we get home?"

"Come. Let us return to our lodge. Put on your clothes."

Manly Heart pushed him away. "The only way you will get me to go home is to carry me. Naked as I am. I will not go otherwise."

Greatly embarrassed, while his beloved brother Raincrow sat by helplessly, Red Daybreak carried his naked wife home in a robe.

The moment the doorflap was closed, Manly Heart leaped out of his arms. She stood chubby and strong before her slender husband. She picked up a stick from the edge of the nearly dead fire in the hearth and broke it in half and threw the broken pieces at him. "Listen. I have had you for a husband long enough. Depart."

His mouth fell open.

She saw in his manner that he had been planning on divorce, too. She had beat him to it. He had verily been thinking of turning her over to the youth of the village but he hadn't quite had the courage to do it.

"Must I break another set of sticks at you before you will understand? Take your clothes and your weapons with you." She glared at the single eagle feather hanging sideways at the back of his head. "Perhaps it is time for you to catch another eagle at Eagle Rock up on the Blue Mounds. You need a fresh feather."

Broken, craven, he gathered up his possessions and left her. He went to his mother's tepee.

Manly Heart lived alone in her lodge for a time. She could do as she wished anytime she wished. She could go about clothed or go about naked without having to worry what anyone else might say.

◄ 4 ►

MANLY HEART

ONE EVENING AT SUNDOWN, AS SHE STROLLED ABOUT THE ENCAMP-
ment, she decided on impulse to drop in on her father's cousin,
an old woman known as Rattling Wings Woman. She lived with her
young son Sunny Day Walker. Sunny Day Walker was one of those
who, on a clear bright day, liked to look at his own shadow.

Rattling Wings Woman was glad to see her. She and her son had
dined but she offered to fix Manly Heart something special to eat
anyway, some fresh Yankton salt bread, or what was left of some
deer foetus soup. Rattling Wings Woman was known to make a
most delicious concoction out of a foetus boiled in its own bag of
waters. She said that Sunny Day Walker had brought down a doe
heavy with young in a clump of chokecherries near the Buffalo Rub
Rocks.

Manly Heart shook her head. She said she'd had her fill for that
day. She said she had just dropped by for a chat.

The tepee of Rattling Wings Woman was an old one. The whole upper half was darkly smoked over. There were several rents in the buffalo hide along the bottom. It was time her son went along on some of the buffalo hunts so that he might bring home a new set of buffalo hides for his mother to make into a new tepee. Even the clothes Rattling Wings Woman had on were in tatters. With her heavy jaw, on which grew some gray hairs, and her long sloping nose, and very wrinkled brow, she resembled a scarecrow. It was astonishing that she should have such a handsome son. What was even more unusual about mother and son was that she had had him without benefit of a husband. The event of his birth had been a scandal at the time and the band had seriously considered banning her. Chastity was a highly prized thing among the Yanktons. The council finally sent Person In The Moon to question her about it. Her reply astounded them. "Do you remember the night of the great windstorm a year ago now, during The Moon of Dark Cherries? My son was begot by a flash of lightning." The council could do nothing about it. Person In The Moon said her claim that her son was of virgin birth was entirely possible.

Sunny Day Walker was a slender fellow with long thumbs and thick lips. He fancied himself a woman chaser. Mothers in the camp hated him because in some instances they were not sure but what he hadn't picked the bloom off their daughters. He liked to catch the maidens along the paths to the two springs and lure them into the shadows under overhanging red rocks or under clumps of chokecherries.

Sunny Day Walker sat back at ease in the master's place opposite the door. His clothes and the lazyback under him were the only new things in the tepee. He smiled superiorly at Manly Heart and every now and then quite casually let his glance drift down to her bosom. There was a look about him that if someone were to cross him he could become a berserker. He lacked having been guided by a wise father.

Manly Heart asked bluntly, "Old mother, have you ever been sorry you did not marry?"

Rattling Wings Woman lifted her head. She looked down her huge nose at her. "Never. I've had my own way. And I've had a son."

"Well, old mother, as for me, with my second husband gone, my hearth is without talk or song."

Rattling Wings Woman pursed out her old cracked buckskin

lips. Her mouth resembled the blunt end of a chafed quirt. "Then marry again."

"I have been thinking that the next time I shall take a younger man. I've had one old man. I've had one of middle age. It's time I had one at the other end."

Rattling Wings Woman saw Manly Heart glancing at her son. She humphed up a sniff. "Perhaps at the next sundance, when all the sister bands of the Yankton Dakota come together, a marriage can be arranged for you." Rattling Wings Woman darted a blackish look at her son. "The eligible young men in this camp are mostly your kin, and marriage with them is forbidden. Ae, there is a poverty of males here for you."

"But what if I decide to be struck by lightning by one of them?" Manly Heart had often wondered why Rattling Wings Woman had kept the secret of who the father of her child really was. Perhaps it was Manly Heart's own father who had struck Rattling Wings Woman with a lightning. "Tell me, old mother, when your lightning struck, did you sing like a man?"

"I have my son."

Manly Heart nodded. The old woman had had her lightning and she'd had her son.

The moon had just come up. Looking up from where she lay on her sleeping robe, Manly Heart could see clearly where the tips of the lodgepoles stuck out through the smokehole. Sight of the soft moonlight on the smoked poles made her feel lonesome. She shivered. Life was done. There was nothing left to live for.

She rolled on her side to find sleep.

She had lain still for a little while, nuzzling her nose in the musty buffalo fur, when she was startled to hear a flute at her door. What? A young man come to court her? She sat up. Her breasts suddenly hurt her.

The quavering tones drifted in through the door like the sweet-smelling smoke of a sage fire. The tune spoke of love. The flutist said he was so lonesome that his heart was going to break if someone didn't soon come to assuage him in the night. "Listen," the quavering flute sang, "you there on your sleeping robe, I hear the beat of your heart very clearly. You are lonesome. Your hearth is without talk or song."

Manly Heart knew who it was. Sunny Day Walker. Lightning stood outside her door.

"Come," the flute cried, "the song of love, it is a good thing to have. The gods have given this to us and we are fools to deny it. Come. It is a sweet thing to be lost in song."

Trembling she got to her feet. The warm night air touched her like mink fur. She held her naked breasts in her hands as if aiming them. They ached all the way up into her head. She stepped to the door and poked her head out.

Sunny Day Walker stood in the moonlight. He was blowing on his flute, head tipped back, eyes closed, slender body swaying back and forth. He was handsome. He was handsome enough even to be forgiven it. "I have a swollen heart for you," he sang. "It rides about in my breast like a cattail. A cattail is a beautiful thing. When will you come with your clamshell and open my cattail to let the seed ride on the wind?"

Manly Heart shook. But she managed to speak matter-of-factly. "But we are kin and we cannot."

Sunny Day Walker lowered his willow flute. He smiled in the moonlight. For once he did not smile with a superior air. "We are related only from the waist up." He smiled beseechingly.

She smiled. What he'd just said was often laughed about around a hearth or at a social dance. "Perhaps what lies below your waist is an enemy of what lies below my waist."

"Does not the doe invite the arrow?" He opened his walking robe and sought to capture her in it where she stood in the entrance to her tepee.

She sidestepped him. She smiled in the moonlight. "You have your bow with you, I see."

"Will you help me nock the arrow?"

"Your bow will not break when it is fully drawn?"

"I will turn the bow in my hand."

"Ae. Then the arrow will soon be in flight."

He found her yielding and in a moment pushed his way into her tepee.

His song was soon sung.

Her song though was never quite sung. She couldn't find the right note to begin on.

He visited her a half-dozen times after that. When she discovered that even with young male flesh she still couldn't sing like a man, she became despondent. There had to be more than just the pleasure of listening to a young flute quavering in the night.

She was on the way to get water from the springs, when she saw an old swallow and a young swallow swooping through an opening in the trees. They were gobbling up the morning mosquitoes.

They swalved and dippled and rose. The sun shone a glossy blue over their wings. She stopped to watch them. It was most pleasurable.

A heavy yellowblack bumblebee droned past her. It looped heavily from one pink prairie rose to another. It poked around for honey and finding none buzzed on. It bumbled up finally in the path of the dippling swallows. The old swallow ignored it. But the young swallow, thinking sweet insect flesh, dove for it. Then, just as it was about to catch the bumblebee, the young swallow brought itself up short with a strong banking of wings, afraid of the bumbling stinger's yellow threat, and dipped off.

"Eii. It is a sign."

From that day on she refused to unfasten the leather thongs to her doorflap when Sunny Day Walker came calling with his quavering flute.

Rattling Wings Woman said to her one evening, sarcastically, "Ae, I see you have at last discovered that you are also related to my son from the waist down, ech?"

Manly Heart held up her hand in gentle remonstrance. "Peace, old mother, let not his heart become bad towards me."

Manly Heart did not feel dejected for very long. Her body kept waking up in the mornings full of energy. She did her tepee chores and felt better after them. Sometimes she heard a low whispering at the back of her head. The whispering said for her to eat well and to sleep well and to take courage.

Manly Heart attended most of the dances. She had little to say at them. She sat on a red rock behind the front row of spectators. As time went on, from what she'd gone through, what with two unnatural husbands and a young lover, she was more sure than ever that many women were being wronged in the camp.

Presently she started sitting in the front row with the resting dancers and making sarcastic remarks about who paired off with whom. While other women sat with lowered eyes, under skin capes, she took off her skin cape and looked around at everything and everybody as a man might.

No one appeared to object. They knew about her hard lot.

She became very bossy. She told the men what women they should dance with, and she urged the women to get up and pick out the man they wanted instead of waiting for the man to ask them.

She noticed that Seven Sticks, the most venerated chief of the camp, never danced. Seven Sticks was one of those who always built his hearth fire with no more than seven sticks of wood. He did this out of reverence for the seven directions. The name also went well with the knowledge that the Yanktons were one of the seven friendly Dakota tribes. Seven Sticks rarely spoke, preferring to keep the peace with a minimum show of personal force. Yet, when aroused at last, he could inspire as much awe as the young and powerful Turning Horse. Manly Heart thought it regrettable, even a dark shame, that Seven Sticks did not mingle with the people. Some maiden would think it a great day in her life if he would dance with her, if only for a few shuffling steps.

One night the camp drummers worked themselves into a great wild rout of thumping. The singers shrilled ecstatically, until it was feared the red rocks would shiver in pieces. The whole camp was beside itself. All flesh clattered like cottonwood leaves.

Yet there sat solemn old Seven Sticks, alone on a stone at the end of the dancing circle, almost asleep, as though there were no pretty maidens in the valley, let alone middle-aged women, who might like to become his second or third wife.

After a pause in the dancing, the drummers changed the tempo by starting up a popular grass dance. It was one where all the males, young as well as old, were expected to ask a woman to dance beside them in the soft grass.

Seven Sticks continued to doze on his easy stone.

Burning a little, Manly Heart got to her feet and walked over and stood in front of Seven Sticks. "Old father, are your knees broken that you do not favor a young woman by asking her to dance at your side?"

Seven Sticks started. For a second he resembled an old turkey gobbler disturbed on its roost in a tree. "Ech? What? Who is this?"

"Do you not dance?"

Seven Sticks righted himself. He composed his old wrinkled face until it smoothed over. His rheumy grayish eyes became piercing black eyes. "Woman, these bones of mine were dancing long before your father played the flute for your mother."

"Then why not dance? Come." She held out her hand.

Silence swept through the dancers who'd just begun a slow bird step, as well as through the spectators sitting on the ground. The singers almost stopped singing. The little children sitting up on the various ledges of the red rock wall clapped a hand to the mouth.

"Come." She lifted her forefinger and swept it in an easy motion to her face. She smiled.

"Ugh. Ech. Well." The old chief glared at her a moment longer with a haughty taciturn expression; then, breaking into a turtle smile, rose to his feet, took her hand, and led her out into the center of the circle.

They danced.

After a while his old joints loosened up and he began to dance like a young man again. She responded in kind. Soon they were swalving over the grass in graceful majestic birdlike dips. The red light from the four fires at the corners of the dancing area lighted their faces clearly. All could see that the two were at ease and happy together.

What before had been a rout of wild thumping became a riot of dipping and shrilling brown birds. The Yankton Dakota loved to dance.

Later, when other dances were called, Manly Heart assigned other young girls to dance with the old turtle Seven Sticks.

Manly Heart took a walk over to Eagle Rock one day. She strolled past Boiling Rock where Sunny Day Walker lay lolling on its smooth fleshen rock, past Solitary Mound where a gopher poked up its head, past Chokecherry Rocks where she helped herself to some puckerish cherries. She hardly knew why she took the walk. Her body had just got up of itself in her tepee and began walking.

She climbed Eagle Rock. It was about as big and as tall as a tepee. From it she could see everywhere, to all horizons. No wonder her uncle, her father's brother, Happy One, spoke of it as The Top Of The World. Happy One as a young man used to sit on Eagle Rock as a lookout.

She looked south to where The River Of The Red Rock angled northeast down a dim far valley. She looked east to where a line of hills resembled a vast forearm covered by a rash of mosquito bites. She looked north to where their encampment lay along Blue Mound Creek. She looked west to where the vague outlines of three successive heights-of-land could be made out. Truly it was The Top Of The World. An enemy could be seen a good half-day away.

The day became quite warm. After a while she felt sleepy and she stretched out on the cool rock. It was soothing to lie alone on the high red rock on the high place. Her thought became dream and soon she fell asleep.

A golden eagle looped down out of the sky from the white north.

It settled on the very point of the high red rock, only an arm's length away from where Manly Heart lay. It settled itself down with the composure of an old chief. The toes of its great claws made light ticking sounds on the hard glinting red rock. It shuffled its feathers into place until it had made a perfect shape.

Manly Heart was very afraid at first. Eagles were known to think of human eyes as a great delicacy. She was sure he had come to pluck out her eyes.

The eagle sat looking off into space.

Manly Heart waited. Her heart throbbed like a scared mouse.

The golden eagle yawned, wide, until his beak looked like a pair of scythes.

Manly Heart breathed lightly. Her nose held as still as a rabbit.

At last the eagle turned a coolly benign eye upon her. It winked at her solemnly. "I see you have come to my rock seeking a vision. Yet you wear the clothes of a woman."

Manly Heart trembled. What was coming?

"When you return to your tepee make yourself the clothes of a man and put them on."

"Why is this?"

"You are being given the vision of a man. You are in a vision at this very moment."

"I await what you have to say."

"After you have put on the clothes of a man, come back to this place. Hurry to do it. Do not wait. And then, once you have come back to this rock, continue on to the south and push your feet slowly through the deep grass until your toes strike a long row of stones."

"I have seen this row of stones many times. What is it?"

"It is a row made by The Old Ones a very long time ago. It was built by very wise men who wished to lay down for all time the true path to the east and the true path to the west. The sun rises and sets over this row of stones during a certain day in The Moon Of Sore Eyes."

"Then the row of stones is wakan."

The golden eagle glared down at her. The hint of yellow showed along the outer rim of his eye. The eagle did not like being interrupted. "Follow this row of stones in the grass to the east, all the way to where it ends. Follow it over and past the large rocks. When you come to the end of the row of stones, it will be given to you. You will find your helper."

"I shall find a helper even though I am a woman?"

Again the golden eagle glared down at her. "At times you sound as though you have only a handful of pebbles for brains."

"I await what you have to say."

"After you put on the clothes of a man, it will be given you. Also, after you return from having found your helper, walk as a man does, sleep as a man does in the man's place in the tepee, make yourself a bow and learn to shoot it like a man—"

"—But revered one, I already can shoot a bow like a—"

"Awwk!" the golden eagle belched. "Can you not make your tongue lie quiet in your mouth? And wait until this vision is finished?"

"Ae, revered one."

"Also, go about your village and look for a wife who can cook for you. She must also be able to make moccasins for you as well as hang your shield and bow in the honored place of the true warrior."

"I hear, revered one."

"It will be given to you to recognize her. Your helper will speak to you."

"But I have not fasted in the true manner of the young brave seeking his vision."

"Are you not unhappy in your village?"

Manly Heart fell silent.

"You do not need the fast. You have been proved and tested many times. Otherwise I would not have come to you. Accept the vision. Do not protest it. Did not your uncle Happy One call you his manly-hearted niece a long time ago?"

"Ae. I hear you."

"You will do all this?"

"Yes, strange father."

"Remember, the gods will be watching. They fret over the destiny of The People Of The Blue Mounds. Your people need a manly-hearted woman to save them. There is danger nearby."

"Yes, strange father."

The golden eagle nodded. The golden eagle ruffed its neck out and then shook its feathers. It got ready to fly off. Its great black wings slowly began to open.

"Strange father, I have yet a question to ask."

"What is it, my daughter?"

"You say I should now be the man of the lodge. Must I still go to the separation hut at the usual appointed times?"

"Awrrck!" The golden eagle becked its beak four times and abruptly dropped off the rock. It caught just enough air under its great wings to become airborne and then drawing up its black talons and dippling its white tail soared off into the east.

Manly Heart lay breathing very lightly for a long time.

At last the huge cold red rock under her shook a couple of times, so that she bounced. It caused her to bump her head, and she awoke.

She sat up. She looked around to all sides.

It was all different. Her nostrils felt big. Her eyes saw all things with great sharpness. She could see hogback ridges in the blue distance beyond those she was used to seeing. A new weather had widened in her head.

She stood erect on Eagle Rock and looked back to her camp. She saw the children playing mock war games in the grass below the springs. She saw the smoke-blackened smokeholes of all the tepees. She saw the cornplots down in the bottoms along The River Of The Red Rock. She thought she could even see the green leaves of the melons and the squash glinting in the sun like wet skinks.

She knew what she had to do. She ran down the long slope of the Blue Mounds toward her tepee. She avoided the people in the horns of the camp. She skirted past the council lodge in the center.

Once inside her tepee she tied down the thongs of her doorflap to make sure no one would interrupt her.

She dug out her first husband's clothes and spread them out on the floor. She removed her woman's dress. Once more, as she'd done for the buffalo hunt, she put on her old husband's clothes, new ones she'd made for him which he hadn't had a chance to wear, shirt, clout, leggings. His moccasins were a little too big for her and to make them fit she had to take in several stitches over the ankle. Done, she put away her old clothes.

She undid her hair and combed it out with a buffalo tongue. Then carefully, trying to recall how her first husband used to fix his hair, she worked up her hair into two fat braids. She wove bits of fur into them so that at the end the braids appeared to be covered with a coat of hair. The two braids hung down her back like a pair of sleeping weasels.

She ducked out of the camp, taking a secret route through a labyrinth of red rocks and deep slough grass. She still didn't have a helper and still didn't quite feel free to go about openly as a man.

When she got back to Eagle Rock again, she was surprised to find she wasn't a bit tired. It was being given her to be strong and tireless. The wise eagle had told her a true thing.

She pushed her feet through the grass until she came upon the row of stones in the grass, running from east to west. She followed them east. A summer sun warmed upon her. All of the stones, both little and big, were covered with an old lichen. She followed the row over a little drop-off, then to where it butted into a huge rock almost as large as Eagle Rock, picked it up on the other side where the row of stones appeared to be placed as though to form a wall. A few steps south of the line stood The Sundered Rocks, which, legend said, had been split by a bolt of black lightning. The Later People had tried to use the row of rocks to drive buffalo with, instead of respecting it as a sacred thing.

As she followed the row of rocks she kept a sharp lookout for sign of her helper. She was puzzled as to what it might be. Her eyes kept wanting to look ahead to the end of the row where the golden eagle said it would be given to her, but she knew too she had better wait until she got there.

There were blooming cactus everywhere, yellow cup flowers with strange blue pistils. She carefully padded around the patches of the prickly lobes. There appeared to be four kinds, one as small as the size of a baby finger, one the size of a fat plum, another the size of a human ear, and finally, largest of all, one the size of a buffalo liver. The larger cactus had prickles as big as awls.

A large puffball stuck out of the grass between two long rocks. It resembled exactly the swollen scrotum of a man.

She stopped. She listened. No voice came to her. She wried her head around to listen very carefully. Still no words came to her.

Sighing, she moved on. It was not being given her that the puffball was to be her helper. She was also relieved. Who would want a puffball for a helper? It would vanish in a day.

The row of rocks ended beside an oak and a huge boulder. The row began no particular place and it ended at no particular place. The buffalo drop was still a short stone's throw away.

Ahead through the trees on the cliff she could see sloping land far below. Where she stood truly was The Top Of The World.

Then, as she stood musing, and wondering, she spotted a grass lizard squirting ahead in a series of zigging and zagging dashes. She stared down at it. In a moment another grass lizard appeared from the same place, out from under the shadow under the last rock in the row. It followed the path of the first grass lizard exactly.

"Follow the lizards," a voice said to her. The voice was slightly above and behind her parted hair. "Quickly. Or you will lose them. They will lead you to your helper."

She ran after the two grass lizards. The second one followed the path of the first one exactly. She ran so fast she almost stepped on the nearest one. In a moment they were within a few feet of the lip of the steep cliff. For a second she was sure they were going to leap off the cliff and she would have to follow them.

But then, only the length of a footfall from the sharp red edge of the great cliff, the two lizards, one after the other, vanished into a slim red crack. For a second she thought their disappearance a ludicrous thing, even lewd, until she spotted something in a bare place on the red rock.

It was a large spearpoint. It was made in the ancient manner. It resembled a large willow leaf exactly.

The spearpoint spoke from where it lay on the pink rock. "I am the one you are looking for. I am your helper at last. Take me up. There is a little hole in my tail. String me to a leather thong and wear me between your breasts. With me hanging on your chest you will be a man. No longer will you need to fret that you are only a woman."

Trembling, hardly believing it, yet knowing it was a true thing, Manly Heart picked up the spearpoint. The spearpoint was a light brown flint, almost transparent, and when she held it up she could vaguely make out the sun through it.

The spearpoint spoke to her again. "It can be seen you are one of those manly-hearted women that are sometimes given to a band. Thus the name they know you by, Manly Heart, is a good name. But now, and listen carefully, now you shall also have a secret name, just as all true warriors have. Listen. Attend. Your secret name from this moment on shall be Point From The Clouds."

"Eii. Then you have fallen from the clouds?"

"Return to your lodge. Sit in your doorway and watch the maidens pass by. It will be told you which one shall be your wife."

"A wife? Shall I father a child?"

"Have you made the thong on which to string me?"

"Ae. I hasten to obey."

She started to run for the village.

Her helper spoke to her gently from where she held it in her hand. "Do not run. Walk. You are now a hunter and a man both. Walk with the bearing of a grave man. You have much to think upon and much to do."

She slowed down to a walk. She thought of her father and tried to step along exactly like him. She stiffened her hip muscles to cut down on the woman's swing in her buttocks.

She smiled a funny smile to one side. She wondered in what

manner it would be given her so that she could mount a woman.

"Listen," her helper said, "mark this. Do not sneer at what is being given you."

"Will I sing like a man?"

"Have courage."

She reentered her tepee. From her scrapbag she dug out a tough bit of buckskin. She cut off a slim strip around the edge of it until she had a fine leather thong. She strung the stone point on it and hung it around her neck. The stone point fell exactly between her breasts. She was surprised to find that it felt warm on her skin.

"I have found my home at last," her helper said. "I have waited many winters, beyond all counting, for this good place. Ae. Wear me always and it will be given you to be renowned in all future times. Even take me with you to the grave."

"I hear you. Wana hiyelo."

She sat in the entrance to her tepee, knees apart, boldly choosing not to sit in the ancient Sioux way with both legs tucked to one side. She watched the maidens go by.

It was water-getting time. As the village girls passed by, they smiled at her sitting in her doorway. They saw right away that she was sitting like a man. They did not appear to think it out of place for her. With a hand to their heads where they held their clay vessels in place, they swung gracefully along, their soft moccasins padding in the beaten grass.

Most of the girls who walked by were kin, and them she couldn't consider at all.

Presently five virgins came strolling up from below. They had been bathing in the lower pool. Their hair was wet and shone like black rubstones. Four of them had always been friends. The fifth one, Prettyhead, had only recently begun going around with the other four. Prettyhead walked a little behind the other four as if she still wasn't sure she belonged.

Prettyhead wasn't kin.

When Prettyhead was still a baby she had been found by a scout, lost and crying beside a rapids in The River Of The Red Rock. The scout had looked everywhere for her people. He thought perhaps she had fallen out of a cradleboard unbeknownst to the mother. He found it hard to believe that a mother would abandon a beautiful child. There was no sign of struggle about, no sign of any kind in the grass, neither human footprint nor the scuffling of horse hooves. It was mysterious.

It happened that a couple in the band had recently lost their firstborn child to a pestilence. They were still in mourning, and every night at sundown went out to the scaffold on which they'd placed their dead child and wailed their grief. It was decided at a council meeting that the gods had placed the lost baby in the path of the scout so that he might give it to the grieving parents to replace their dead child. The grieving mother, Clear Eyes, was overjoyed; and she went out and buried the bones of her dead child, and then came back to take over the orphan child. Her husband, Charms The Grizzly, smiled to see his wife happy again.

While yet a little girl, Prettyhead soon understood she was different from her playmates. She had lighter skin. There were whispers in camp that she was a half-breed, part white and part Indian. Half-breeds had no true people. Some of the little boys, for something to pick on because she was a stranger dropped in their midst, nicknamed her White Plum.

Prettyhead hated her lighter skin and each day sunned herself as much as she could to darken her skin to the proper hue.

Her skin paid no attention to all the sunning. It remained a light brown.

It was soon noted that none of the young braves cared to court her, even though despite the lighter skin she was considered by many to be quite pretty. When she was seventeen winters old she still had no suitor. Not a single man had brought a pony to the door of her parents to signify he wanted to marry her. They shied away from strange blood.

Her foster parents went about with heads bowed. They grieved. They considered leaving the band and throwing in their lot with their sister band The People Of Talking Water living to the north.

Manly Heart had heard all the gossip about Prettyhead. She understood why the girl felt offish. It was another instance of the sad life given to some women.

A voice spoke from between Manly Heart's breasts. "Listen, Point From The Clouds. Look Carefully. There she is. The girl last in line. The fifth one."

Manly Heart stiffened. Ae? What? Prettyhead was to be her wife? What was this?

"Do not sneer. I am your helper and I am telling you something. Prettyhead is a lovely girl. Also, she is very lonely. She too wishes she had a mate."

"But her poor grieving parents, they already are sad enough that she does not have an ordinary husband."

"Foolish one. You have been told you have a manly heart. You have conducted yourself in a brave manner as a hunter. You have been given a vision in a dream by the golden eagle. You have been given a helper. You wish to have the lightning? Then listen."

"She will run away in fright."

"Tonight when the sun sets, fetch up White Hooves from the lower meadow and tie him to a stake in front of the tepee of Charms The Grizzly and Clear Eyes. They know the horse. They will remember that it was the favorite war pony of your departed old husband He Is Empty."

"But—"

"Do it and then wait in your tepee. She will come."

Manly Heart could feel her helper tugging at her where it lay on her bosom. The tugging was very strong. Also her helper felt quite warm, having almost the heat of a live coal.

Manly Heart did as she was told to do. She got her favorite war pony White Hooves from the meadow and took it to the door of Charms The Grizzly and Clear Eyes. Then she retreated to her tepee.

Manly Heart waited. It got dark. The stars came out.

Prettyhead did not come.

Manly Heart heard her neighbors talking about her. They had seen her take her hunting pony to the lodge where Prettyhead lived. The women grumbled about it, but the men, especially the hunters, didn't think it out of the ordinary. They had been present when she'd driven White Hooves again and again into a herd of buffalo, dropping animal after animal with her daring markmanship.

Prettyhead did not come.

Manly Heart fell asleep to the sound of the night wind softly ruffling the smokeflap above her.

Manly Heart slept fitfully. She dreamt of crazy happenings. Once the point hanging between her breasts changed magically, before her very eyes, into the head of a stinging snake. Later in the night the stinging snake changed into the phallus of a stallion. Toward morning she was appalled to discover in dream that the vine of a squash had encircled her body, gripping her like a lariat, and that at its very growing end there hung a single pendulous fruit.

The camp crier calling out his morning cry at the four corners of the camp awakened her. "Listen!" Wide Mouth cried. "Attend! Already the meadowlark sings. It is time for the morning bath. It is time to air out the sleeping robes."

Manly Heart sat up with a start. She looked around.

Too bad. Prettyhead had decided not to come.

Narrowing her eyes, expecting the worst, Manly Heart leaned over to peer out underthrough the doorflap. She was sure that her offer to marry Prettyhead had been rejected and that she'd see that White Hooves had been brought back to her door.

Manly Heart didn't see any white hooves stomping in the grass outside.

Manly Heart bounded to her feet and unfastened the thongs to the door and peered outside. She looked down the curving circle to where Prettyhead lived with her parents. Ae. The horse boys were just then leading White Hooves away from the door of Prettyhead's parents to put it out to pasture.

"Eii. They have accepted me as their son-in-law."

Quickly, happily, Manly Heart grabbed up her clothes, as well as her walking cape, and ran down to her private place along Blue Mounds Creek where she liked to bathe. It was above the camp, a gravelly spot with ribs of fine pink mushy sand. She scrubbed herself with the pink sand until her dark brown body turned a warm rose brown.

Back in her tepee she put on her best man's clothes. She redid her fat braids and re-covered them with strips of weasel fur. She painted a red line back from each eye to give her face a more manly look. She was careful to hang her helper, the ancient spearpoint, between her breasts.

She thought the village unnaturally quiet as she strode stiff-hipped across to the tepee of Prettyhead's parents. But no one appeared to be looking her way. Those outside their tepees kept themselves busy with their own affairs.

She paused outside Prettyhead's tepee. She noted the decoration painted on the outside of the tepee. It depicted a warrior chasing a grizzly. She cocked her head to see if she could hear them stirring about inside. She couldn't. Finally, nervous, she coughed to let them know she had arrived.

After a decent interval, Charms The Grizzly stuck out his old gray head through the slanting doorflap. "Our daughter awaits you," he said mildly. He held the doorflap open. He was a slender man with sagging chest muscles.

Manly Heart paused. She almost clapped hand to mouth in surprise. The mother hadn't come to the door to greet her but the father. They were accepting her as a man. A mother-in-law always avoided looking at or talking with her daughter's husband. Only the father could talk to the son-in-law.

"Come." Charms The Grizzly made plenty of room for her to pass by.

Manly Heart ducked down and slipped inside.

Charms The Grizzly closed the door behind them.

It took several moments for Manly Heart's eyes to adjust to the dark. She saw with pleasure that Prettyhead and her mother kept a neat lodge. A little twig fire burned in the hearth. Clear Eyes, the mother, sat in the woman's place on the left, next to her leather storage bags. She sat with face averted as was the custom. She was a heavy woman with breasts like squash.

Charms The Grizzly gestured for Manly Heart to be seated in the visitor's seat and then went around behind her to his own place at the head of the hearth, facing the door to the east.

Manly Heart seated herself on a folded buffalo fur just inside the door. After a moment she looked over to where Prettyhead sat beside her mother.

Prettyhead had braided her hair in the manner of a married woman. The loose rust-splashed hair flowing over her shoulders was gone. At the same time, though, she still hadn't painted her forehead. Like her mother she sat with both legs tucked to one side.

Manly Heart could hardly believe her good fortune. Life in felicity with such a lovely person? She thrilled to the thought of new and strange adventures ahead.

Prettyhead flashed her a quick look, then bowed her head.

Charms The Grizzly picked up a gossip pipe from its little rest in front of the fire. He slowly filled it, lit it, and puffed on it. He passed it across the fire to Manly Heart for her to take a puff too.

The pulse in Manly Heart's throat pushed at the root of her tongue in strong even surges. She almost flushed. The old man was accepting her as a man with whom he might sit and pass the time of day. Manly Heart took a slow leisurely puff and then handed the gossip pipe back across the fire.

The old man took another puff. He brooded to himself some more; then at last spoke up. "We have had a good talk with our daughter Prettyhead. We have told her that soon she will be an old woman. We have told her that before that time comes she should get herself a husband and go live in her own lodge and raise some children. We have said that perhaps she can do what we did, accept an orphan from some other tribe."

Manly Heart nodded. "When I awakened this morning I looked

outside. I saw that my buffalo pony had not been returned to me. Yet when I looked in my sleeping robe there was no one."

Charms The Grizzly nodded and took another puff.

Manly Heart spoke boldly like a man. "When my bride did not come in the night after my pony was accepted, I wondered what was wrong. That is why I have come."

"Prettyhead will come tonight after it is dark. She has told us that she wishes to spend one more day with her foster parents."

Manly Heart suppressed a tremble. It was about to happen. Soon she would truly live as a man.

"Also our daughter wished to talk with her mother about what shall be eaten at your wedding feast."

Manly Heart suppressed another tremble. There would be guests at such a feast. Ae, truly, it was all coming about as her helper had told her.

"Further her mother still has some counsel to give her."

Manly Heart got to her feet. She spoke down to Prettyhead. "I await your coming." Then she left.

It was dark when Manly Heart at last heard light footsteps outside her tepee. She had left the thongs to her door unfastened. She waited. After a moment she heard someone slip inside her tepee. She sat up. "Who is there?"

The slender shadow in the doorway said nothing.

Manly Heart picked up several dry twigs and tossed them on the still hot ashes in the hearth. There was a sizzling and then four tiny little flames jumped up. The flames cast up a soft orange light.

A scared Prettyhead looked tremulously down at her. Prettyhead had finally painted her forehead and done it in the manner of the virgin bride.

"I see you have come," Manly Heart said gently. Manly Heart opened her sleeping robe. "My helper tells me it will be given to us what to do. I trust my helper."

Prettyhead darted a look at the opened robe, then looked around desperately at the rest of the tepee. "I see you do not have two sleeping robes." Her voice was so pinched in fear it squeaked.

"My love, marrieds always sleep together under one robe. It is the custom of our people."

Prettyhead hardened herself. "It is true I am married to you. But we shall raise orphans. How can we have children of our own?"

"I am as puzzled as you are as to how it shall be. But already my helper has shown me several miracles. Perhaps he will now show me another. I do not know."

"Oee."

A wild ruckling jumped about in Manly Heart's breast. Pretty-head was truly scared to death. At the same time Prettyhead was one of those who would be stubborn.

A whisper arose in Manly Heart's bosom. "Attend. It is a strange thing we are asking of Prettyhead. Let her become acquainted with us first. Be gentle with her. Abstain from affection at first. After a time she will make a fine wife."

Manly Heart's pulse steadied. She drew up her sleeping robe to make sure her naked body was covered. Manly Heart recalled how gentle her first husband, old He Is Empty, had been with her. At first he'd only asked her to serve as his sit-beside wife. It was two months before he ventured to mount her and make her his true wife. Even with her second husband, that brute Red Daybreak, there had been a slight delay before there'd been the taking of pleasure. Manly Heart smiled, trying to ease the feeling between herself and Prettyhead. "Well, as you are now my wife, you will have to make your own bed if you wish to sleep apart." Manly Heart pointed to her largest storage bag. "In there you will find another sleeping robe. It is a new one. I think you will find it has been freshly perfumed with the leaves of the sage."

Prettyhead stared down at her until her eyes glittered like a pair of shiny arrows. She shivered. She almost darted back outside. Then at last, sighing, Prettyhead went over and got out the extra sleeping robe. She spread it out in the guest's place on the other side of the hearth. Still darting occasional glances at Manly Heart, she slid into the sleeping robe. She undressed under the robe, slowly, and placed her garments neatly on the grass floor. Then, once again shivering, teeth chattering, she turned her back on Manly Heart. Stiffly she nuzzled her head in the fur robe. At last she lay still.

The dry twigs burnt out with a little whup of a sound. It became dark in the tepee.

Manly Heart said in the dark. "Sleep well, Prettyhead."

Prettyhead spoke sharply. "We will do as my foster parents did. We will find us some orphans and raise them."

"That had also been my thought, love."

"Oh."

"How else? Unless, as I have said, my helper shows us a special way."

Prettyhead breathed unsteadily for a while. Then, apparently satisfied with what she had heard, she stirred at ease in her sleeping robe and at last composed herself for sleep.

The next morning Prettyhead was the first up. She went out to take her morning bath. When she returned she quietly but swiftly awakened the little fire in the hearth and prepared the breakfast.

Manly Heart heard the soft swift rustling in the tepee. It pleased her immensely that for once she did not have to get up first. So that was what the men had. Well, they hardly deserved it. It was very sweet to lie a moment longer in a warm robe.

Presently Prettyhead was standing over her. "Have you not heard the camp crier calling the morning bath?"

Manly Heart rolled over and looked up at her mate. She smiled. She was careful to smile in a reassuring manner. There was still a chance Prettyhead might bolt. "No, I did not hear him. Thank you for telling me."

"The sun awaits you. It will be a good day."

Manly Heart waited until Prettyhead had turned around, then swung back the sleeping robe and got to her feet. She threw a walking cape over her nakedness and slipped outside. Others in the camp were also stumbling sleepily down to the stream to take their morning dip. Manly Heart took her time. She even let herself stumble on the red rock trail several times to show she was like any other sleepy husband in the morning.

The big family pot was a steaming over the fire when Manly Heart got back. Licking her lips in anticipation, she settled cross-legged in the husband's place.

Prettyhead filled a small bowl with buffalo meat soup and handed it across to Manly Heart. She also set out a clay platter of parched corn. There was a prim air about the way Prettyhead served her husband.

They sipped in silence together. Occasionally they gave each other a sidelong glance. They were careful not to meet eyes. Their chewing of the parched corn made a lot of noise.

Finished, Manly Heart yawned elaborately, lay back on her willow backrest, and rubbed her stomach in satisfaction.

About three weeks later, as they sat at supper together, still cautious with each other, they heard a cough at the door.

Manly Heart looked up. "We have company." She called out, "Enter, the thongs to the door hang free."

The village shaman, Person In The Moon, poked his old head through the door. "I have been sent by the Soldier Society."

"Sit in the favored place."

Person In The Moon continued standing. He'd become quite bent in the last years and the odd purple shadows under his eyes had turned a ragged black. As usual a fat yellow tear trembled in his lower eyelids. "The Soldier Society wishes to know something." He coughed delicately. He threw a glance in the direction of Prettyhead. "It is a private thing."

"As man and wife we have no secrets from each other."

"Well. It is not a good thing to question the kind of life a husband and wife have together. Yet it seems it must be done."

"The Soldier Society had a meeting and I was not told?"

"They met quite by accident in the lodge of our old chief Seven Sticks. Each soldier was asked to come by his own private helper."

"Ae, old Seven Sticks did not like it then that I made him dance with me."

"The Soldier Society says it must know something." Person In The Moon's wide lips curled back at the corners as if he were about to bite into something bitter.

"Speak. My ears wait."

Again old Person In The Moon coughed apologetically. "Are you not still one of those who every moon must retire to the separation hut?"

A pinched sound escaped from Prettyhead. "Oee." Then Prettyhead hid her face.

"It was seen that your wife went the required five days to the separation hut. That was expected of her." Person In The Moon shillied about on his old willow legs. He truly hated what he was doing. Yet it had to be done. "It was told us that six weeks before this, before you were married, you still were one of those who customarily repaired to the separation hut."

Manly Heart slowly clapped a hand to her mouth. It was true. She had skipped the last moon. What was this? The Soldier Society was right to wonder. It was the duty of the Soldier Society to keep order and proper decorum in the tribe.

Many Heart's helper spoke from her bosom. "Be not afraid. You have not broken the law. It was given to you to be a husband. Since when have husbands had to repair to the separation hut? Be of good cheer. Speak calmly. It will be given to you what to say."

Manly Heart looked the old shaman in the eye. "Old father, ask Turning Horse if I did not hunt with the best of his hunters."

"Turning Horse spoke of this."

"Old father, ask our old chief Seven Sticks if it is required of one that he go to the separation hut after he has been given a vision. Ask him also if such a person must go after he has been given a helper."

Person In The Moon held his head to one side. "You have had a vision?"

"An eagle came and spoke to me in a dream on Eagle Rock."

"You have a helper?"

"Even so, old father."

Person In The Moon looked down at the floor. He chewed on his old lips as though they were intractable buckskin.

Prettyhead continued to sit with her head bowed. Her light brown cheeks burned a deep purple. She resembled a nighthawk hen sitting on a hidden nest in the grass afraid of being stepped on.

Manly Heart smiled at Prettyhead. "Wife, from what you know of our life together as married, can it be said that I have invited the wrath of the thunderbird by ignoring the custom of the separation hut?"

Prettyhead sat very still.

"Wife?"

Prettyhead's eyes finally fluttered up. "You say you have a helper who tells you what you must do? I have not heard him speak to you."

For the first time Manly Heart became impatient with her. Manly Heart's lips curled at the corners. "A helper is not a true helper if everyone can hear what kind of advice he gives. In the presence of the enemy it would mean certain death."

"I am one of the enemy then?" Prettyhead asked.

"But," Manly Heart continued, daringly, "to prove to the unbeliever that warriors all have a secret helper, I now call on my helper to speak out so that our shaman as well as my wife may hear." Manly Heart was careful not to look down at the point hanging by a thong between her breasts lest Prettyhead as well as Person In The Moon would know where it lay hidden on her body. It was important only that they hear her helper, not see him.

But she must have blinked once in such a way that Prettyhead caught on where it lay hidden. "Is that why you have the strange vanity of wearing an arrow between your nipples?" Prettyhead pronounced the word nipples with some irony.

Manly Heart glared at her. What? So the good wife had a sharp tongue, did she? Manly Heart chose to ignore the question. "Listen. You shall hear."

The point between Manly Heart's nipples spoke up, loud enough for all three to hear. "What? Is there someone in this lodge who dares to question one of the revelations of Wakantanka?"

Person In The Moon's old eyebrows lifted at the corners.

Prettyhead clapped a hand to her mouth. Stunned, she bent down as though to weather out a storm.

The little stick fire in the hearth burned with soft tonguing sounds.

Manly Heart waited with a bold black look.

Person In The Moon at last nodded. He turned and with quiet hieratic dignity left the tepee.

Manly Heart had known all along that her helper would speak up for her when needed. But now that it actually had, she too sat a little shaken by the power of the world of helpers.

It amazed her that Person In The Moon had behaved as if it was an old thing for helpers to speak up in the presence of strangers.

Neither Person In The Moon nor the Soldier Society ever questioned her again about her not having to visit the separation hut.

For a miraculous fact, after her vision on Eagle Rock, she did not have to go to the separation hut. The gods had given her a manly heart.

Several weeks later, cowed, Prettyhead folded up her sleeping robe and put it away. She slipped quietly into bed beside Manly Heart.

Manly Heart smiled in the dark.

Manly Heart once again recalled her old first husband and his leisurely manners in bed. If he could wait she could wait. She would not rush Prettyhead.

At first Prettyhead slept with her back to Manly Heart. But after a further couple of weeks, when she realized Manly Heart meant her no harm and that Manly Heart truly loved her, she relaxed around her. And within two moons she began to cozy up to Manly Heart in the dark.

Manly Heart's helper, meanwhile, delayed in telling them the special way in which they might truly become husband and wife.

◄ 5 ►

FLAT WARCLUB

WIDE MOUTH THE CAMP CRIER CAME CALLING THROUGH THE four corners of the camp. He announced that all the braves who'd been selected for the war party, both those of the home camp as well as those of the sister camp, were invited to a feast in the council lodge.

Manly Heart got to her feet immediately, threw a walking cape over her shoulders, and stood ready to go.

Flat Warclub did not move. He lay smiling to himself. It was going to come to pass.

Manly Heart furrowed her brow at him. "Are you not coming?"

"Presently."

"You will miss the opening smoke?"

"I am waiting for my helper to tell me when to go. It is all in his hands now. It is fated."

Manly Heart nodded. She cast a soft look of love at Prettyhead and then left without further word.

Flat Warclub stretched out at his ease on the willow backrest.

Prettyhead sat as still as a red rock. She didn't once look up. It was only when the little fire died down and was in danger of going out that she at last stirred to throw on a handful of twigs.

Flat Warclub watched the little fire take hold again. He enjoyed the crackling sounds. Still smiling, he threw Prettyhead a searching look. He tried to catch her eye and get her to look at him.

Prettyhead stolidly ignored him.

"You are like the tall prairie rose," he said at last. "Very beautiful. And the smell of you brings back memory of The Moon Of First Eggs."

Prettyhead tittered scornfully and at last broke her silence. "I have heard of the tall prairie rose before. Ehee. It has a blossom that lasts but a single day."

"But, maiden, where would the world be without the prairie rose?"

"I think it a better thing to look for hips in the fall."

Flat Warclub smiled to himself. A wonderful pleasing thing was fated to happen very soon.

Prettyhead said, "By now the braves are surely busy with the feast. Can it be that you are not licking your lips?"

"I am not hungry. I will think of food when the right time comes."

"Braves who fight must eat."

"My helper will tell me when to go to the council lodge."

Prettyhead tossed her braid back over her shoulder. "Well, I am hungry nevertheless and I shall eat. May our guest forgive me."

"Fret not, maiden. Do as your heart tells you."

Prettyhead ate a chunk of boiled buffalo meat with a handful of parched corn. She smacked her lips quietly to herself so as not to offend Flat Warclub. She built up the fire twice while she ate.

At last Flat Warclub's helper was ready. It whispered, "Some children are playing nearby outside the tepee. Ask Prettyhead to call in the oldest boy."

Flat Warclub nodded. He turned to Prettyhead. "What is the name of the oldest boy playing outside your door?"

Prettyhead leaned over to look out through the doorflap. "Swift Afoot."

"Call him."

Prettyhead went outside and called up the boy. The two whis-

pered together for a moment outside the door, and then she reappeared with Swift Afoot beside her. "Here he is. He is a good boy."

Swift Afoot stared down at the stranger Flat Warclub. The boy
stood very stiff ready for what was coming.

Flat Warclub gave the boy a good smile. "Will you deliver a
message for me?"

"I am already hurrying. What is it?"

"Go to your old chief Seven Sticks and tell him to send the lance
bearers of the Soldier Society to the lodge of Manly Heart. Tell
him that when they arrive Flat Warclub will tell them what to do."

"I am already running," Swift Afoot cried and was off, ducking
out through the leather doorflap and darting across the commons.

Flat Warclub waited, smiling.

Prettyhead took a seat on the woman's side and waited too. The
usual troubled look on her face was replaced by a bewildered look.

Swift Afoot came running back out of breath. "Seven Sticks says
—he wonders why—you cannot come on your own two feet—and
tell him what it is you want."

Prettyhead tittered nervously from the woman's side.

Flat Warclub reached out a hand and placed it warmly on Swift
Afoot's knee. "Tell him that the message comes from my helper
and not from me."

"I am already there to tell him." Again, boyish and very serious,
Swift Afoot was off for the council lodge.

Prettyhead looked at Flat Warclub as if she thought him a visitor
from the other world.

Presently there was the sound of muscular men walking on
beaten grass. Four times the doorway darkened and four strong
braves stood staring down at Flat Warclub. They waited for him
to speak.

Flat Warclub looked across to Prettyhead. "Do you have there
in your parfleches a newly cured bull robe? One that has never
been used?"

Prettyhead thought a moment. "I will look." She got up and
rustled through various leather boxes. At last she hauled out a
splendid brown bull robe. It had the fine black ruffed neck of the
true buffalo bull. "I had forgotten this one. It is the one my husband Manly Heart brought down on a hunting party." Prettyhead
smiled up at one of the four lance bearers. "Turning Horse, you
remember the time, do you not?"

Turning Horse stared down at the robe. After a time he nodded.
"It is the very one."

Prettyhead handed it over to Flat Warclub. "May Manly Heart not be angry with me."

Flat Warclub leaned forward. He unfolded the robe and looked it over. "It is a good one. It will be strong enough." He smiled up at Turning Horse. "Open the robe on the floor of the tepee. Then I will tell you what my helper has said."

It was done. The robe was spread out neatly next to the hearth.

Flat Warclub made a little sideways motion with his hand. The gesture came easily to him, as though all his life he had been used to being waited on. "Pick me up and place me on the robe."

Turning Horse stared at the clamshell ornament in Flat Warclub's loose flowing hair. He said, lips thinning, "I see you have counted coup on the lowly clam."

Flat Warclub continued to smile. He knew something and thus could tolerate sarcasm. "We must all listen to what my helper has to say. Wana hiyelo." He cradled his flat warclub in his arms.

Turning Horse made a shrugging motion; then together all four men took hold of Flat Warclub, one at each limb, and lifted him onto the new bull robe. "We wait."

"Now carry me into the council lodge and place me before your chief."

Again, somewhat reluctantly, Turning Horse and the other three lance bearers picked up the robe at the corners and lifted him up between them. Prettyhead got to her feet and held the doorflap aside. The four men carried him outside.

Almost instantly little children came running to see a strange thing. A young man in apparent good health was being carried across to the council lodge. Something remarkable was afoot. The little children formed lines on both sides of the path to the council lodge. Women too appeared at the doors of their lodges to look at what was happening. They watched with quirked black eyes.

The boy Swift Afoot followed the procession. When they came near to the council lodge in the center of the camp, he ran ahead and held the door open.

The four lance bearers carried Flat Warclub into the dusky gloom inside. Grunting as they stepped around the hearth, they lowered Flat Warclub to the dirt floor in the center of the lodge. Then they returned to their places in the circle.

Flat Warclub cradled his warclub in his lap.

The feast was only half-finished. Warriors sat with a partly eaten piece of meat in their hands. Some chunks of hump meat and slabs of buffalo steak were sizzling on green sticks at the edge of the fire.

All the braves stared at the handsome young fellow suddenly set down in their midst. He surely was a bold one to ask for the privilege of being carried on a special robe into their meeting.

After a silence, Seven Sticks stirred in his seat of prominence. "Did you not hear Wide Mouth make the call to the feast?"

"My helper told me to wait until you were well into the meat."

"What is it that your helper tells you?"

"Finish the feast first and then my helper and I will tell you how to win the war."

Seven Sticks glanced at the still sizzling meat. "Will you not take at least a token bite?"

"I will accept a token bite though my helper is not hungry."

Manly Heart sat near the door. She stared at the new bull robe Flat Warclub sat on. She was angry to see it.

Seven Sticks mused his old wrinkled lips together. He shifted his ancient limbs about. Finally he nodded to himself. "Give our guest a goodly portion of the meat. He may be hungry later."

The meatkeeper arose from his seat and plucked up one of the broiling steaks. He placed it on a strip of leather and handed it to Flat Warclub.

Flat Warclub accepted the meat with a nod and set it to one side.

"Let us now finish the feast," Seven Sticks said.

All except Flat Warclub pitched in. There was the sound of chewing as well as the sound of a crackling fire. Juices flowed. Eyes softened. Soon there was talk again, and it became hearty. The feasting made every one feel they were having a great merry day together.

Flat Warclub sat smiling gently to himself.

After a time Manly Heart quit eating. Manly Heart couldn't keep her eye off the splendid bull robe Flat Warclub sat on. Her favorite robe was getting dirty on the grease-spotted floor.

Finally the last piece of meat was eaten and the warriors leaned back to give their stomachs room to work. A few had eaten so much their eyes glazed over.

Seven Sticks picked up the war pipe. He filled it in the ritual way and then lighted it with a coal from the hearth. He blew smoke in honor of the seven directions. It could be seen as he inhaled that the smoking of the pipe was for him a deep thing. He was a sincere and true smoker. He handed the pipe to Flat Warclub.

Flat Warclub accepted the pipe. He looked at the fire-darkened red bowl. He cleaned his lips with the back of his hand and took a puff. He exhaled toward the smokehole. Once more to his own astonishment a perfect smoke ring floated upward like a ghost hoop.

All the braves watched the smoke ring commingle with the other smoke rising from the hearth fire and then disappear. "Houw! Houw!"

Flat Warclub passed the pipe back to Seven Sticks.

Seven Sticks in turn sent it down the line to his left. The long pipe moved mouth by mouth to the last man by the door and then was returned and started anew with the man on the other side of the door.

When all had smoked, Seven Sticks set the pipe down on its little rest again. He sat a moment in thought. At last, stirring his old bones about a little and resettling his flat hams on the floor, he looked at Flat Warclub. "Has your helper told you why it is that you must do things in a singular manner?"

"What does my venerable friend mean?"

"Legbone has told us that even on the way out to our camp here, you left the party and climbed alone to the top of the ridge where there lies the stone effigy of a man chasing a buffalo. Legbone also tells us that you often dream alone by yourself out on the prairie. Is that true?"

"It is all true, my father."

"And now in this camp you continue to do things in a singular manner. When our camp crier called up the warriors you did not come to the war feast, but instead waited until we were almost finished."

"It is as I have said. My helper told me to wait."

"When I was a young man my father taught me that no man ought ever to try to do a single thing alone for its own sole sake, in play or in earnest, but always, in peace as in war, to go where the leader of the war party led me, to keep him always in sight, to take my motion from him in the least detail."

"Houw houw!" the braves in the circle all cried in unison.

Flat Warclub sat smiling. "My helper hears you, old father."

Seven Sticks pushed out his lips in thought. Deep wrinkles showed alongside his nose. "I was taught to halt or to advance, to drill or to rest, to bathe my limbs or comb my hair, to dine or to fast, to keep wakeful hours in the night as sentry or to be tireless as a runner, all at my leader's bidding. In the stricken field itself it was asked of me that I neither pursue nor retire without my leader's signal. This was done to teach my soul the habit of never thinking to do one single act apart from my fellows. This was done that I might make of my life here on these wide plains, to the uttermost, an unbroken circle, of circles within circles, of family, of band, of tribe, of nation. For the circle is wakan. That is why our tepees are built in a circle. That is why our encampments are always set in a circle. A wiser and better rule of life no man has ever discovered, nor ever will, nor a truer art of victory or of happiness."

"I hear you. My helper hears you."

"We have all been taught, even from the very cradleboard, to think first of our neighbor and last of our belly."

"We hear you."

"It is only when we go to seek our private vision of life that we are permitted to go alone to some solitary hilltop. The enemy respects the custom and he will not touch us. Just as we will not touch him when he seeks his vision. The seeking of the vision is sacred for all peoples everywhere."

"Houw!" all the warriors cried together.

"At all other times we hunger to take our true place in the circle."

"Yelo! Yelo!" the warriors cried together.

"My son," the old man continued, "reach into your heart and tear out, by the root, this thing that causes you to do things against the circle."

Silence.

All sat hunched over with legs crossed.

Flat Warclub continued to smile in the manner of a man who was dead sure that what he was doing was the wakan thing to do.

Bitten Nose could not resist it. He looked with vast sneering contempt at Flat Warclub's weapon where it lay in his lap. "If Flat Warclub is permitted to come with us against the Omaha, perhaps we can let him kill one of their little four-leggeds. If he can kill a beetle with his flat weapon he can kill a louse with it, ech?"

Red Ant also had a vast sneer for Flat Warclub. "Have you lost your feather?"

Flat Warclub smiled. He turned his head to one side. The clamshell in his hair gleamed, then glittered.

Seven Sticks waved the sneers aside. "And now you have asked us for the singular privilege of being carried on a bull robe into our midst. We have agreed to give you this privilege because you say your helper asks this of us. What does your helper want?"

"Grandfather, may I speak as my helper tells me?"

"Speak. We listen."

Flat Warclub got to his feet slowly. He stood in the middle of the beautiful bull robe. He shook his slender shoulders and brushed down his new buckskin shirt. He cradled his weapon in his left arm. He looked lovingly down at where the little black stone from the clouds lay hidden in a knot. He ran his thumb over the knot.

His helper awoke and whispered up at him. "Now is here. Speak. Wana hiyelo."

Flat Warclub lifted his hand. "Attend. It is true that I do not yet wear the tail feather of an eagle. When I went to seek my vision, it was not given me at that time to seek the enemy warrior. Instead I was told to look for the clam. As Legbone can attest, I found many clams and saved our village from hunger at a time when we were short of meat."

Legbone nodded, once, from his honored seat. His single eagle feather tipped around and back.

Flat Warclub said, "I was much distraught that I should only be a finder of clams, like some woman. I went to our medicine man to ask if perhaps I should not go to a high hill once more to seek a different vision. After much thought, he said it would be in vain. The gods had spoken and there was nothing he could do about it."

"Houw."

"Our village girls tittered at me. The boys I used to play with laughed at me in derision. They told me to put on a woman's dress and go hunt more clams. I was alone much of the time. It was no use. There were times when I thought I was related to no one. Only my mother loved me. But a young man cannot live with his mother forever. It was all dark."

Not a muscle twitched in the circle of men.

"Then one day, as I was walking alone, the thunderbirds sent me my helper."

"Eii."

"It is not for me to tell you the nature of my helper. No man reveals the nature of his helper, not even to his loving mother. And certainly never to his loving wife. I was very happy."

Seven Sticks paid him close attention.

"At first I was surprised at what my helper told me. I had hoped he would send me out to help the hunters right away. I had hoped he would send me out to help the raiders immediately. But he did not. My helper said to wait for the right time." Flat Warclub could feel his helper, the little black pitted stone, exuding warmth in its hiding place. "Then on the very morning when your runner Light-foot came to our village, my helper spoke to me and told me the time had come. He said that my father Driving Hawk, who now lives in The Other Life, needed me very much and that he had asked Wakantanka to send me on. My helper said that Wakantanka had promised him that I could come and that this should happen at the moment when I would give my people my most precious possession."

"Eii."

"It is fated, therefore, that I shall soon leave you. It is fated that I am not coming back from this war trail against the Omaha. I have been told by my helper to leave my body amongst the enemies. Wana hiyelo."

The faces of the warriors around the circle opened like sunflowers at dawn. Seven Sticks sat with his eyes especially wide open.

"My helper tells me it is time for me to throw my life away. He tells me that before I fall in death, I shall bring down seven of the enemy with this club." Flat Warclub suddenly leaped up and shouted a great warlike cry. He flourished his flat warclub about in such a manner that all the braves nearest him ducked back and gave way for fear of being hit. "Oh, I have heard the sneers and the scorns of my fellow warriors, yes. That a flat warclub is not much good for cracking enemy heads open. That it is only good for whacking beetles with. Even lice. But my helper tells me that for this one time, yes, it will serve as a mighty weapon, even as mighty as any of the best weapons ever known to man."

Red Ant's mouth dropped open.

Flat Warclub was surprised himself at his ferocity and eloquence. He had never even dreamt he could be a fiery orator. "You speak of me as behaving in a singular manner. Am I alone in this? Was it not strange that the people of the Blue Mounds should let me sit alone on my horse in their midst after we first arrived? Only the little children had time for me with their sweet innocent wonderment. Where was the famed good heart of the Dakota at that moment? Ee-ka. I wonder."

Seven Sticks pursed out his old lips until the inner pink showed. He said slowly, "But do you not know that the good of the whole is always more highly valued than the good of the single soul?"

"Listen. Attend. Know this. For this one time at least it is fated that the road taken by this single soul will be the salvation of the whole."

"We hear. We listen."

"And was it not strange that it was one of your strange braves who should be the only one to welcome this soul to a camp lodge?"

"Perhaps the gods arranged it thus."

Flat Warclub resisted the impulse to wrinkle his nose.

The braves waited.

"Ka-he kamon," Flat Warclub cried. "Therefore I have done this. I have come to this war council to tell you that I am willing to throw my life away against the Omaha."

Silence.

Flat Warclub looked carefully around at every face in the circle. Now was here. They had listened gravely.

Seven Sticks looked across to Legbone. He spoke reflectively, as well as in admiration, of all he had just heard. "It is not often that a young brave will offer to throw his life away against the enemy. I can remember but one such in all my winters. I was but a lad and my father came to the lodge to tell my mother of it. This brave also offered to throw his life away. It was because he had lost his wife and his only son in a flood. My father counseled him to wait a little on the pleasure of the gods, that perhaps the gods were only testing him, but that they would soon give him another wife and son, and he could live happily again. But the spirit of this brave had fallen into a deep sinkhole. He said, 'When I look forward I see nothing but blackness ahead. I am nothing.' Our medicine man also counseled him, saying, 'Do you not know that a circle is larger than a single brave?' For four days the brave sat in blackness, neither eating nor drinking. Nor did he sleep. On the fifth day he told the war council that he had decided to throw his life away on the next raid. Ae, well, it was done as he requested. He led the next war party and so eagerly did he try to throw his life away that he sent the enemy flying. And when he saw at last that he could not get killed, that he was going to live no matter what he did, he broke free from his melancholy, and returned to his band rejoicing. And it was given him to have a new wife, and with her a new son. It was a story well known to my old fathers."

Legbone nodded. His single feather nodded. "I heard my father tell of him. Was his name not Many Wounds?"

"The same. And he shall never be forgotten." Seven Sticks noticed that the fire in the hearth had about died out. He reached around and picked up a handful of sticks, selected seven of them, and set them up in the shape of a tepee in the warm ashes. Then, taking a deep breath, he blew on the ashes. In a moment the ashes turned pink; and then a yellow blue flame jumped out of them. "Ah."

All the dark eyes in the circle pricked out with points of yellow light.

Seven Sticks looked each man in the eye around the circle. "Eii, it is an honor that we should have once again such a man in our midst. Should Flat Warclub leave his body amongst the enemy, we shall be free of the Omaha who wish to rob us of our buffalo jump. Wana hiyelo. A great day has come." He turned soberly upon Flat Warclub. "Is there anything we can do to make your life happy before you die?"

Flat Warclub's helper spoke to him secretly from its hiding place. "Now is here. Ask for the favor we spoke of earlier. It will now be granted you. It is the wish of the gods that your seed shall be scattered over the prairies like the down of the thistle. Ask. I have said."

"Ech?" Seven Sticks queried.

Flat Warclub said, "When will the war party leave?"

"Four days from this night."

"Four days. Ae. Grant me then the favor of permitting me to talk to any woman in this band, young or old."

The braves stared at Flat Warclub. They sat checked as one man. Eii. What? When Yankton custom did not tolerate such a thing? When Yankton fathers and husbands were very strict and the Dakota woman were well known for their virtue? Talking to a woman meant taking his pleasure with her.

Bitten Nose was the most astonished. He was continually being taken aback by the surprisingly bold Flat Warclub.

Seven Sticks pushed out his tongue as though he had just bitten into a rotten plum. "Is not this again a singular thing to ask, my son?"

"My helper tells me what to do."

"Did you not have a good father to tell you what was expected of you?"

"My father died when I was only a little boy."

"And you had no good uncles after whom you might follow in the true path?"

"My mother was an only child."

"Well, but did your mother remarry so that you might have a father to tell you about the true path?"

"My mother had several new husbands. But each time they broke a stick at her, complaining that she had a vagina equipped with sharp teeth."

"Eii, one of those."

Flat Warclub looked down at his weapon. He sighed. "There was no one after whom I might shape my life."

Seven Sticks twirled his old tongue around in his sunken cheeks.

"Well. Again I am remembering that we once had amongst us such a man. He was known as Suckabone. He was a very brave warrior. He had a silly tongue when we smoked the war pipe. But out on the field, whether it was on the hunt or during raid, he was brave and cunning. And it was because of this bravery and cunning that we permitted him many liberties. When it was a time of peace, he was always talking with some girl or other, or with certain unhappy wives. One girl even took her life because Suckabone had talked with her and had fathered her baby. People sometimes spoke of him by his other name, The Man Who Talked With Girls And Made Them Mothers Against Their Will. Our whole village began to have a bad name because of him. Yet our old chiefs did nothing about him because he brought in the meat and stole many horses from the Pawnee. Someday though, the old chiefs said, the thunderbirds would either teach him to behave or take his life. They said we would all have to wait." Seven Sticks fell into a reflective silence.

"What happened, old father?"

"He was struck by lightning while spying on the Pawnee horse herds from a high hill."

Legbone meanwhile sat pondering to himself, slowly swelling up with dark thought.

Seven Sticks cleared his throat, harshly. "This thing you ask, it is a hard thing, my son."

"My helper knows this. Yet he asks it."

Manly Heart spoke from her seat at the end of the circle near the door. "Listen. Attend. You all know that Flat Warclub is my honored guest. Well, it is my wish that he be granted this request." It was apparent that Manly Heart had decided to overlook Flat Warclub's having used her best robe without her permission. "Since my honored guest is giving his body to the enemy and has only a short time to live, we truly cannot refuse him. What he asks is but a trifle compared to winning the war against the Omaha. So say I. Houw."

Silence.

Legbone sucked in a deep sigh; then let it out slowly. His swollen face settled back to normal. He shot a look at Flat Warclub. "Must you have this?"

Flat Warclub nodded. It was inevitable. "My helper speaks and I listen."

Seven Sticks then hardened into it. "It must be done. We cannot refuse a warrior's helper." He turned to his camp crier Wide

Mouth sitting across from Manly Heart near the door. "Go make the rounds and announce from the four corners of the camp what Flat Warclub is going to do. Announce that it is the wish of this Soldier Society as well as the wish of this war council that no father or no husband shall interfere with the young man's lovemaking. Tell them that Flat Warclub is going to throw his life away to help us save our buffalo jump and for this no gift can be great enough. Ka-he kamon. Therefore I have done this." Seven Sticks looked across to Turning Horse. "Let our lance bearers carry the young brave back to his tepee on the bull robe."

The four braves carried Flat Warclub back.

Wide Mouth went about announcing the favor that was to be given Flat Warclub.

It was also decided by Turning Horse and Legbone not to invite Manly Heart to join the war party. It was enough that they had one spirit-touched warrior with them.

That night there was a great feast and much dancing. It had been decreed by the gods. Yelo. In four days a war party would go against the enemy and they would win. They had a new champion who would lead them to victory.

FLAT WARCLUB

THE NEXT MORNING FLAT WARCLUB GOT UP EARLY TO TAKE HIS morning bath in the stream below the camp. He put on his best clothes. He painted himself, carefully tracing stripes over his face, black for death and pink for childbirth. The black death stripes drooped at the ends and the pink birth colors lifted at the ends. He fastened his clamshell in his hair. He also painted his horse Many Spots, placing a black dot in the center of each of its white spots. He fastened pink roses in its black mane and black tail. Then he jumped on his wonderful horse and rode around inside the circle of the camp, flat warclub in hand, singing his death song:

> *"Ho, a voice I send everywhere,*
> *   hear me, people of the land.*
> *Ho, a voice I send everywhere,*
> *   hear me, people of the world.*

> *Ho, four times the sun will sink*
> *before I go to die.*
> *Ho, I have said it. I will die.*
> *I will throw my life away.*
> *Pity me."*

The old women stood listening beside their drying racks. Some held their head sideways and smiled as they remembered an old lover. Some looked down and wept a little as they recalled a dead husband sweetheart. For once the little children did not tag after the parading young blood. Their fathers had mentioned Flat Warclub's name in a certain way that forbade roisterous play. Young wives and young girls stayed coyly inside their tepees.

The second time around the circle Flat Warclub sang another song:

> *"Yelo, here am I crying my life away,*
> *soon the long long sleep.*
> *Yelo, here all is dark,*
> *the light of my eyes is wiped out.*
> *Yelo, I am very alone,*
> *no father and no uncle to help me.*
> *Yelo, I must give my life back,*
> *I am finished using it.*
> *Pity me."*

Soon some of the less modest maidens appeared in the doorways of their tepees. They smiled admiringly at him. It could be seen in their shining black eyes that they thought him very handsome as he rode his wonderful horse Many Spots around in the camp.

Flat Warclub circled the inside of the camp a third time, singing a winsome lament:

> *"The people of the leather lodges*
> *advance*
> *on the people of the earthen lodges, kola.*

> *Seven shall fall by this club,*
> *advance,*
> *the remainder are already fleeing, kola.*

Listen, the white rising of the man,
> *attend,*
> *the yellow softening of the woman, kola.*

The maidens come to drink of my white blood,
> *advance,*
> *think of all the unborn yet to come, Kola."*

Manly Heart stood watching Flat Warclub from her doorway. Behind her stood Prettyhead. Manly Heart looked on with glittering black eyes. Prettyhead stared with shining eyes.

Flat Warclub paraded about a fourth and final round. His voice pealed over the smokeholes:

"Yewa yelo, I have sent the bird of warning,
> *telling them who move against the stream*
> *one comes who will throw his life away.*

Wa yelo, I have caused them great shock,
> *their horses run away from under them,*
> *one comes who is finished with his life.*

Yelo, here I am with my flat warclub
> *looking for an enemy to kill.*
> *Have you a soft spot for me?*

Ho, here I ride around on my wonderful horse.
> *I want to throw my life away.*
> *I long for the lightning death.*
> > *Pity me."*

Sighing, affecting the airs of the languishing lover, he dismounted and led his horse out to pasture. Then carrying his weapon in his right hand and with his helper directing him, he went down the path through the wild plum thickets to greet the girls as they came to get water from the stream.

He took up his first position beside the great pink Fleshen Rock, which the old chiefs said had once been used by a race of giant people. It was some twenty steps long, three steps wide, and was perfectly shaped, with such a sharp edge that none of the little children cared to sit on it.

He could hear the girls teasing each other back in the camp. They pushed and jostled each other to see who'd be the first to go down the path and dare the lover Flat Warclub to make his advances.

At last one of them, Goodlick, said she would go. Her mother had been scolding her because the water supply in their tepee was low.

Flat Warclub, seeing Goodlick come smiling toward him through the shadows, thought her beautiful.

Goodlick's long flowing hair was brown, not the usual black. Her skin had the bronze hue of the blossom of the finger cactus. Her merry eyes were like ripe cherries. She wore a dress decorated with the design of a large sunflower. She was eighteen winters old and should long ago have been married. But she liked many boys, not just one, and could not make up her mind which one she wanted. Three times her parents had accepted ponies from suitors, only to have Goodlick run away for a few months to a sister band living near Falling Water, and each time her parents had to return the ponies. She was one of those who smiled at almost any movement around her. She was known even to have smiled at the flourishing black tail of a horse. And she knew about the lightning.

Flat Warclub's heart began to beat like a bird's. The first time was about to come to pass. "Help me," he whispered desperately down at his helper, "what shall I do now? How shall it be done? How?"

"It will be given to you. Fear not. Advance."

Flat Warclub discovered too late that he'd left his flute back in Manly Heart's tepee. He had thought to play a sweet tune to the girls, and then, as they were fainting from the beauty of it, mount them.

"Tell her she is wearing a pretty dress," his helper told him. "Tell her that the sunflower on it is well quilled. She will like that."

Flat Warclub tried to wet his lips. But his tongue was too dry. He stammered, "Your flowers are pretty."

Goodlick tried to give him a cross look. She was carrying the waterpot on her head, holding it up with one hand. She glanced down at the quilled sunflower design on her dress. Then she gave up trying to look severe and smiled instead.

"I am sorry. Have I said something wrong?"

"What do you want? Can't you see I am in a hurry to get water for my mother?"

"Oh. Well, if your mother needs her water right away . . ." he said lamely. He stepped to one side. He brushed into a clump of chokecherries.

She laughed a merry laugh at him. "You are a strange one. Eii. It was announced by Wide Mouth that all the girls must let you talk to them, and yet here you step aside."

He flushed.

She studied him with smiling lips. "Can it be," she said, "that you have not talked much with the girls?"

He flushed some more.

"Ae," she cried, softly, "then you are one of those who is still innocent as a colt."

He looked down at his left hand where he should have been carrying a flute. He was an innocent all right. He hated to admit it.

"You have a strange warclub. Must you come armed with it to help you talk to the girls?"

Again he flushed. Finally he said, "Pity me."

Her face softened. Her merry smile became a woman's giving smile. She took the pot from her head and set it to one side of the path. "Poor boy. Here, come, this way. There is a place behind Flesher Rock where no one can see us. Come." She took him by the hand and led him through a screen of black raspberry bushes. Both had to skulk down to keep from getting scratched. They emerged into a small cozy glade. "Come." She led him to a spot of thick green grass under the long square edge of Flesher Rock. She drew him down with her.

He lay panting beside her as if he'd just finished a long hard run. Images of horses raced past the front of his eyes. He had trouble seeing. He lay as stiff as a board.

"Come," she said, and she lifted her hips and wriggled her doeskin dress up, exposing her thighs. She parted her legs and made little motions with her little mound of a belly for him to mount her.

His eyes rolled. The limbs of an ash tree overhead appeared to flourish about like nervous horsetails.

"Come," she said, and she took his flat warclub from him and set it to one side in the grass. "You have more than one weapon, do you not?"

He still couldn't get his limbs to move. "Oh," he cried, "I am as one dead. I know nothing."

She laughed indulgently. She pushed up his shirt and undid his clout and leggings. "Ae," she cried, upon seeing his manhood, "you have two flat warclubs. This second one has the head of a bullsnake. It becks its head about as though searching for a victim. By the gods, it will bring me the death."

He watched her as in a dream.

She tugged at him. "Advance. I am fleeing."

He stared at the patch of hair where her legs lay divided. It was shaped like a tepee. The wings of the door were open and awaited. It moved about as though a gentle wind were riding through it.

"Enter," his helper whispered to him from where it lay in the grass to one side, "the favored place for the guest awaits you."

Then he knew what was wanted and he mounted her.

It seemed but a moment and she began to gallop under him like a mad horse and she made strange bird cries in his ear; and then yet another moment and he began to gallop like Many Spots going hot after a cow until the rider should safely deliver the arrows to the heart. And when the arrows were loosed, he grunted a deep guttural rutting sound, and fainted dead away.

Presently she stirred under him. She touched her nose against his. "Now you know about the lightning. Did you like it?"

"Eii," he whispered softly. "I am as one dead. Yet I cannot wait to be alive again."

They lay languorous together for a time.

When they heard other girls giggling not too far away from Flesher Rock, they parted, and got to their feet. They smiled at each other in secret knowing.

Goodlick smoothed down her dress and flourished her hair about her neck. Then, ducking down, she crept back to the path. She picked up her waterpot and, laughing merrily, joined the girls as they strolled down to the stream.

Flat Warclub straightened out his buckskin clothes too. He picked up his flat warclub. He stared down at the little knothole near his thumb. "Now I know what it is I am being given. Now I shall want to die a little many times before I throw my life away. Ka-he kamon. Now I have done this."

He strolled down the beaten path to look for another place to waylay the girls. The path wound over a low tumble of small rocks and pierced through a thicket of tall wild roses. A small pink cliff projected over the wild roses. Two great cottonwoods towered over the lip of the cliff.

"Ae," he thought to himself, "it is a wonder no one ever noticed

it before. Up on the lip of that little cliff is an excellent place for
talking with girls."

He didn't have long to wait. A girl named Dress That Swishes
came wandering down the path alone. She had just finished doing
some household chores for her mother and was out enjoying the
flowers of the morning. She had a curious way of walking. Her hip
moved first and then her knee followed. It sometimes caused her
dress to thresh at the hem. It also gave her a stylish swing. Her
cheeks were fat and her eyes wide set. There was a look about her
as if she might have come from another nation.

Flat Warclub fawned his best at her. At last he knew what he
should have known long ago. "Where is your waterpot?"

"Eii!" Dress That Swishes jumped back, crying out in mock
fright. "Are you not that stranger who wants to talk to all the girls?
Would that I were now sitting in a separation hut."

Flat Warclub gave her a severe look. It was dangerous to mock
the gods, especially those gods who sent the woman to the separation hut. Being around a woman during those times could be
deadly. He flushed with some heat.

"Eee. Now he is angry."

Flat Warclub turned to go.

She was instantly contrite. She came up and placed her hand on
his elbow. She had a strong square hand and her grip was firm. "Do
not be angry with me. The girls of this band all consider it an honor
to talk with a brave who is going to throw his life away. Where shall
we talk?"

He melted. He smiled a little again. He threw up a look at the
lip of the pink cliff. "Can you climb? Here, I will help you."

She said stoutly, "Oh, I know my way up there. There are certain
toeholds that I've known about ever since I was a child. Come."
Smiling large lips, she started up ahead of him. "One must be
careful of the cactus. Especially the little round balls of them. As
well as the finger cactus."

He followed her footing exactly. The toeholds as well as the
handholds were shiny from much usage. It was an old ascent. It
could be seen that it had been used by The Old Ones in The Old
Time.

On top of the pink lip lay a fine carpet of buffalo grass about the
size of a tepee floor. It was yellow green in color and was as
comforting to the foot as the buffalo robe. A few cactuses of the
long spear kind grew out of the fissures. In another week the
cactuses would be blooming. Some of the Yankton people called

them the sundance cactus since they always bloomed during the sundance rites.

He knew now what to do. He smiled thickly upon her and pushed her down on the grass and helped her raise her dress. He undressed himself.

"You are blunt and flat," she cried, "and not conical like the other boys."

"You have been here before with some other boy?"

She clucked. "A girl does not admit such things."

"Well, I can smell the suds of the yucca root on you. Did you just have your morning bath?"

"Eii. A wild one. I can smell the pink down of the thistle on you."

"It has a will of its own."

A little breeze moved through the tops of the two tall cottonwoods above them. The leaves claddered as though they were a multitude of little leather bells. The shadowed air they cast upon the two lovers tasted as sweet as springwater.

A storm rose in his head. His whole spirit bent all in one direction. It made him press himself upon her.

She opened under him and received him.

Yet through it all she lay inert under him. She hardly sighed. From her he heard no bird cries.

He didn't faint like the first time either; only turned numb for a moment. The second time was not the same.

As he lay dimly in lassitude, listening to the leaves of the cottonwoods belling above him, enjoying the tingling in his toes, he came to know it was a rich thing to be a man.

He whispered to his helper, "Ae, had I known all this, perhaps I would not have agreed so quickly to throw my life away. Instruct me."

His helper lay in his weapon on the grass. It whispered just loud enough for him to hear. "Listen. The gods are giving you a few extra bones to suck to make up for throwing your life away. In ordinary life they would not have been given to you even scattered over many years. Thus be happy. All is well. You shall live a very juicy life in the next few days. It shall be given to you. Even now other girls stand along the path waiting for you to talk to them."

"But this last girl did not have the lightning."

"For some it is not easily come by."

Dress That Swishes under him gave him a push. She said with a wondering look up at him, "What is all this whispering I hear?"

"It is nothing," he said.

"Are you one of those crazy ones who talks to himself?" Dress That Swishes said under him, "Oee, get off." She gave him yet another push.

He resented the push. At the same time he discovered he desired her again. Looking past his curved nose, he cried, "What is this?" Every time his heart beat his new friend bobbed. "I thought we were to save a charge of seed for each girl."

"Get off!"

Suddenly, growling at her, as a dog might with a little bunny in its mouth, he grabbed her by the shoulders, and kept her legs apart with his knees, and began to talk with her again. "Waku welo," he whispered huskily, "I return."

"Eii," she cried. "I am doing more than my share."

"Yelo. It is. It is."

As he lay in swoon again, she took advantage of his momentary weakness, and gave him a very hard shove, and rolled him off her. "Now you have given me twins," she said sorrowfully. "When it is the Yankton custom to destroy one of the twins at birth. Oo-wei." Distressed with herself, she got up with a little groan. She straightened out her clothes, then turned her back on him and quickly descended the ladder of toeholds down the little pink cliff.

He lay in wondering thought about it all for a while.

There was a rustling in the cottonwood leaves above him that was louder than usual, and then suddenly a young maiden dropped out of the leaves upon him. She came down like a pouncing fox squirrel. Her name was Chattering Leaves. Chattering Leaves was always climbing the high places around, treetops, cliffs, even drying racks. When she was a little girl she liked to shin up her tall father's body and sit on his shoulders. Her playmates sometimes called her Snake because she could slim herself around an object like a grapevine.

"Eli," Flat Warclub cried in fright. "What is this?"

"I sat hidden in the leaves and saw you talking with Dress That Swishes. Twice it was. It is a wonderful thing that you did with her and I want it too." She hugged him.

"But," Flat Warclub cried, "I am now unable. As you can see it has fallen."

"Nevertheless, I want what she had, and I will have it." Chattering Leaves drew up her dress and vined herself on top of him.

"Tato keya! This is against the winds."

"Talk to me."

"Please. I thank the gods you are not a bullsnake."

"Talk."

"But is it not unbecoming for a Dakota maiden to be envious?"

But she took hold of what was left of him and somehow managed to place it where it was warm.

His helper encouraged him. "Fear not. These little deaths will only make you stronger for the great death to come when you destroy the Omaha. It will be given to you. The Dakotas are in need of children who can climb trees. Just as they need children who can throw their lives away when the proper time comes."

His nose became stuffy. Then his ears began to crack. And lo! and behold! it was given to him by the gods to talk to her.

Both cried out in surprise at about the same time.

After some moments, he smiled up at her. "Is it not a strange thing to see the stallion bearing up the mare?"

"The gods sometimes choose wondrous ways to work their will."

He smiled some more, and shook his head in pleasure. "Were you not taught to respect the privacy of lovers, that you crawled up into the tree to spy on me when I was talking with Dress That Swishes?"

Chattering Leaves got to her feet. She straightened her dress. Then, smiling over her shoulder at him, she climbed back up into her cottonwood loft.

Again for a while he lay in wondering thought about it all.

At last he fell into a sound sleep.

A bluejay cawed near him and awoke him. It stood on some rubble only a couple of steps away. It cocked its head at him. It waited a moment, and then, becking, hopped four times toward him, and cawed again.

He blinked. He looked up through the cottonwood leaves to see where the sun was. "Eii," he said in astonishment. "I have slept across the noon hour. The sun is almost halfway down. I do not have much time."

At the sound of his voice the bluejay flew off.

He picked up his flat warclub and clambered down the side of the pink cliff.

He hurried to the stream. He found a little pool with a dark bottom and looked at his reflection. His bobbed hair was in disarray. Sweat had made his paint run some.

He washed himself thoroughly. He got out his little kit pouch from where he kept it tucked inside his breechclout and repainted himself. He brushed out his hair.

Refreshed, he toed down the path looking for some more girls.

He felt light. He considered himself a bird. He was a love-struck thrush.

He walked all the way to the end of the path and found no girls. While he had napped on the high pink rock, the girls had finished getting up the water for the day.

As he sauntered back toward camp, sighing at the folly of his having fallen asleep when he had so little time left, he spotted, off to his left, movement on the slope of the slanting Blue Mounds plateau. He held a hand over his eyes. He made his eyes pierce the distance. In the late afternoon sunlight he at last made it out as a woman digging. The woman had a slender form. Ah. There was yet one girl left to talk with before the evening meal. The magic fourth.

He turned up a path that led to some worn stepping-stones across the flowing creek. He hurried up a little draw.

Silver sage waved underfoot. The daytime breeze had almost died down. There were stretches of yellow green buffalo grass everywhere. A patch of very bright yellow brown daisies shone like sunlight out of the ground. Pink wild roses, of the short kind, perfumed the soft moving air.

He came up out of the draw and looked ahead. It was a woman all right. She carried a parfleche in one hand and a digging stick in the other. She was slowly digging her way south toward the great cliff. She was looking for tipsinna. The Dakota turnip helped to give meat soup a pleasant edge.

He caught up with her at Boiling Rock. The sun struck the wakan rock in a slanting manner and brought out all its swirling colors, pink and orange and red and brown. Boiling Rock resembled a heap of frozen flames.

The woman heard his footfall and turned. "Ah," she cried, "it is the brave who has been granted the right to talk to any girl that catches his fancy." She was very pleased. She placed her digging stick and parfleche on the ground.

Flat Warclub was disappointed. The woman was slender, yes, but she was almost forty winters old. She was the wife of grumpy Heavy Cloud. Her name was Bad Moccasins, and she was as ugly as an old hammerhead mare. Her name had been given her because she couldn't sew. She handled an awl as if it were a tepee stake. A few coarse black hairs grew scraggly on her chin. Her nostrils flared out like a horse's after a hard gallop.

Flat Warclub stood numb.

Bad Moccasins laughed, her tongue coming out like a buffalo

cow's, broad, flat. "You wish to talk to me? Eii, it is a miracle. Truly. I did not expect you to talk with this old one. Especially not when there are so many pretty girls in camp." She began to rattle on and on. "My husband and I do not have any children. Did you know that? We tried many times. We painted our faces pink many times even. Still and all, Eii, the gods did not bless us." She smiled. Her lips opened wide enough to have swallowed a puppy all in one gulp.

Flat Warclub shuddered. Take pleasure with her? After having talked with Goodlick and Dress That Swishes and Chattering Leaves?

Bad Moccasins prattled on and on. "My husband and I tried adopting twice. But again the gods were against us. Both children died from the colic. A boy and a girl. The little girl was very beautiful and my husband and I thought she would make up for my ugly horseface. When an old woman raises a pretty child it helps make up for her ugliness. Ehh?"

Flat Warclub didn't have quite the heart to turn away from her. He felt sorry for her and thus could not be cruel to her.

His helper spoke up from under his thumb, whispering, "Stand quietly a moment. Do not run off. It will be given to you to help her and her husband."

Flat Warclub was astounded. What kind of advice was that? Had his helper gone over to the enemy?

"Nevertheless," his helper whispered further, "you were given something happy to do before you were to throw your life away. It is the wish of the Dakota gods that your seed shall live after you in all their generations. Ae, you shall be the father of many generations. Do as I say."

Bad Moccasins quirked her merry eyes at him. "What is all this whispering I hear?"

"Nothing."

"Well." Bad Moccasins settled herself coquettishly on the many-colored slab of rock. She patted a place beside her. "Come. It is pleasant to sit on Boiling Rock. I have taken many a nap on it in the sun. Come."

Somewhat stiffly he sat down beside her. He laid his weapon to one side. The gleaming rock was as smooth as well-licked ice. Despite its extreme hardness it was easy to recline on. It felt cool to the touch.

She picked up his hand and turned it over palm up. "Ah," she said, a happy catch in her voice, "what a slender thumb you have."

She took his long finger and bent it down toward the lower pad of the hand, then measured the distance from where it reached back to its tip. "Ah, you have a long hand." She laughed, almost coarsely. She lay back and, arching up her hips, pulled up her tattered leather dress above her breasts.

Flat Warclub stared. He was surprised. She might have the face of a horse, and her neck might be wrinkled with age, but her body was young. The skin was smooth and tight, the limbs slender and shapely, the breasts small and firm, and the belly as slim as that of a red ant.

"You will give me the fresh seed?" she asked, arching herself up off the glistening smooth rock several times and swaying her slim hips about seductively. Then, with a self-wise laugh, she flipped her leather dress even higher, covering her face. The act reminded him of the prairie hen throwing up her tail to make a flat place for the cock to stand on.

He readied himself, slowly.

"Come, hurry," she cried, muffled under the folds of her dress. "Hurry. I await you."

When he found he was ready, he talked with her.

After a time she wept like a horse and then bugled loudly in his ear.

He lay spent.

She moved slippery under him. It caused him to retreat a little. He could feel the sun striking him from the side. Soon his host Manly Heart would be having supper.

He made a move to get up.

Bad Moccasins wouldn't let him go. She clutched at him fiercely, hugging him to her breasts until he was almost smothered in her turned-up dress. Her dress had the odor of wild sage in it. It made her smell remarkably clean. She took liberties with him he had not believed possible. She rolled with him over and back and over on the bone-smooth Boiling Rock, until, finally, to his vast surprise, he was ready to talk with her again.

She bugled even louder the second time. It made his eardrums crack. It was the lightning all right.

After a while the smooth rock began to feel hard and uncomfortable to them both. Her spine ached and his elbows stung.

She got up and dropped her dress and smiled her thanks with wide horse lips, and went back to digging tipsinna.

He got up, greatly sobered, and headed directly for camp. At the first spring he washed his face of its markings.

As he entered the horns of the village, he saw that most of the people had eaten and had come outside to sit in the cool of the evening air. Some had formed impromptu circles. Fathers were smoking their gossip pipes and telling stories to their oldest sons about the old Dakota days. Fathers were entrusted with the histories of the tribe. Should any father wander off the true road of the past, an older man sat nearby to correct him. The little children, their bellies full of meat and roots, wilder than ever, skirled around and through the talking circles, playing their war games, the boys the fearsome attackers and the girls the shrieking victims.

Flat Warclub ducked into Manly Heart's tepee. He stood a moment to let his eyes adjust to the gloom. His flat warclub hung heavy in his hand.

After blinking his eyes several times, he made out two figures, Manly Heart in the place of the husband and Prettyhead in the place of the wife. There was a most pleasant smell of buffalo hump cooking on the little twig fire in the hearth.

Manly Heart gestured toward the guest lazyback. "Sit. We welcome your return to our hearth."

"Have you not eaten?" Flat Warclub asked. "You did not have to wait for me. I am sorry to be so late. There were just too many to talk with."

Manly Heart nodded. "You have been given a special mission to perform. We are grateful. Our home is your home. Your least hunger is our hunger. Therefore we waited with the supper."

Flat Warclub sank wearily into his lazyback. "And I in turn am properly grateful that you have waited." His belly fetched up a huge sigh. His eyes closed a moment. His hooked nose quivered. "Ahh, the meat and the soup smell good." With the side of his hand he made a sawing motion across his belly as though to cut himself in two. "I am hungry enough for seven nations."

Manly Heart looked across the fire at Prettyhead. "Well, wife?"

Prettyhead quickly undulated up off her robe and settled on her knees before the pot. She ladled out the food into three bowls and passed the bowls around.

Manly Heart and Flat Warclub ate with proper Dakota smacking sounds.

Prettyhead helped herself only after her husband and the guest were nearly finished eating. Then she chewed quietly to herself. She cast several wondering looks at Flat Warclub.

When they were finished, and after they had licked their fingers clean, Manly Heart gestured that both she and Flat Warclub should light up their after-supper pipe of tobacco.

Both smoked in leisurely fashion while Prettyhead put away the food and the bowls.

Flat Warclub was the first to tap out his little red pipe on a hearthstone. He sighed, and again lay back on his willow rest.

Manly Heart also emptied out her pipe on a hearthstone, rapping it smartly to get out a bit of stubborn dottle. "Well, kola, did you have a good day?" There was a tiny hint of sarcasm in Manly Heart's tone, but not enough for Flat Warclub to take offense at.

Flat Warclub became aware that Prettyhead would every now and then cast a sly wondering look at him. Flat Warclub was dead tired, but at the same time he felt good about sitting at the same fire with a beautiful woman. That she had lighter skin than usual made her quite appealing. Flat Warclub said, "I listen to my helper. I have to do what he says."

Manly Heart nodded. "Ae, we must always listen to our helper. It is something we have done in this lodge."

Prettyhead quirked a look at her husband. "We? Since when has it become a Dakota custom for the wife to have a helper?"

Manly Heart gave her an irritated look. "Are we not husband and wife and as one together?"

"But, my husband, it was you, not me, who had the vision." Prettyhead lowered her head. "I am only the humble wife who receives what her husband pleases to give her."

Flat Warclub caught the showing of teeth between husband and wife. He worried that they might break into a squabble. He wished husband and wife would go sit outside as the other couples in camp did. He wanted to go to bed. He deliberately heaved a vast sigh, then let his shoulders sag as though about to roll out of his backrest. His eyes were the most tired and they closed of themselves.

Manly Heart caught the hint. Manly Heart had also become a little disturbed about the wondering looks the good wife was giving their guest. Manly Heart jumped to her feet. "Wife? Come. We will go visit Shooter our neighbor two doors down the circle. Shooter tells great stories in the evening over his fire. He is my cousin and good to visit."

Prettyhead got meekly to her feet.

The door darkened twice as husband and wife left the tepee.

Flat Warclub removed his clothes and crept naked into the sleeping robe his host had provided for him. He nuzzled his ear and cheek into the fur. The old animal smell deep in the fur was comforting. His limbs ached sweetly. His spine ached. His new-found friend ached like a thumb used too often to pull the bowstring. There were also two places in the middle of his belly where empty aches turned like a pair of little whirlwinds.

"Wa yelo," he whispered to himself, "I have caused. Now let the sleep come."

There was a ruffling sound up in the smokehole where an evening breeze, rising, had begun to tug at the smokeflap. There was also another sound somewhere in the tepee, something like an insect sawing at leather. He was trying to figure out what kind of insect it might be that could make such a noise, a cricket, a woodroach, when a cloud of nothing rushed across the sky inside his head and in an instant he was engulfed in sleep.

A wisp of steam, wavering off the pot on the fire, drifted past Flat Warclub's nostrils. His eyelids popped open. Eii. The second day had arrived.

When he went to stir his limbs he discovered he was everywhere as taut as dried buckskin. There was also in the sleeping robe with him a little monster gorged with blood.

He groaned.

"Ah, our guest is awake," a voice said.

Flat Warclub raised his head. He saw Manly Heart sitting in her usual place and smiling at him. Manly Heart appeared to be in a good mood. Flat Warclub let his glance drift toward the steaming pot. Behind the pot sat Prettyhead, also smiling at him. Husband and wife appeared to be the best of friends again. "Waku welo," Flat Warclub said, "I return from a place where there were not even dreams, neither good nor bad. Taku sni. Nothing."

Prettyhead's smile opened even more. She was very beautiful in the morning. "Are you not hungry mornings?"

Flat Warclub stirred around stiffly. What was he to do, get up with his friend standing erect like a listening gopher? To do so before his host and the good wife would be a shame that would never be forgiven him even if he were to totally destroy all the Omaha. He wished Prettyhead had a pot of ice-cold water about. That would settle his friend in a hurry.

"Come. Get up. It is time to refresh oneself with good hump soup, my friend," Manly Heart smiled at him. "The sun is out. The meadowlarks sing from their hummocks on the other side of the stream. Today will be another good day to talk with the girls."

Flat Warclub groaned some more.

Manly Heart said teasingly, "Ho. If you are going to be like this on the day of the raid, stiff and full of groans, you will not kill the seven enemy braves you promised. Not even with a round war-club."

Flat Warclub decided the best thing to do was to slip on his breechcloth under the sleeping robe, as best he could, and hope they wouldn't notice anything wrong with his appearance.

At that point his helper whispered up from his weapon lying near to hand on the grass floor. "You have nothing to fear. Every-one knows that you must talk with girls for four days and everyone will be wondering anyway what it is that helps you talk so well. Stand up. Be not ashamed. All Dakota braves desire virtue but, because of what the gods have decreed, this is a special time. Also, perhaps this husband and the good wife will be polite and look the other way."

A self-wondering look spread in Flat Warclub's eyes. "I hear, my friend," he whispered back. He flipped back his sleeping robe and, with some soft pleasant crackings in his joints, stood up.

But Manly Heart and Prettyhead, not knowing of his troubles, didn't have a chance to be polite and look the other way. They saw him standing erect.

Prettyhead's mouth dropped open. Then very quickly, in red-dened modesty, she lowered her eyes.

Manly Heart stared. And stared.

Flat Warclub's helper whispered up at him some more. "It is good. It was the design of the gods that they saw what they saw. It will be revealed to you why they had to see. Now, clothe your-self."

Flat Warclub put on his clout and his shirt and his leggings and his moccasins. He discovered when he had finished that he could move about quite easily after all. He stretched himself several times, and feeling relaxed again, went down to the stream to bathe himself.

All three had their breakfast together. No one had a word to say.

Presently Flat Warclub, licking his fingers and his lips, went down to the stream to repaint his face and to comb and decorate his hair. He also redecorated his horse Many Spots much as he'd done the day before.

Flat warclub in hand, riding his wonderful spotted horse around inside the camp circle, he sang his death chants again. That second day his voice took on the gruff ruckling edge of a herd father.

"Ho, here I ride around on my wise little horse.
I want to throw my life away.

I long for the lightning death.
Pity me."

Finished singing, he took his horse to the meadows and released it with a loving pat on its rump.

He decided to take up his stance along a different water trail to catch a different set of girls. The best spring of all was some distance down the stream, on the south side, near a thicket of yellow plums. The old chiefs sometimes called for the better water on those mornings when they felt gimpy.

He jumped the stream under the first waterfall and strolled up a slight rise. He'd noticed the evening before, upon returning from his talk with Bad Moccasins, that a patch of wild tobacco grew in a little glade. Their tiny pink flowers had caught his eye, and he was curious to see what the leaves looked like. He strolled into the patch. The leaves were quite broad, larger than he'd ever seen. Ae, it was hardly a wonder the people of the Blue Mounds could boast of their tobacco. Such wide thick leaves made for a tasty aromatic smoke.

There was a whirr above him and then a loud whoop close to his ears. He ducked instinctively, fearful of being struck on the head. Wings beat air immediately in front of his eyes and then the thing swooped up and away. A marsh hawk.

"Eii," he cried low to himself. "The gods are trying to tell me something."

His helper spoke up from under his thumb. "Attend. It is nothing. It is not a message of any kind. You almost stepped on that marsh hawk's nest. You cannot blame her. She means to protect her young. They have just broken out of their eggs. Please step to one side. The mother will feel better."

"I hear," Flat Warclub said and quickly stepped out of the patch of wild tobacco.

The marsh hawk continued to circle above him, though no longer with its eye on him. "Eeeeck, eeeeck," it went, floating and dipping around in the sky, "eeeeck, eeeeck."

"Attend," his helper said from under his thumb, "in a moment you will see something. You will see that even among the predator wingeds there is family love."

Within moments a speck appeared in the sky ahead. It grew into a father marsh hawk. The father hawk circled several times above where the nest was secreted and called out stridently. "Aeck! Aeck!" He was carrying something.

The mother hawk cried back in joy. "Eeek! Eeek!" She swalved back and forth under him. "Ekk!"

"Aeck!" the father hawk responded and let fall a field mouse. The field mouse was still alive, and as it fell it clawed and scratched at the air and flipped its little length about, white belly showing, trying desperately to find footing. In a flash the mother hawk swooped under the father hawk and turned over on her side and caught the mouse. "Eek!" the mother hawk cried. Then the mother hawk swalved down to a certain place in the patch of wild tobacco. In a moment there was the sound of tiny rendings of flesh and the dying squeaks of the field mouse. Meanwhile the father hawk, hearing the welcome sound of his children feeding, circled ecstatically above their nest, several times rolling over on his back. "Aeck! Aeckk!" And then the father hawk was off for another mouse.

Flat Warclub spoke softly in recognition. "Ae, truly, even among the predator wingeds a family is a great thing to have."

"Attend now," his helper said. "Such a family you will never have. It has been decreed that you shall throw your life away. Therefore you have been given many girls to talk to before you die. This is done to assuage your loss. Also, the Dakotas have need for your singular seed. Now, go down to the better spring and talk to the girls. Go."

"Pity me," Flat Warclub sighed, then continued down the water trail toward the thicket of yellow plums.

The first girl to be sent by her old father to get the special spring water was Lastborn. She was the runt in her family but she was lovely. She barely came up to Flat Warclub's chest. She was well shaped in all her points and was known to run as swift as a dog. She had an open face with lively inquiring eyes. She was game for anything novel. When she spotted Flat Warclub waiting for her, she let out a delighted squeal, and without a hint of coquetry, let him lead her deep into the plum bushes, to a little plot of green grass the size of a buffalo robe. Her talking, however, was not like her running. She liked to linger along the way. She had a momentary tiny dream that perhaps, somehow, someday he would marry her.

The second girl for the day was known as Sulk. She talked out of a crouch, as though she had hidden something in her navel which she didn't want anybody to find, and with her chin tight down on her chest. She was difficult. But since it had been decreed, she submitted to him. Well, she exhausted him. He had to go sit by himself afterwards for a while. She made him pant.

He slept in the thicket of yellow plums all through the noon
hour.

The third girl he talked with was Long Tongue. She had gone
looking for him. She had guessed he'd be hungry from all his
labors and brought him cooked meat and some roots and seeds.
He was happy to see the food and invited her to come sit with him
on the grassy plot of grass the size of a buffalo robe. Her family
had said of her that she'd been born with an extra long tongue.
She'd always had trouble keeping it all in her mouth. Otherwise
she was lovely. In talking with her Flat Warclub had to avoid
looking at her mouth with its protruding tongue. It almost made
him unable.

Next he talked with a girl known as Molest. Her longer name was
Molest Me The White Men Have. She was crying bitterly to herself
as she came down the trail to get the special water. Her plaint was
short:

> *"My life was taken from me.*
> *The bearded white braves took my virtue.*
> *Struck by the white soldiers many times.*
> *Pity me.*
> *How shall I ever be able to brag*
> *That the great Flat Warclub talked to me?*
> *Pity me."*

Flat Warclub, while tired, felt sorry for her and called her over.
He had heard about her though until that moment he hadn't seen
her around camp. Molest had been captured by the Omaha who
in turn had traded her to the Kansa for a white stallion who in turn
had carried her with them on one of their visits to a village far to
the south on The Great Smoky Water. The village had a wall of
logs around it and it was filled with a strange people who had hair
all over their faces like wolves. These bearded braves had the usual
copper skin over the cheek and the brow, but when they undressed
they were all white. Their whiteness was like grass that had grown
under a log and had remained pale. These strange pale people
lacked the sun. Some of the bearded braves took Molest and
brought her into a great square lodge and removed her clothes.
When she struggled to retain her modesty, as well as her virtue,
they tied her to the four corners of what they called a bed. Then
they had knowledge of her. There were a dozen of them. And then
they untied her and threw her out of doors. Weeping, she skulked
around in the shadows of this strange village, and somehow

managed to climb the wall of logs despite their sharpened points, and then slipped away into the forest. It took her months to find her way back to her people on the Blue Mounds. On the way she caught mice and ate them. She dug roots and ate them. She ate willow bark and twig tips. Sometimes in the night she was heard to scream in her sleep.

Molest hadn't heard him call the first time and Flat Warclub had to raise his voice to get her attention. "Where are you going?"

She paused, and looked around guardedly. She was still afraid from that old time in the walled village. She was carrying a stick and held it up in front of her. Her eyes glittered back and forth in fear. Her eyes worked the shadows until she spotted him standing in the yellow plums. "Yes? What is it?"

"I heard your song."

"Oee." Her face opened with a little smile. "Are you not the great Flat Warclub?"

"Come. Do not be afraid. There is some grass here as soft as a buffalo robe."

She wanted to come yet was afraid. Her lips were crimpled along the edges like a fish's mouth.

He smiled kindly upon her. "Where are you going?"

"My mother has sent me to the cornplot to guard it against the crows." She shook her head sadly. "All I am good for is a scarecrow."

Flat Warclub found himself staring at her. So this was the poor maiden who had been raped by the savage whites.

"I have been tainted by the whites." Molest sighed a double sigh. "Forever."

"I have a helper and he tells me to talk to you. Come." He held out his hand to her. "It is cool here under the yellow plums."

"Truly?"

"Truly."

"Eii. Well, then it is fated. Then there is nothing I can do but come to you."

With his free hand he drew her close to him. He rubbed noses with her.

"Is this truly happening to me?"

"Does not your nose tell you it is?"

He drew her down on the grass. He set his weapon to one side. He talked to her. She was as the cowrie shell.

When they were breathing quietly again, she whispered, asking, "Did the savage whites ruin me?"

"The crows would never take you for a scarecrow."

She mused up at the twittering leaves of the yellow plums. "Perhaps now the braves of our band will consider me of some value as a woman. A great man has touched me and I have been made whole."

Flat Warclub thought of the terrible white that had touched her and wondered if perhaps it had not whited her spirit as he had seen in milkweed plants.

"I have the hope again," Molest said. Then she got up and went her way to the plot of corn.

He was tired from all his labors and loves. He lay back on the grass. He stretched his limbs several times. He mused up at the plum leaves above him. The green plums bounced up and down like little soundless bells.

A single prairie clover grew out of the grass beside him. Its pink conical flower head was speckled over with bits of gold and purple pollen. He rolled on his side and, reaching, picked the single flower head on its long stem. He twirled it between two fingers. Some of the gold and purple specks spun off and drifted across his face. They made him sneeze. He laid the flower head to one side.

He fell asleep for a second time that day.

When he awakened, the sun was more than halfway down the western sky. He sat up.

To his surprise where before he'd seen but a single clover growing there were seven clovers growing, all touched with gold and purple specks, all vividly conical.

"Aii," he cried. "I have done a bad thing. I have picked a thing that was wakan."

His helper spoke. "You did not do a bad thing. It was intended that you should pick the clover. The gods wished to show you that for your one death there shall be seven deaths. Pluck the seven and go home and put them in a medicine bundle. They must go with you when you fight the Omaha and it shall be given you. Now you will not have to purchase a sundance bundle from some old retired brave. You will have your own war medicine bundle."

Flat Warclub stared at the clovers awhile. At last he said, "Forgive me, but I must take all of you. My helper has told me to do this." He leaned forward and pulled up all seven clover stems by the roots. He fashioned them into a bunch with the first one he'd picked.

His helper continued. "Your host awaits you. Supper is ready."

Weapon in one hand and the eight clovers in the other, Flat

Warclub pushed his way out of the thicket of yellow plums and headed up the path for the camp circle.

Prettyhead had another savory meal ready for him, buffalo meat soup, a handful of sunflower seeds, and a couple dozen dried buffalo berries.

Again Flat Warclub went to bed early, while his host Manly Heart and wife Prettyhead went to visit some kin.

When he awoke in the morning he found Manly Heart looking intently at him from her sleeping robe. Apparently Manly Heart had been staring at him and thinking about him for some time.

Flat Warclub couldn't hold up to the look and rolled over the other way. He glanced sideways up at the smokehole. The sky outside had just begun to lighten up. Dawn was coming.

Manly Heart's intent look made Flat Warclub wonder what was wrong. The look was lowering, black-centered. Perhaps Manly Heart had heard something bad about him the night before. Or maybe Manly Heart hadn't liked it that he'd talked to the white-tainted Molest.

Then anger flashed in Flat Warclub. Who was this Manly Heart to stare at him like that? He rolled back on his right side and looked Manly Heart in the eye. Their stares met head-on. Each looked the other exactly in the center of the eye. Hard and black they stared and stared.

Flat Warclub thought: "Where is my helper? Let him tell me what to do next."

The light in the tepee slowly turned brown. The air resembled the exploded dust of a dried puffball.

Flat Warclub thought: "Helper? Where are you? Hurry, and help me in this staring contest with Manly Heart."

Manly Heart's black eyes slowly became blacker and blacker.

A rustling noise arose beside Manly Heart. Without moving his eyes, Flat Warclub could make out, in the margin of his sight, that Prettyhead was waking up. She stirred as though she were moving in water. She groaned deliciously to herself. She murmured several words. She moved and moaned sweetly some more. It appeared she was singing a little love song in her sleep. Then she singsonged aloud, quite clearly:

> "Ho Kuwelo,
>   He comes home howling.
>   When will the great man talk to me?"

Flat Warclub started. What? Had Prettyhead wanted him to take his pleasure with her? Out of good manners he had not entertained the thought. Yet he'd liked her the very first time he saw her, that time when she came up the water trail with four other maidens. She was the last girl in line and she hadn't quite smiled like the others. There'd been a troubled look about her and she'd kept herself apart. He remembered now that he had whispered to himself at the time that it was fated he would soon talk to her.

Still staring hardily back at Manly Heart, Flat Warclub became aware that Manly Heart could also see in the margin of her sight that Prettyhead was stirring in their sleeping robe. Without moving their eyes from each other, both were paying closer attention to what Prettyhead was up to than they were to their staring.

Flat Warclub thought: "Yes, and my helper will tell me how to get Prettyhead to smile like any other happy girl."

Suddenly Manly Heart sat up. She held the sleeping robe up over her bosom. "Well, I see you are too good for us."

Flat Warclub sat up in turn. What? That had not been his thought at all. He didn't know what to say. At the same time another thought came to him. Ae, Prettyhead was surely one of those who could use the seed too, seeing she was married to a manly-hearted woman.

Prettyhead popped up in bed beside Manly Heart. "Oee," she cried. "I see now that I have done some bad thing."

Manly Heart continued to glare malevolently at Flat Warclub. "So you are too good to lie and gossip a little in the morning before you get up, ech?"

"Wa yelo," Prettyhead wailed. "Yes, yes, I see that I have given my husband cause to have a bad heart against our guest." Prettyhead dropped back into their sleeping robe and slowly pulled the robe up over her head. She began to sing to herself in a low key under the robe as though to ward off punishment.

Flat Warclub's helper finally awoke. "Attend. Smile upon them. As well as weep a few tears because you know the future. It is fated that Prettyhead shall have a son by you. Talk to her."

Flat Warclub whispered, "But it is not mannerly—"

"It is fated. Do it."

Flat Warclub sighed. And sighed yet a second time. After a moment he bent a little smile upon Manly Heart. At the same time, on signal, his eyes began to weep copious tears. "I have just now been told by my helper that I must talk to your wife," he cried softly. "But listen. I had no thought of it until my helper spoke of it. I did not think it proper. Unless you as host offered it first. According to old Yankton custom there cannot be adultery. It is only after the husband decides to make a gift of his wife's favors that it becomes the right thing to do. I await your word. Though my helper has spoken."

Manly Heart stared a moment longer; trembled; finally said, as though listening to an inner voice of her own, "It is a good thing. My helper agrees. It is fated. Perhaps we shall now have children. Eii!" With that Manly Heart jumped up and covered her body with a fur walking cape. "I go now to take my morning bath. I am very filthy and it will take a good while to cleanse myself." Then with firm resolve, because it was fated, she added, "Take your pleasure as you wish. There is no need to hurry. We need the seed." With a short brusque motion she brushed out through the leather door-flap.

Flat Warclub sat in wondering silence. He rolled his eyes from side to side.

Prettyhead lay inert. She had fallen silent under the sleeping robe.

"Truly," Flat Warclub said, more to himself than to Prettyhead, "I did not know."

Prettyhead stirred. She rubbed her legs one over the other, very slowly, under the sleeping robe. Her face was hidden but it was evident that she was smiling to herself.

"Perhaps I am not ready to talk to you," Flat Warclub said across to the form under the buffalo robe. "I have not bathed and I have not painted my face for love and I have not yet ridden my wonderful spotted horse and sung my death song."

Silence.

Outside the camp crier awoke. Wide Mouth came trudging around the circle of the camp. "The sun is about to come up. It is a great day to be busy with the morning chores. Cleanse yourself. The Blue Mounds stream runs pure. The water is a piece of the sky. Attend. Attend."

Prettyhead flipped back her sleeping robe and, naked, sat up. Her breasts sloped into puppy noses. Her breasts were brown on the underside and a very light brown on the upper sides. She had a slender neck and slender shoulders and slender arms. "I think I should stir up the ashes. My husband will want meat and soup when she returns." But Prettyhead didn't move. After a moment she turned her head and smiled at Flat Warclub. Her face was a little swollen from sleep.

"I remember the first time I saw you," he said. "You were trudging behind your four friends when we rode into camp."

"And I remember you riding your spotted horse. There was a clamshell shining in your hair."

"I knew we would soon walk the same road."

"You were slow to take it." She smiled. Her lips drew back pink at the corners. She thickened with desire. She waited for him to talk. Slowly she became more and more swollen.

He said, "I had a good sleep."

"I heard you breathing hard in the night after all your labors," she teased.

"Well, it is being done because my helper told me it must be done."

"Why did your helper wait so long to speak to me?"

"I cannot say. Such things are for the gods. Such things are hidden from us."

"Are you afraid to talk to me?"

"What is this?" And he threw back his robe and on hands and knees went over to her.

"Aii," she cried. "What a strange weapon." Then she shivered. "My husband has nothing like that." She lay back and with a little squeak flipped the fur robe up over her head.

He laughed. He pulled the robe away from her little by little until he had bared all her body. She had skin the color of a well-tanned doeskin just barely smoked.

"I am afraid the bullsnake will eat up the mouse."

He slimmed himself beside her. He fondled her belly. He played with her breasts and made as though to make the puppy noses fight with each other. He pretended to growl for each of the puppies, giving each a slightly different voice. "See," he said, "they too wish to talk."

She shivered. She rolled back and forth under his hand in anticipation. Her little mound of a belly began to hop involuntarily. Something longed for was coming.

"You are like the prairie rose," he said. "The tall rose growing by the first water trail. The pink blossom is especially large and its scent makes me swoon."

She whimpered a little. She laughed a little. "You have spoken of the tall prairie before. What shall I do?" She shook her head to herself. "My lover compares me to the tall prairie rose. Aii. The day will come when I shall have withered in his hands and then he will leave me."

"The smell of you is like the time of The Moon Of First Eggs."

"That too you have spoken of before. What shall I do?"

"Let me talk to the tall prairie rose. In the fall you can gather the hips."

"Why is it," she said, "that the women of our band complain that, when their husbands wish to talk to them, their husbands talk suddenly and without notice? Even the dogs talk for a little while."

"This I do not know."

"Who are you that you are different and prefer to dally?"

"That is something for the gods to say."

"It is what every woman longs for from her husband. To tarry along the way and dally and fondle. All women love the touchings." She threw her arms around him and hugged him. She moaned. Ardently she rubbed noses with him. It gave her an inexpressible beauty. "Hiyu ye! Come here. Now I am ready for the assault."

He talked with her.

"Yelo!" she cried in his ear.

"Wana hiyelo!" he cried. "Now is here."

"It is." She shivered. She shuddered. She fainted dead away.

He noted how dead she lay under him. "What is this?" he whispered. He too lay almost dead upon her. "Have we both died?"

At last she stirred under him. "Where am I?"

"Ae, I too was lost for a little while."

"What happened to me?"

"You have been struck by the lightning that all lovers long for."

She lay still a little while, eyes closed, thinking out loud. "Yes. That is what it was. It has at last come to me. What I had before in girl play was only a little spark, of the kind that jumps between one's finger and a fur robe after one has rubbed it for a while."

Flat Warclub's eyes rolled in his head. He could not get a clear picture of what she meant by girl play. Yet whatever it was it had to be a good thing, otherwise the gods would not have permitted it.

Prettyhead let herself pour out flat to the ends of her body. "Ahh. Now I am fulfilled." She lolled a little under him. "I can feel you retreating."

Flat Warclub nuzzled his head against her head. He rubbed ears with her.

She turned her head and placed her lips against his ear. She whispered to him. "Now it can be told. That first day, when you began to talk with the other girls, I was crushed that you did not choose me for the first one."

"Well. Had I known of it I would have talked to you first. You were the first."

There was an impatient cough outside.

Prettyhead jerked tight under him. "It is my husband. She has been waiting for us to finish our talk." She pushed him away and quickly scampered to her feet and dressed herself.

Flat Warclub smiled at her concern. He himself did not worry. His helper had told him what to do and therefore it could not be wrong. Poor Prettyhead had no helper to tell her what was right or wrong. She was not connected with the gods and so would sometimes not know what was proper. He stretched himself indolently on the fur sleeping robe. Out of good manners he covered his belly and his thighs with the tip of the robe.

There was another cough outside and then the door flipped open and Manly Heart brushed inside. Her black eyes shot from Prettyhead to Flat Warclub and then back to Prettyhead.

Prettyhead busied herself at the hearth. With a little stick she stirred around in the blue ashes until she found a pink ember. She dropped a curl of dry grass on the pink ember and blew on it until little flames spurted up. Then she piled on slender twigs and after a moment built a little fire in the shape of a tepee. "Welcome, my husband," she said with downcast eyes. "In a moment I shall have the soup and meat ready for you to break the fast."

"Well." Manly Heart strode sturdily over to her place in front of the fire. "You better take the morning bath first. Have you forgotten?"

Prettyhead clapped hand to mouth. "I have forgotten, yes. Oee." Prettyhead grabbed up her walking cape and ducked out of the lodge. Not once had she looked at Manly Heart.

Flat Warclub reached out as far as the tip of the robe would allow and picked up his clout and drew it toward him. He slipped it on. "I too have forgotten about the morning bath." He stood up. He gathered up his toiletries and with a side smile at Manly Heart left for his favorite bathing place along the cool running stream.

◄ 7 ►

MANLY HEART

IT WAS MANLY HEART'S TURN TO FEEL CRUSHED. SHE'D HEARD Prettyhead speak of the lighting that all lovers long for. She had done wrong in marrying Prettyhead. Prettyhead deserved a man husband.

The odor of lovemaking lingered in the tepee. Semen had the fume of fresh corn pollen. Manly Heart remembered it from her first husband.

It made Manly Heart feel sad that Prettyhead hadn't been able to look her in the eye. She heaved a sigh, and let her shoulders slump down. She loved Prettyhead and wanted her to be happy. After Flat Warclub, eii, Prettyhead would never be the same wife again. It was too bad that Flat Warclub had promised to throw his life away against the Omaha. He would have made Prettyhead a fine husband.

Manly Heart slowly sat down beside the hearth. She picked up a little stick and dropped it in the little crackling fire. The little stick first turned black; after a moment spurted a long sliver of orange flame.

Manly Heart cried to herself. "Why wasn't I born a man? Why was I given these breasts? They are of as much use to me as empty cornhusks. Why was I given these wings? Only one man, an old man, enjoyed them. They are as useless to me now as an abandoned parfleche."

Manly Heart picked up another stick and dropped it in the fire. It too first turned black; then licked out a long thin flame.

The smell of cooking from other tepees drifted in through the door. Some of the children had already begun to play their endless game of hunting and war.

Manly Heart didn't know who she was the more jealous of, Flat Warclub for being able to enjoy Prettyhead, or Prettyhead for being able to enjoy Flat Warclub.

Manly Heart considered the idea of seducing Flat Warclub. It would be delicious to talk to this young man for once. Flat Warclub was very handsome. He had the springiness of the willow in him and the toughness of the oak. Yes, he was both supple and tough-fibered. He could give her a noble child, one who could become as brave a hero as her own noble brother Stalk.

The spearpoint hanging on its thong between her breasts spoke up. "It is foolish for you to think of mating with Flat Warclub. Have I not made you a husband?"

Manly Heart looked down past her nose into her bodice. She could just make out her helper. It moved like a trembling willow leaf. "I hear you. Yes, it is foolish. Forgive what was once a full woman's heart. I know I am now a manly-hearted one."

Her helper had more to say. "Do not disturb the two lovers in your tepee. It is our wish that they shall couple until the seed is firmly planted."

Manly Heart asked, "After he has taken his morning bath, will he not ride around on his spotted horse and sing his death songs and then go seek out more girls in our camp?"

"He will be given the desire to stay solely in your tepee until it is time for him to go against the Omaha and throw his life away."

Manly Heart was greatly startled. "How will he know this?"

"Even now his helper is telling him."

"Eii. I did not know that the helpers knew of each other."

"They have lives in the higher world, yes."

"They have kin?"

"Even so."

"Are they also born? Do they die?"

Her spearpoint spoke wearily. "Those are old questions asked as a child might ask them. We stand ready behind the sun at all times, and when a young man receives his vision on a high place we quickly enter his chosen fetish and become his guardian spirit. Even as we did at last with you. And we remain in his fetish until it is fated that he dies. After that we return to our old places behind the sun and wait for the next call to earth."

"Eii. It is all wakan." Manly Heart closed her eyes. "I bow my head. After I have broken the fast I will go and become a lookout on the Blue Mounds and keep my eyes open for drifting buffalo."

Prettyhead was the first to return from the morning bath. As she hurried to get the food ready, she never once glanced at Manly Heart.

Manly Heart watched her for a time. "What are you afraid of?"

Prettyhead jerked so that she almost tipped the soup she was stirring with a wooden ladle. "Nothing."

"Did you not hear that our old chief Seven Sticks requested it? Who are we to deny Flat Warclub? He has been given permission to talk to any maiden in our camp."

Prettyhead settled herself in the place of the wife. Gradually her face composed itself. It became a mask.

"It is a favor we are to allow him. Why do you act so skittish?"

Prettyhead fell perfectly still, thinking to herself. Her pulse beat regularly across her temple. Her pulse was like a line of angleworms undulating down the same path.

"Well, wife, there is news. My helper has told me that from this morning on, yes, ae, until the morning we leave for the Omaha two days hence, Flat Warclub will talk to no other maiden but you."

Prettyhead clapped a hand across her mouth. She rolled her eyes from side to side.

"It is decreed, wife."

"Will he know this?"

"His helper is telling him even now."

A tiny smile pulled at the corners of Prettyhead's mouth. She strove to hide it from Manly Heart. Quickly, with utmost delicate tact, she lowered her head. She did not like to hurt her husband.

Manly Heart continued. "I will now eat."

"The soup is ready, my husband."

"Afterwards I will go and become a camp lookout for the buffalo."

Prettyhead nodded, once.

Presently Flat Warclub returned from the bath. It had refreshed him. There wasn't a hint about him, neither in his eyes nor in his fingers, that he had been engaged in exhausting labors. He moved about with the springiness of the quick red fox. He sat himself easy before the fire, knees akimbo.

Prettyhead gave him a bowl of soup.

Flat Warclub looked at the bowl a moment, then said, looking Manly Heart in the eye, "Before I break the fast, it must be told that my helper has some news for you two."

Manly Heart returned the frank look heartbeat for heartbeat. "Speak. Our ears are yours. We attend."

"My helper spoke to me suddenly as I was bathing. I did not expect him to be awake so early."

"Ho ye ya. Send your voice."

Flat Warclub's black eyes continued to bore straight into Manly Heart's black eyes. "My helper says I have now scattered enough seed amongst the other Dakota maidens. My helper tells me that today and tomorrow I must talk to only one woman. The gods want to make sure that my host and the host's wife have at least one child. The gods say that the two of you will make fine parents. The band of the Blue Mounds needs a child raised by the two of you. Many strange things are going to happen in the tomorrows to come and against that time we must prepare ourselves with a generation that can meet any kind of friend or foe." Flat Warclub paused. For a fleeting moment the light in his black eyes dimmed over. "My helper spoke to me as if he had been talking with your helper. It was a strange thing."

Manly Heart nodded. "Yelo."

"There is then another world behind us."

"Ae, and it is also ahead of us."

"Ae."

Flat Warclub broke off looking at Manly Heart. "It was a strange thing. When my helper spoke to me this morning, he called me by my secret name. It was the second time that he had done this."

Manly Heart started. "Eii. Mine did not call me by my secret name this day. Had he done so it also would have been the second time."

"Well, perhaps your helper will call you by your secret name for a second time later."

"It is a strange thing." Manly Heart held up two fingers and spiraled them upward.

"These are great times. A wakan thing will shortly come to pass."

Manly Heart jumped to her feet. "Eat. Much lies yet ahead. I go to scout for buffalo." Manly Heart fixed Prettyhead with a piercing look. "Attend to the needs of our guest." Then Manly Heart pushed roughly out through the flaps of the tepee.

Manly Heart went to the tepee of Turning Horse to tell him she was willing to be one of the lookouts for the day. Turning Horse was the current master of the buffalo jump. He told her where to go. There was a rock shaped like a considerable lazyback on the farther edge of the Blue Mounds. She was to sit on it, if she wished, until she spotted buffalo drifting out of the northwest, and then she was to quickly signal to the next lookout over on The Row Of Stones that she'd seen game, and he in turn would signal Turning Horse back in camp.

Manly Heart left the horns of the camp briskly.

It was a good day to be alive while a son was being engendered in her wife's womb. Ka-he kamon.

About halfway across the flat top of the Blue Mounds, she couldn't resist a look back at the camp. She climbed a tumble of rocks for a better look. She had just barely got herself set steady on the slippery tip of the highest rock, when she spotted Flat Warclub. He had mounted his pretty horse Many Spots and was riding around inside the camp circle singing his death chants. Strain her ears as she might, she couldn't quite make out his voice.

Manly Heart watched him as he finished his fourth circuit of the camp circle and led his horse out to the pasture. Then seeing him return to her tepee, Manly Heart sturdily, with a small pinch of happiness for herself in the thought that their tepee would soon be blessed with a child, trudged across to her waiting place on Lazyback Rock.

Not a single buffalo appeared on the horizon all day. Nor did Manly Heart see a single deer or antelope. She spotted only one four legged, a long-eared jackrabbit. The rabbit was scooting in easy zigzags toward the place of the many buffalo rubstones to the west.

Twice Manly Heart gnawed on a short strip of dried beef. Twice she went down to a spring below for a refreshing drink of sweet soft water.

Resolutely she kept her thoughts fixed on that time when the raid on the Omaha would be over. It would be a darling thing to see Prettyhead's belly swelling with child.

In the evening she returned to camp. The people were all having supper. Smoke was also drifting out of her own tepee. Prettyhead was a good cook. Manly Heart looked forward to a pleasant time eating beside her pretty wife. She even found herself looking forward to talking with Flat Warclub. She and her wife had indeed been honored that the coming hero of their next war party should be their lodge guest.

Manly Heart darkened the door of her tepee and stepped inside. Her quick eyes took in the scene in one glance. "Waku welo. I return."

Prettyhead was sitting demurely in the wife's place, watching the soup simmering over the fire. Prettyhead gave her a shy cautious smile. "Supper is ready."

"Houw."

Flat Warclub sat in the place of the honored guest. Flat Warclub gave Manly Heart a confident smile. "The day has passed well."

"Eka. I wonder."

Prettyhead continued to give Manly Heart a shy cautious smile. "Will you not sit?" Prettyhead began to fill a bowl with soup. "I have savored the soup with your favorite prairie beans. The mice will be jealous."

Manly Heart settled herself in the husband's place. She crossed her legs. She looked into the little pink fire a moment. "I saw not one buffalo." Then she caught up both their looks with one glance. "Did you talk?"

Flat Warclub had a bold look for her. "Wa yelo. What your helper and my helper had to say was wakan, therefore we followed their instructions."

Manly Heart lifted a forefinger and bent it down in a bowing manner. "It is good. Let us sup together."

After supper all three went outside and sat on the grass to enjoy the evening air together. In the setting sun the pink rock walls threw out long purple shadows. The shiny leaves of the cottonwood trees clittered merrily above them. The soft wind moving up the draw from the southeast tasted of coming rain. Pinkbrown children played subdued in the long purple shadows.

People drifted by, visiting one another. They had smiles and nods and bits of gossip for the threesome. The camp was happy. In a few days a troublesome problem would be righted. They already knew who the hero would be and they were honoring him with their soft smiles and merry small talk.

When it became dark, the threesome reentered their lodge.

Prettyhead went to lie with her husband.

Flat Warclub slept in the guest sleeping robe.

The next morning all three took their morning bath. All three broke their fast together. All three had a merry countenance for each other. They were a happy family.

Finished eating, Manly Heart left to take up her position on Lazyback Rock, Flat Warclub painted his face and got up his horse, and Prettyhead cleaned up the breakfast bowls.

But Manly Heart didn't right away go to Lazyback Rock. She stopped beside Boiling Rock to reconsider. She had to know something. She wanted to see Flat Warclub talking to Prettyhead.

Her helper spoke up sharply from her bosom. "What is this? You were not instructed to watch them."

Manly Heart wept. "Oee, but I wish to know. It gnaws me in my belly not to know."

"Such things are not done. Do your work."

"I fear I am a woman after all." A quiver moved through her. "Ohh. I have a woman's curiosity. I wish to know all things and this thing I must see. Permit me."

Her helper spoke severely. "Get to your lookout."

"But it will drive me crazy not to know. Let me have but a tiny glimpse. It need not be longer than the blink of an owl's eye. But I must know."

Silence.

"My wife knows of the lightning and I do not. Must I go without? There has never yet been a father but what he did not experience the lightning at least once."

Her helper jiggled angrily. Its flaked edge cut her flesh a little. "Go!"

Manly Heart could not make herself go. She tried to make her feet make tracks but they would not. At last she threw herself on Boiling Rock and wept to herself. The smooth cool surface of the pink rock was of little comfort to her.

Silence.

A golden eagle flew by overhead, high, going toward the camp, crying, "Kee-ah. Kee-ah."

Manly Heart sat up. She looked back at the camp.

Flat Warclub had just finished his four circuits of the encampment and was putting his spotted horse out to pasture. He gave his horse a loving pat and then strolled toward Manly Heart's tepee to talk to Prettyhead.

With a hoarse wrenching cry, "Aa-ii," Manly Heart got up off Boiling Rock and headed back for camp.

As she entered the horns of the camp, she was astounded to see two young boys lying on their bellies behind her tepee, their heads poked in under the bottom edges of the slanting walls. When it became warm out Prettyhead sometimes rolled up the sides of the tepee a couple of inches to allow the breeze to drift through. Smothered laughter rippled down the length of the slender copper bodies of the boys. They were spying on the lovers.

Manly Heart clapped a hand to her mouth. She directed a thought at her helper. "See? It was a good thing I returned. The eagle flying north was right."

Silence.

Angry at the disdain her helper was showing her, and furious at the peeping boys, Manly Heart set her teeth, and grabbing first one boy and then the other by their feet, dragged them out from under the edge of the tepee and rolled them over on their backs in the grass.

The faces of the two boys stretched out like wet buckskin, from choked merriment to checked shock. The boys knew that Manly Heart, when aroused, was not one to trifle with.

Manly Heart leaned down at the two culprits. "Why are you not out herding the horses?"

The two lay utterly still. Even their shocked eyes remained fixed on her.

"Go! Or I shall call out our two Dance Whippers."

The boys still couldn't move.

"And you know what they will do if you do not have good manners." Manly Heart whispered harshly at them. "One edge of their whipstock is notched like the teeth of the carp and they will come and saw the back of your neck with it and hurt you very badly. Now go, or I shall call them." Manly Heart gave them a light kick on the soles of their feet.

The kick broke them out of their shock. The two boys scrambled to their feet and disappeared into the cattails on the other side of the Blue Mounds stream.

Manly Heart watched them go, a smile cracking her sober face. She sighed. Ae, yes, no matter how naughty those two boys had been, she still loved little boys. She wished she might have seven of them.

Manly Heart turned back to her tepee. She listened to see if the two lovers inside had heard her chastise the two peepers.

She heard whispering inside. She put her ear to the leather wall. She couldn't quite make out who was whispering or what was being said.

As she leaned forward, her helper touched her between her breasts. "Were you instructed to peep on your wife?"

"I am dying of curiosity and I wish to know."

"Go to your lookout on Lazyback Rock."

"I must know, my guardian spirit. Can you not understand that I have breasts and so am in part a woman? Ae, you lie between my breasts, thus you should know this."

Silence.

Manly Heart looked furtively around to all sides and then, seeing no one looking her way, got down on her stomach and, undulating with the stealth of a knowing grass snake, slipped her head in under the edge of her tepee.

The doorflap was tied shut from within. Soft thrush light came shedding down from the dark-edged smokehole. It took several moments for Manly Heart's eyes to adjust to the leather dusk.

The two lovers were so busy with their touchings, and they were so thick with love, they had not heard her. They were lying on Flat Warclub's sleeping robe. They were naked in play.

Manly Heart placed a hand over her mouth to keep from crying out. She knew all the places where a woman loved to have the touchings.

The slender god Manly Heart saw rearing up out of Flat Warclub's thighs astonished her once again. It was as handsome as a wise old brown bullsnake. It bobbed about as though looking for some opening through which it might seek the mouse. Flat Warclub was aptly named.

Manly Heart's belly muscles tightened against the ground. Hard. She hated him. She loved him. He would debauch her wife. He would give her a noble son.

In her mind Manly Heart cried out to her helper, "Why cannot I have a son from him myself? I have both the mama and the tamni for it."

Silence.

"I wish to have it."

Silence.

Hand over her mouth, Manly Heart watched them.

Prettyhead rippled her belly muscles several times. Prettyhead took hold of Flat Warclub and pulled at him. Prettyhead whispered, "When will the attack begin? I cannot wait any longer."

Flat Warclub pretended surprise. "What?" he whispered. "Plainly you can see he is not ready."

Prettyhead drew at him again, roughly. "Hiyu yeyo. Come forth and make the raid."

Flat Warclub smiled with his eyes almost closed. "Wait until he has put on the warpaint."

"Hurry!"

Flat Warclub pretended to give in. "Well, all right, then it shall be. Hiyu ye. Come here." Flat Warclub lifted himself supplely upon her and, thrusting, began to talk to her. He embraced Prettyhead as though he were a supplejack winding his way up a swamp willow.

Presently the swamp willow began to shake. A strong wind was trying to tear it out of the ground by its roots. Then lightning struck, and rain began to fall. There were two lightning strokes at almost the same time.

Hand still clapped tight over her mouth, and using the noise of the lightnings to cover the rustling sound of her retreat, Manly Heart withdrew her head from under the leather wall.

Manly Heart scuttled backwards across the grass until her heels banged against a slender ash tree. She sat up and leaned back against the ash. She panted. For a few moments her vision was ragged. Her chest pained her.

The heads of the two boys, who had earlier been peeping under the hide walls of her tepee, slowly rose out of the cattails. They stared at her, trying to understand what it was she had seen that they hadn't.

Manly Heart saw the two black heads in the waving brown cattails only dimly.

Manly Heart's lips shaped themselves to say something. But her throat made no sound.

The two dark heads stared at her strange behavior, and finally, not understanding it at all, slowly lowered themselves and disappeared into the cattails again.

The golden eagle reappeared out of the north, a high speck in the sky. Flying south across the encampment, it vanished beyond the rim of the Blue Mounds.

Manly Heart made up her mind. She composed her face. She got to her feet and went back to her tepee. She decided to stand guard for the two lovers inside. There'd be no more peepers. She stood with her back to the doorflap, arms folded, legs set firmly apart in the grass.

Several women from the neighboring tepees, working at the drying racks, cast oblique glances in her direction. They said nothing and went about their work.

Soon the little boy Swift Afoot was called from play in the meadows behind the camp and was sent into the lodge of Seven Sticks. Within moments Swift Afoot reemerged and ducked running toward the lodge of Turning Horse. Turning Horse after a moment sent him running to the lodges of the three other braves.

Manly Heart wondered what was happening.

The three braves appeared and strolled quietly across to the lodge of Turning Horse and stepped inside.

"Eii, what is this?" Manly Heart whispered to herself.

"Remain calm," her helper told her. "You should not be here. But now that you are here, calm, all is well."

"But Turning Horse and the three braves are the lance bearers of the Soldier Society."

"Be patient. You will soon know."

Turning Horse and the other three braves emerged from Turning Horse's lodge and in a dignified manner walked slowly toward Manly Heart. They halted in front of her. Turning Horse held his head sideways a little and asked, with some concern, "What is it? We see you standing guard at the door of your own lodge."

Manly Heart said steadily, "All is well."

"Is your guest happy?"

"He is well content."

"Then why are you not at the place of your lookout?"

"An eagle gave me a sign and thus I returned to camp."

"What did you find?"

"Some rascals were peeping at the lovers. I chased them off and now I stand guard."

Turning Horse lifted his brows. "Were the peepers not children?"

"They were young boys."

"You know that the Dakota are loath to chastise the little ones?"

"Who would know this better than I? I have sometimes wished I had seven sons."

"Otherwise all is well?"

Manly Heart stood her ground. "All is well."

Turning Horse smiled. "Seven Sticks was worried. We need our honored guest. He will defeat the Omaha for us. He must be made happy at all times. Seven Sticks sent us to ask. Ka-he-kamon.

Therefore I have done this. We do not mean to pry. What happens inside the tepee belongs to the people within."

"Tato heya. We do nothing against the winds."

Turning Horse nodded, and then without further words turned and walked back to his tepee. The other three lance bearers also returned to their lodges.

The sun moved up the sky.

Children played in the purple clover. The horse herd frolicked in the pastures across the stream. The arrowmaker up on the east rise continued to teach his pupils how to flake their arrows as well as to shape their lives. Four young men accompanied by an old drummer and a singer went to a grove of ash on the west rise to practice for the coming war dance.

The golden eagle appeared a third time, out of the south. It flew until it was directly overhead; then began to float around in slow ovals. Wings outspread, it looked down at Manly Heart.

Manly Heart stared up at the eagle. "What is it? What have I done?"

The golden eagle, ovaling slowly around, began to talk to itself in low musical tones. The talk was like the sweet evening code of the cock robin.

Manly Heart clapped a hand to her mouth. She shook her head from side to side. Her black eyes rolled around, first to the left, then to the right. "Can this be?"

All of a sudden, the golden eagle soared skyward in broad spirals as though mounting some steps up a steep rock. It went up, up, until it appeared to be no larger than a small marsh hawk. It poised a few moments in the air as though perched on a branch; then, abruptly closing its wings, it dropped headfirst like a falling star. It fell almost to where Manly Heart stood; then, at the last moment, it opened its wings and checked its fall. It swooped up in a loud curve. Shrieking once, fiercely, it began the whole maneuver all over again. It rose and fell and tumbled about, all the while talking to itself in low musical tones. It tumbled twelve times. Then it flew off to the north once more.

"This I have never seen before," Manly Heart whispered to herself. "It is a sign."

Someone brushed through the leather doorflap behind her. Manly Heart turned. It was Prettyhead.

"Oh," Prettyhead said, startled to see her. Prettyhead's eyes shone like polished buffalo rubstones. A sudden rush of blood darkened her face becomingly. "No buffalo up on the Blue Mounds today?"

"An eagle told me to stand guard here."

Prettyhead managed a smile, trying to hide what had happened to her. "Oh. Well. Then we did not know how safe we really were." A deeper flush spread over Prettyhead's face. Prettyhead held up a jug. "We are out of water."

"Are we?"

"Yes."

Manly Heart reflected to herself a moment. "Well. Would you do your husband a favor?"

"Speak. I hear you."

"Get the water at the best spring. The one near the thicket of yellow plums. My bones ache today."

Prettyhead nodded, once; and again managing to smile to make things easy between herself and her husband, departed for the good spring.

Manly Heart waited until Prettyhead was out of sight, then ducked into her lodge.

Manly Heart could just make out in the gloom that Flat Warclub was drifting off to sleep. He was lying upon his sleeping robe. His naked limbs were thrown out with the abandon of spent love.

Manly Heart undressed herself quietly and lay herself down beside Flat Warclub. She nuzzled her head in the fur of the sleeping robe. It was a good feeling to be lying next to a man again.

Manly Heart ran her hands up and down her sides. She noticed she had begun to put on a little weight. It was as though a fillet of snake had been slipped around her middle under the skin.

Manly Heart nuzzled her head some more, hoping the noise of it would awaken Flat Warclub.

Flat Warclub sighed several times in his sleep. He was tired.

Manly Heart looked at his manhood. The phallus had fallen. The whole of it reminded her of several mice sleeping together in a nest.

Manly Heart glanced at her own thighs. Her triangle of hair lay blue in the soft light shedding down from the smokehole.

Flat Warclub's face turned toward her in sleep. He sighed.

Manly Heart studied his curving lips and his hawk nose. Slowly she felt herself warming toward him.

Presently Flat Warclub's eyes appeared to open of themselves. When his eyes finally made out who it was, he asked weakly, "Am I in a dream that I see the husband of Prettyhead lying beside me?"

"Husband? Well, an eagle has told me I am also a woman. This you know as it was already told you."

Flat Warclub sat up on an elbow. "What do you want?"

"I too wish to have a son."

"Eii! A husband to give birth to a child at the same time that the wife does?"

Manly Heart smiled. She hoped she was smiling a woman's soft smile. She had smiled as a husband for so long she wasn't sure she could smile as a woman anymore. "Look at me." She waved a hand along the length of her firm body. "I have the mama. I have the tamni. As you can see it has been given me to calve just like any other woman. Even as Prettyhead. Thus I too want your seed. The Dakotas need your seed for a future time."

"Eka. I wonder."

Manly Heart bounced herself on the sleeping robe in a suggestive manner. "Come. I await the seed."

Flat Warclub sat up straight. He stared at her in amazement. "What! Can you not see that I am tired? I need a nap."

"Nevertheless, I want the seed. Also, I want the lightning. The lightning I have never had."

"Ah. Another one of those." Flat Warclub shook his head. "There are a number of you then."

"There are others?" Manly Heart was greedy to know. "Who?"

Flat Warclub let his eyes close tiredly. "It is not for me to say, even though you are my host."

"Nevertheless I desire the lightning. Perhaps then I shall have a son at last. From neither He Is Empty nor from Red Daybreak could I have a child."

Flat Warclub rolled up his eyes at the smokehole. "Woman, let me have my sleep. I need a short rest."

"What? Is the great lover who desired to talk to all the girls of the Blue Mounds band too tired to finish his mission? What will the gods say?"

With an exaggerated sigh, Flat Warclub let himself flop back onto the sleeping robe. "I need the nap."

Manly Heart asked cunningly, "What does your helper say?"

"Even my helper says I am too tired to talk at this moment."

"I did not see you converse with him. Is he near? Did he call you by your secret name a third time? I did not hear him."

Flat Warclub, thoroughly awake at last, became wary. "I wish to sleep."

Manly Heart thrashed around exasperated. Soon Prettyhead

would be back with the water. At last Manly Heart took hold of him and gave him a pull. "Wake up, sleepyhead. Give me the seed and the lightning."

Flat Warclub cried out in some pain. "Eka! Let me sleep!"

"Perhaps," Manly Heart said, eyes wicking back and forth, "perhaps your nose needs some fresh perfume. Prettyhead forgot to cleanse the air with incense. When I entered I could smell fresh pollen."

Flat Warclub fell silent, embarrassed.

Manly Heart rose to her knees. She reached into one of the smaller storage bags against the wall and pulled out a pinch of yellowed grass. She threw the pinch of grass into the pink embers in the hearth. In a moment the aroma of burnt grass wafted about. It was slightly acrid and had in it the smell of an old time. Manly Heart took a deep sniff, filling her nose with the aroma. "Is it not good? Do you not feel stronger already?" She looked down at his thighs to see what the effect might be. Her own thighs yearned to see a little rising.

Flat Warclub's eyes closed. He appeared to have heard something within himself and was listening very closely to it. Slowly, as he listened, his limbs stiffened.

"Is it your helper again?"

"Ho ye. A voice I hear." Flat Warclub paled. The end of his curved nose turned white. "My helper has just called me by my secret name a third time. Eii. In a very special wakan manner." Flat Warclub shivered. "Eii!"

Manly Heart drew back. No longer was she greedy to know. If Manly Heart spoke his secret name aloud he might be struck dead. With him dead, the Omaha would not be punished. For a man's helper to use his secret name meant that what it had to say was truly wakan. Her own helper had called her only once by her secret name, Point From The Clouds, that time it had helped her select the girl she was to marry.

Flat Warclub shuddered beside her. What he was hearing was dread filled. He lapsed into a faint.

Manly Heart became afraid. She leaned over him. She took his face in his hands. "Eii. Do not die, my pretty one. We need you to destroy the Omaha. We need you to father special sons."

His eyes tried to open but could not. His lips whispered something slowly. "Stone—From—The—Clouds."

Manly Heart jerked back. "That is nearly my secret name. What is this?"

He lapsed into a faint again.

Manly Heart looked at the whole length of him. What did it mean that this handsome brave, this lovely boy with soft curved lips, should murmur what sounded like her secret name?

"Stone—From—The—Clouds," he whispered again.

Manly Heart covered her mouth with her hand. She whispered into her fingers. "He yelo. He has spoken his secret name. Oo-ee. It is against the gods for me to know this." She shook her head from side to side in a slow no-no. "I must never let him know I know it or he will shrivel up and die."

Flat Warclub lay breathing shallowly.

"Yet it was also the wish of the gods that we should very nearly be given the same name. There is but little difference between a stone and a point when they both come from the clouds."

Flat Warclub opened his eyes. He stared transfixed at her. A black cloud formed in the back of his eyes and very quickly it rushed to the front of them. His face became haggard. The skin over his cheeks became like dried buckskin. He appeared to age right in front of her.

"What is it?" Manly Heart whispered through her fingers.

He sat up. "It was given to me to see the manner in which my life shall be thrown away. The gods have let me see myself taking my own last breath near The Blood Run."

Manly Heart continued to shake her head from side to side as though what she had to look at was unbearable.

He stared at her, stared right through her eyes, even through the back of her head. He began to speak as though reading from a winter count on the wall of the tepee. "It shall not be the enemy arrow that shall strike me down."

"What? Shall the thunderbirds strike thee then?"

He continued to read from the invisible winter count. "It shall be one of our own." He shook his head. "The hand of him that shall betray me comes from my own band, from our nation of The Talking Water. I see him. He has already swung his club and I am dead."

"But are we not all kola? Do we not all come from the seven fires of the friendly Dakota?"

Abruptly Flat Warclub rose to his feet. He slipped on his clout, then his walking shirt, then his moccasins and leggings.

"Where do you go?"

He picked up his flat warclub and looked at it lovingly. Then he stepped toward the door.

"Do you go to talk to more girls?"

He turned to look at her. He suddenly had the gravity of an old brave who had taken part in many campaigns. "The gods have now put me beyond all that."

"Then you deny the hunger of my belly for a child?"

"My role as stallion is finished."

Manly Heart got to her feet, holding out a hand to restrain him. "Where do you go?"

"I wish to be alone with my guardian spirit for a last time." He began to weep copious tears over what he knew would come to pass. "Then tonight I shall attend the war feast and the dance."

She held up both arms to him. "Come. Do not leave me. It has been such a long time since a man has embraced me. I have almost forgotten what it is like."

"Friend, with the aid of my helper, I have removed myself forever from the concerns of the flesh." He wouldn't even so much as glance down at her mama or her tamni. "Poor woman."

To be called a poor woman cut deep. It was as though someone had swiped at her belly with a flensing blade. Truly, Flat Warclub was no longer a camp lover only interested in talking to the girls. He was finally one of those who would always be known as a hero.

He smiled at her withdrawn, distant. He bowed, ever so little, and brushed out through the leather door.

Manly Heart let her head fall. She wept.

Presently, collecting herself, she dressed herself before Prettyhead should return with the water.

Manly Heart stepped outside. She looked around to see in what direction Flat Warclub had gone.

He was nowhere in sight.

Manly Heart hurried out through the horns of the camp and climbed a tumble of rocks west above the low pink wall. With a hand over her eyes she peered in all directions. Some little boys saw her looking and they too put a hand over their eyes to look in all directions.

She spotted him at last. He had gone to sit by himself on Boiling Rock. That far away he resembled a stick figure drawn on a winter count robe. He sat leaning forward, chin in hand. Every now and then he reached down at something and then raised the something to his face. She could not make out what it was.

◄ 8 ►

FLAT WARCLUB

A FEW GROUND-CHERRIES GREW BESIDE BOILING ROCK. THEY were within easy reach and every now and then Flat Warclub reached down to pick some. He shelled the yellow cherries out of their wispy bladders and popped them between his lips. With his tongue he broke them slowly into a seedy sweet mush.

He ate several dozen of the ground-cherries.

Behind his eyes lay a burnt black warpath. He was almost blind. Even staring down at the rock he sat on, he could barely distinguish the boiling scarlets and blues and pinks and yellows. It was all black to him.

The black warpath persisted in his eyes like a sunspot. He saw raw wounds flowing blood. The wounds hung before him in the air like shredded red butterflies.

Presently, eating the ground-cherries helped him feel better.

Spit once more flowed. Taste sharpened. Feeling returned to his fingertips.

One of the ground-cherries wouldn't let go of its wispy shell. It squirted red over his fingers.

"Eii. I hunger for death."

He ate the bleeding ground-cherry. It stung him in the belly.

"Ahh!" Grabbing up his warclub, he jumped to his feet and began to run and run.

He ran without purpose. He bounded about like an erratic jackrabbit. He scooted along like a cottontail. He slinked along like a racing hoopsnake. He dodged rocks, leaped over rocks, skimmed past rocks.

"Hanta yo. Clear the way for one who knows the way to a great victory."

He zigzagged in many directions.

"Maka. Maka. Let my earth receive me."

At last he fell flat on his face in light green buffalo grass. Once again he drifted off into a faint. The faint became a deep sleep.

He was awakened by the boy Swift Afoot.

Swift Afoot looked down at him very seriously. His young brow was sharply wrinkled. His black eyes had an extra black spot exactly in the center of them. "Where were you? What has happened? Have you eaten a bad cherry? Seven Sticks wishes to know."

Flat Warclub sat up wearily. A high dusk was about to fall upon the Blue Mounds. The horizon to the south was already brown. Only the horizon to the west and to the north remained silver. Swallows were also about, dipping after the insects, their sweet warblings on the evening air very pleasant to the ear.

"Wa he ye," Swift Afoot continued. "I came and found you as one dead. What has happened?"

Flat Warclub managed a dry smile. His teeth also felt dry. "Hanto yo. Run and tell your chief to clear the way. I am coming." Flat Warclub licked his teeth to make them wet. "Now that I have slept some I feel a little refreshed."

"Seven Sticks worried that what the gods had promised for us tomorrow would not come to pass after all. He did not wish for you to offend the gods."

"Hanto yo."

Swift Afoot broke into a smile, much relieved, and with a quick boyish nod darted back toward the camp.

Flat Warclub saw that his zigzagging had carried him well out of sight of the camp, just above where Many Buffalo Rub Rocks stood gleaming in the rusty dusk. He spotted a pool of water in a creek below. Picking up his warclub, he made his way down through the glistening rocks to the pool. He washed his face and bathed his arms. He combed out his tousled hair with his fingertips. Then, more refreshed, he headed back for the leather village. Even as he walked he began to hear quite clearly in the still evening air the sound of drummers warming up under the trees.

Coming to the rim of the pink rock wall, Flat Warclub stopped a moment to look down upon the encampment.

The camp had suddenly come alive with joy and celebration. That afternoon a small hunting party led by Turning Horse and Bitten Nose had come upon several buffalo in a swale off to the northwest. The buffalo couldn't run in the gucky lowland, and it took but a moment for the hunters to drop them. There were two cows and four yearling calves, all prime meat. The hunters managed to bring in all the slaughtered meat. Person In The Moon, the shaman, pronounced the killing a happy omen for what was to come. On the morrow the war raid would be successful. Members of the Soldier Society built a huge fire in the center of the camp, using grass and twigs and branches as well as the old sun-dried bones of former butcherings. Soon meat of all cuts were broiling on green sticks along the edge of the bone fire. The aroma of singed meat and the sound of crackling fat made the mouth spit little sprays of saliva.

The children were specially wild with joy. The mothers gave them their servings early, and they chewed as they ran in and out of the circle, warm plasma and fat sliding down their chins. Sometimes the boys squabbled over a large chunk of meat like dogs. The more the children ate the wilder they became. The camp dogs followed the children about, ears and tails alert, hoping to snatch up a dropped piece.

Parents smiled indulgently at their happy yelling children. The little ones knew better than anyone else when a notable time had come.

Flat Warclub watched it all with a gentle smile. He loved all the people. They were good people to die for.

He saw an unoccupied stone behind Seven Sticks. It had a small backrest. Flat Warclub picked his way down through a crevice in the rimrock and slowly sauntered over to the free stone. With a pleasant groan, he settled down on it. He set his feet apart and leaned back.

The older people were fed next. They sat two deep around the bonfire, taking the meat as fast as servers handed it out. Both the men and the women had the custom of catching hold of a corner of meat between their teeth and of slicing off what was in the mouth with a rough-edged stone knife. Sometimes the stone knife struck the teeth with a slight cracking sound. Some people preferred boiled meat from the camp pots and several servers handed out boiled pieces as large as a fist. Sliced turnip and toasted corn kernels and boiled prairie beans were also served.

Right in the middle of the happy feasting, Turning Horse abruptly stood up.

"O yeh he tu!" he cried out. "I wish to announce the name of a hero and what he has done. Ae, great it was. It was Bitten Nose who heard the strangled cries of the buffalo as they sought to escape the clutches of the swamp. We listened too but we could not hear the cries. Only Bitten Nose had the ears sharp enough to catch the sound. He heard it carried on the soft wind. We decided to follow him and thus we found the meat we now eat. Had it not been for Bitten Nose, this war feast would have been a mockery. Yelo epelo! I have said."

Cries of praise erupted from all around the bonfire.

Bitten Nose was too busy to acknowledge tribute. He was gnawing on a good legbone. Besides, he hated to hear praise. It was said he even hated to hear praise about his favorite daughter.

Swift Afoot attended Seven Sticks where he sat, bringing him choice cuts of well-broiled meat, a clamshell of softened corn, and a bowl filled with well-boiled tipsinna.

The maiden Chattering Leaves, who also loved to do good, filled several leather bags with boiled chunks of buffalo meat and took them out to the women confined to their separation huts.

Swift Afoot also attended Flat Warclub, bringing him sizzling strips of hump meat caught on a green stick.

Flat Warclub nibbled at the food. He wasn't very hungry. He ate only because he knew that in the next life his spirit would need the food while it traveled to The Other World.

When all had eaten until their bellies hurt, until their eyes were a little crossed, they retired to get ready for the dance.

Young men painted themselves each according to his own fancy. Some drew lines down the centers of their naked bodies, starting at the crown and ending at the breechclout, and then painted one half of the body red and the other black. Some painted the figure of a bird on their chests. Some painted the design of a fish on their bellies. Some placed a hand in black paint and made handprints all over their bodies. Older men were content to put on quill-decorated war jackets and set a feather in their hair.

Suddenly there was a loud Boom! and in a moment four powerful men, Soldier Society warriers of high repute, led by a singer named Jaw, came stepping into the light of the bonfire, thumping out a heavy slow beat on the taut leather of a wide drum. Every backbone cracked erect.

The four drummers sat down in a circle near the fire. They drummed a little. Jaw sang a few snatches of songs. Gradually they worked themselves into the proper mood.

The little children swirled around the drummers, eyes as bright as spearpoints. They would hover a moment, watching the drummers intently; then, with a wild cry like that of young eagles, would whirl off into the farther reaches of the firelight.

Soon young men appeared along the sidelines dressed up in their dancing gear, their heels and hips hung with tinkling clamshells. Some masqueraded as four-leggeds, some as two-leggeds. Maidens came laughing out of their tepees, wearing their newest dresses decorated with their best quillwork.

Old people reminisced aloud about the great times they used to have when they were young.

The firekeeper heaped on more old buffalo bones, branches, twigs, old discarded clothes, bluejoint grass tied in tight knots. The smell of singed fat and belched gall and burned marrow hung bracing on the hot evening air.

Flat Warclub's glance fell on Bitten Nose. The next day Bitten Nose would do a certain thing. The gods had decreed it. There was no escaping it. A smile turned up the corners of Flat Warclub's soft lips.

Bitten Nose, having already painted his face with black stripes from the corners of his lips up across his cheeks, was busy fitting on the crown of a buffalo skull and horns. When he finally got it on, it gave his mouth, already cruel, the look, truly, of an enraged buffalo.

There was a pause; then the drummers beat out the rhythm of a new song.

Bitten Nose jumped straight up and let out a shattering war whoop, "Wah! hoo. Wah!"

The drummers responded over their drumming with an equally loud war whoop, "Wah! hoo. Wah!"

Bitten Nose then swung into a song, the four drummers beating softly below the words:

"A pipe they mentioned
as they walked many times
looking for the buffalo.

We have offered the pipe
many times as we walked
looking for the buffalo.

Yeh he tu. Yeh!"

Young men along the sidelines instantly charged into the arena, dancing and bounding about, imitating the actions of buffaloes, wolves, eagles, hawks. They leaped up and down with their hands on their hips, striking the soles of the maccasins so hard upon the light green grass they left footprints in the ground.

"A small herd of buffalo we found
as we walked the land hungry.
Bitten Nose heard them.
We ran. We saw them. We rushed in.
We killed many. We killed plenty.
We relished the raw liver. Yelo.

Yeh he tu. Yeh!
With our lips we suck at the raw liver. Yelo."

Older men joined in. They too danced hard and resoundingly on the ground, bending up and down, shaking their heads vigorously in the old Dakota style. Their old dusty maccasins could not resist the dance.

The little boys came next out of the shadows. They followed their elders around in the dance circle, imitating this or that war hero exactly, so intent on doing it right their eyes bugged a little and their lower lip set out.

Finally the young women began to dance along the outer edges of the dancing arena, in a slow double sidestep. Their voices quavered over the men singers, high, trilling.

And last the old women, standing in one place, rocking back and forth from one foot to the other, added their own shrill falsetto to the wild jamboree.

When the song was finished, a short silence rose up from the encampment. And then Turning Horse stepped forth and danced the tail of the song, going around the circle once, slowly, singing a short phrase:

> *"We charged them;*
> *U pelo.*
> *The friends charged them. "*

Song after song drummed into the still hot evening air. The red rimrock and the low cliff walls compressed the sounds, deepening the beat of stick on leather drum and the jouncing stomp of powerful legs into the ground.

Ever so slowly, but with the pull of a deepening whirlpool, the tempo became faster, the bodies swirled swifter, the male voices widened and the female voices heightened. Dakota hearts pumped the blood riotously.

When the drummers and singers swung into the war songs, the frenzy of the dancers mounted even more:

> *"Wah! hoo. Wah!*
> *Wah! hoo. Wah!*
> *Omaha!*
> > *Make sure your lookouts*
> > *have clear eyes.*
>
> *Omaha!*
> > *Tomorrow we take the warpath.*
> > *We charge your village on the Blood Run.*
>
> > *He! He! He!*
> > *Beware.*
> > *Hunh. Hunh. Hunh. "*

The singers drew the beat along, quickening it. The beat deepened the time. The time widened the place. The place became the top of the world.

Several of the pretty maidens, Goodlick and Lastborn and Long Tongue, birdstepped up to Seven Sticks, toe down first and then the heel, and gestured for him to join them in the dance, if only for a few steps around his sitting stone.

Smiling, the old chief hunched his old bones upright and jounced a little with them.

Next the three maidens birdstepped up to where Flat Warclub

sat and invited him to dance too. Flat Warclub indulged them.
They had accepted his seed. He danced beside them with the slow
dignity of a god from the other world. Then he sat down again.

Bitten Nose charged out of the revolving melee and came at Flat
Warclub with his head down as though to butt him off his stone
seat. He pawed at the earth. He roared at the skies. He bellowed
and grunted. Again and again he thrust his horns at Flat Warclub,
almost into Flat Warclub's eyes. Finally Bitten Nose, snorting and
pawing, butted into Flat Warclub, unseating him, causing him to
fall upon the ground.

Flat Warclub laughed. It was all part of a ritual. It had to be. Flat
Warclub righted himself and got to his feet and took his seat again.

The drummers and singers, pleased to see that Flat Warclub had
not taken offense but had accepted what had happened as a playful
act, broke out into even more frenzied song:

> "Haugh! A god has come into our circle.
>   Tomorrow he will lead us to victory.
>   A god has taken flesh in our camp.
>   Haugh! Haugh! Haugh!
>
> He! All the Dakota will hear of this.
>   All the enemy will hear of it.
>   A god has taken flesh in our circle.
>   He! He! He!
>
> Hiyelo! He sits apart at our fire."

Flat Warclub sat smiling to himself. It was fated.

The male dancers thumped the ground harder and harder in
their joy for tomorrow. The women pitched their trills higher and
higher, until the dogs couldn't stand it any longer and joined in
with their shrill tremolos.

"Aii!" Flat Warclub cried suddenly.

Four bullsnakes wound slowly out of a clump of wolfberries
beside the stone he sat on. The powerful stomping of the warriors
had bumped them awake. They were stiff with sleep. Even their
tongues flittered slowly. Their brown spots appeared to move one
at a time. A motion like the sticking out of a human tongue began
at the nape of their neck and then moved like a slow swallow down
the whole length of their bodies.

Some of the nearby dancers next spotted the slowly sliding bullsnakes. They danced back and away a few steps. Their voices softened. Even their glinting clamshells fell to a muted tinkling.

Flat Warclub smiled down at the four tan brown snakes. "Ae, truly," he cried, "our dancing has awakened the whole earth in this place."

Then nearby dancers took courage and bounded even more powerfully on the ground. They sang with their mouths wide open. Their tongues ululated like the quivering anthers of swamp lilies.

Up beyond the camp circle the women in their separation huts poked out their heads to hear the better, an ear and a braid showing.

All the Dakota danced snakelike in friendly fashion until the speckled bullsnakes had vanished into the cattails.

Again the three maidens came begging to Flat Warclub and asked him to dance with them. He was a god. If he would dance with them yet once more, they could all be gods for a short time.

With a languid easy air he consented again. He danced very lightly, as a tiny wren might, light toe down first, then an even lighter heel.

Bitten Nose pretended to be vastly jealous. He danced harsh circles around Flat Warclub and the three girls. It appeared that now he intended to butt Flat Warclub backwards into the bonfire.

Flat Warclub accepted the play with a gracious air.

The Dakota rejoiced. Tomorrow would be a great day to die.

Finally Manly Heart came dancing up to Flat Warclub. She grabbed him by the waist and danced him hard and furiously around the bone fire. Her entire head was covered with the feathers of birds, stuck down with buffalo grease. She resembled an outraged grouse, ruffed, ready to peck. "Yelo!" Manly Heart cried. "It is a great thing to dance on top of the world."

At last the singer Jaw came over and asked Flat Warclub if he would please dance the tail of the night.

Everyone seated themselves. The drumming continued lightly.

Flat Warclub was greatly surprised. Dancing the last tail of a whole evening's dance was always an honor reserved for a warrior who had acted nobly while doing some brave deed. "But we have not yet fought with the Omaha."

"We trust your fate."

Flat Warclub sat in grave thought a moment.

"Haugh! He! Come."

Flat Warclub's helper spoke up. "Do not deny the people their pleasure. They wish to honor you for what has already been painted on the winter count robe of the gods."

Flat Warclub jumped up. "I go. I will do it."

Flat Warclub danced around in a little circle. He danced alone. He sang a few short phrases:

> *"Bitten Nose himself and*
> *I helped the Blue Mound people*
> *beat back the Omaha.*
> *He said this.*
> *Bitten Nose himself said*
> *I helped the living*
> *when I did what the gods wanted.*
> *He yelo."*

Boom!

The wonderful war dance was finished.

Everyone trudged off to bed.

◄ 9 ►

FLAT WARCLUB

THE DREAM ENDED AND A VOICE ASKED IF IT WAS NOT TIME FOR him to get up. The dream had been a beautiful dream. He had seen himself swimming with many beautiful girls in a pool of water behind a beaver dam. The water was as clear as amber gold and their copper limbs had appeared to be a soft red. They had all been touching each other with drifting gestures.

"Get up, get up," the voice cried again, "it is time to hit the Omaha."

Flat Warclub popped up from his sleeping robe. He was instantly awake. He looked up at the smokehole. Ae, the sky above had just begun to lighten a little. He pawed around for his clothes.

Manly Heart heard him from her bed. She sat up and tossed several tags of fat on the embers. In an instant blue flames licked up, then flared into a sharp little yellow fire.

Flat Warclub got to his feet and stretched to his full height. He slipped on his walking robe. He threw a look down at Manly Heart. Prettyhead was still sleeping, curled up beside Manly Heart like a red squirrel. Flat Warclub whispered, "I go to take the morning bath."

Manly Heart nodded.

Flat Warclub pushed his way out through the hanging leather door. The earth was dark at his feet. He let his bare feet find the path. His feet had got used to picking their own way through patches of cactus and protruding sharp rock. He threw back his head, sucking up the fresh predawn air. The sky very high up had become grayish. Stars were slowly turning yellow.

He tossed his fur toga onto a ledge of rocks and bathed himself carefully in the sliding creek. The water was chilled from flowing over the cool rocks. He shoveled up a handful of pink sand and gave his body a good scrubbing.

Refreshed, he swung his fur over his shoulders and picked his way back up the path. The earth was still darkish underfoot but the stars had turned to a dull yellow in the lightening sky.

He poked his head into Wide Mouth's doorway and called in a low voice, "Wide Mouth? It is a great day to die. I will awaken Turning Horse. Will you stir up the others?"

Wide Mouth was already up and his face with its great lips was suddenly in front of Flat Warclub. "Where do you wish them to assemble?"

"In the center of the tribal circle."

"It shall be done."

Flat Warclub next sought out the tepee of Turning Horse. He again poked his head into the doorway and spoke down at the floor. "Friend, it is a great day to die."

Turning Horse sat up in the dark of his lodge. He shook his head, rubbed his eyes. "There are no thunderbirds about?"

"None. Even the fireflies have gone to sleep for the day."

"It is a good omen."

"Will you come?"

"We have named you the leader of our war party and I obey."

"Remember. I will have to rely on you for the best route."

"I will be there to help."

Flat Warclub started back across the camp circle. He saw Wide Mouth quietly going from tepee to tepee to awaken the other members of the war party. Flat Warclub looked around at the great camp circle with tears of love. It was a great thing to die for such a noble band of people. He saw that some of the young children, wishing to sleep in the cool night of the outdoors, had climbed up onto the drying scaffolds. They lay with their heads nuzzled on strips of drying buffalo meat. Beyond and in line with them, on the far slope above the first spring, two bodies lay decomposing on burial scaffolds.

By the time Flat Warclub got back to his own tepee, Manly Heart and Prettyhead had taken their morning baths. Prettyhead was busy getting the breakfast ready over a crackling fire. Manly Heart was busy rolling up the leather wall on one side to improve the draft.

Flat Warclub went over his gear to see what he should take with him. The war party would travel light. He set out his club, a tightly rolled up fresh breechclout, a new leather jacket, a full quiver of arrows, and his father's famous shield made out of the triangular front of a buffalo bull's head. He also checked his medicine bundle to make sure the seven clover heads and the one clover head were intact. They had dried out some but their gold-dusted purple color persisted.

Prettyhead dug out something from a storage bag. She said with an arch look to one side, "While you were busy talking to all the girls, I made these for your warpath against the Omaha." She handed him a freshly made set of buckskin moccasins. They were sturdily made, designed for rugged wear. The only decoration on them was a blue arrow quilled over the big toe. The two blue arrows pointed straight ahead. "May they lead you to victory."

Flat Warclub didn't know what to say. When all was fated there was little need to offer thanks to donors. He finally said, "I thank the deer for this gift." Then he said down to the buckskin moccasins, "Buck, help me lead. Buck, help me be a man."

Manly Heart had something to give him too. With a dark yet happy look she removed a leather thong from around her neck and handed it to him. A large spearpoint hung from it. The point was made in the ancient manner and was about as long as a large willow leaf. Her manner of handing it to him was like that of a shaman handing over a strong medicine. There was also the suggestion that she was handing over one of her most prized possessions.

Flat Warclub guessed instantly what it was. Manly Heart was giving him her helper. He recalled her remark that his secret name was nearly like her secret name. His secret name was Stone From The Clouds, which meant that hers had to be Point From The

Clouds. No wonder the gods had thrown them together. And no wonder that the gods had decreed they should wive the same Prettyhead.

"Perhaps," Manly Heart said, "perhaps the extra helper will help you overcome the Omaha as well as bring you back safely to our hearth."

Flat Warclub allowed himself a little curling smile. "It is a great honor to hold your helper in my hand." He held it up daintly. "Ae, two helpers are better than one. But remember, what is fated is fated, and it may very well be that I may never return with your helper. You may never see it again. Are you ready to live without a helper?"

Manly Heart nodded numbly.

"It could mean you may have to return to a former way of life? And give up Prettyhead?"

"I am ready. Let the gods decide."

Flat Warclub listened to himself a moment. Then he said, "Wakantanka heyaya. The gods have advised me. I cannot take it. It is yours. You are the husband and the husband must have a helper. But I will take the spirit of it with me." He picked up one of Prettyhead's stone knives and cut off one of the ends of the leather thong attached to Manly Heart's helper. Turning his back on them and picking up his warclub, he secreted the thong where his own stone helper lay hidden. He turned and handed Manly Heart's helper back to her.

Manly Heart took back her helper minus one of the ends of the thong. She bowed her head.

Prettyhead served up a sumptuous breakfast. There was broiled hump and a delicious root soup flavored with wild onions and a loaf of salty frybread and a handful of the first of the wild crab apples.

Flat Warclub was very hungry and ate until his mouth turned dry.

A single drum boomed outside.

Manly Heart got to her feet and poked her head out to see what was up. In a moment she stepped back. "The people are gathering in the center of the camp. They are getting ready to give the war party a great send-off. It is a curious thing, but did anyone in this lodge hear Wide Mouth call the people together?"

"The people are gathering out of their own free will," Pretty-head said. "Last night I heard several speak of doing this."

"It is a strange thing," Manly Heart said, wonderingly, "when it is the custom for a war party or a raiding party to leave the camp quietly."

All three washed themselves with warm water poured from the same pot and then stepped outside. Flat Warclub carried his war gear. Prettyhead carried a small parcel of dried jerky and some seeds for him. Manly Heart did Flat Warclub the honor of carrying his bow and quiver of arrows. They pushed their way through milling children and old people and happy weeping wives. Dawn was slowly turning pink. Everyone appeared to be fat with sleep. Everyone was smiling. Even Bitten Nose managed a friendly grimace.

A single drummer took up a position in the deep part of the camp circle. Members of the war party hurried to form a line behind him. The people meanwhile gathered along both sides of the parade line out to the horns of the camp. The little boys ran out to the pasture to get up the favorite warhorses as well as the riding horses of their war heroes.

Turning Horse beckoned Flat Warclub over to take up the lead position. The other braves, both those from The Nation Of The Blue Mounds as well as those from The People Of The Talking Water, were eager to go and were waving to the boys to hurry up with their horses.

All were dressed light for swift travel. Turning Horse of the Blue Mounds band and Legbone of the Talking Water band carried special war bundles. The bundles were held in much dread by everybody, and even the men in the war party made it a point not to stand too close to the two leaders. Turning Horse's war bundle was made of the birdskin of a hawk to which were attached four scalps, one of them fresh. Legbone's war bundle was made out of the birdskin of the great-beaked woodpecker to which were tied four dried fingers taken from a very brave enemy. Jaw carried with him the bones of a revered dead uncle wrapped in the dressed skin of a mink. The mink skin was decorated with red and blue porcupine quills. It was said of Jaw that when he took with him the bones of his dead uncle, who was named Whitenose Fox, he never failed in his mission.

Finally the boys got all the horses up from the pasture and on a signal from Flat Warclub the warriors mounted their riding horses and grabbed the lead rope to their war ponies.

Seven Sticks the old chief and Person In The Moon the shaman approached the line of mounted men. Seven Sticks carried a long pointed branch. He held it up for all the people to see. Then he ceremoniously handed it over to Person In The Moon. ·

Person In The Moon held the branch aloft for a moment, then pointed it toward the east.

At that very moment the red rim of the sun pushed over the far bluffs on the other side of The River Of The Red Rock.

A shock of recognition, a check on the spirits, silenced the people.

Person In The Moon cried out, in a loud singsong, "Zuya iya yelo! He is gone to war!" Person In The Moon next stuck the pointed branch in the ground, hard, so that it stood up by itself. Then he jumped back to make room around the branch.

"Houw! Houw!"

Flat Warclub gave his riding horse Old Gray a light touch in the flank, and Old Gray reluctantly set herself in motion. Many Spots pranced around at the end of the lead rope. In a moment the whole line of mounted men were following Flat Warclub, the riding horses as well as the war ponies bucking and rearing and snorting. The people too broke out of their reverent silence and began shouting for joy, and singing, and filling the air with the praises of their heroes. Flat Warclub led the line of mounted men around the branch stuck in the ground seven times. And seven times he struck the branch with his warclub and seven times the people shouted. The pink rock walls around the encampment rang with sharp echoes. The pointed branch stuck in the ground represented the enemy. Seven would die at the hands of Flat Warclub alone.

Flat Warclub then straightened out the head of Old Gray and started her toward the horns of the camp. With an old inherited dignity Flat Warclub led a joyous and riotous parade out toward the hard world.

The lone drummer, marching to one side of the line, began singing short bursts of song, recounting the great deeds of former war heroes, chanting old tribal legends of victory:

> *"Hanto yo! Clear the way!*
> *The manes of the old ones*
> *go prancing forth in victory.*
> *They lead the way.*
> *He! He! He!*
>
> *Hanto yo! Clear the way!*
> *The spirits of the young ones*

go prancing forth in victory.
    They point the way.
    Haugh! Haugh! Haugh!

Remember Whitenose Fox!
    Eka! I wonder!
    Can we find his footprints in the grass?
    He is my friend.
    Kola wayelo!"

Young boys ran down the length of the parade, shaking rattles, calling out the names of their living heroes. Turning Horse. Jaw. Legbone. First Standing. Bitten Nose. Red Ant. Raincrow. Stalk. And loudest of all they called out the name of Flat Warclub who would shortly lead them to victory over the Omaha.

Young girls also tripped along both sides of the parade line, their strings of clamshells tinkling. They lilted the names of their favorites in soft sweet accents. Occasionally they ran up and bedecked the tail of a war pony with a wild flower.

Older women wailed with a strange animal sound, mingling sobs of joy with racks of fear. Old men mumbled warnings in the background.

The wild barking of countless dogs added to the din.

The morning sun emerged whole out of the horizon, a great bloody red egg, then bounced on the horizon a couple of times.

In the red sunlight hints of brilliant pink glinted in the black manes of the war ponies.

Turning Horse raised a powerful red arm. "The war drum sounds!" he cried. "It is time to fight!" He flexed the muscles of his mighty forearm. "O people, we hear your whoops resounding off the red rock walls of our little valley. Tomorrow we shall be painted for war. We promise! Then the gods shall see me fighting side by side with our new hero Flat Warclub! With my right arm bared for the battle and with my trusty wakan shield glittering on my left arm making the enemy blind—eii! I shall prevail! We shall all prevail!"

Huzzas rent the air. Women ran up offering gifts to the warriors snaking back and forth in the parade. They gave them tasty sweet-meats, twisted stems of sweet sorrel, little bags of special parched sweet corn. The warriors, leaning down from their horses, and laughing with much pleasure, accepted the gifts as just due.

Flat Warclub rode as though he had paraded in glory many times before. He had looked upon the winter count of what was to happen given to him in the vision of his deep faint.

"I was only a floating body," Flat Warclub thought to himself, "until I learned what was to happen. After that I knew I was truly of this earth."

Just as Flat Warclub was about to pass out through the horns of the camp, the girls he had talked to came running alongside him, crying out his name in love, singing his praises. Goodlick and her light brown hair. Dress That Swishes and her chubby square hands. Chattering Leaves and her tree-climbing ways. Bad Moccasins and her young body topped off with an old woman's face. Lastborn and her tiny doll body. Sulk and her way of talking out of a crouch with her chin tight against her chest. Long Tongue and her thick manner of talking. Molest and her cowrie shell. Even Prettyhead came running alongside praising his name. All were glowing with pride that in the past several days he had chosen them so that they could bear his children for the good of the tribe. Each tried to outdo the other, each claiming that Flat Warclub had been the nicest to her, each announcing that when he had talked to her there had never before been such a copious overflowing of seed:

> "*Eka he miye!*
> *Well, it was me*
> *to whom he gave all his love.*
> *He talked big to me.*
> *He talked me to death.*
>
> *Maku welo!*
> *He granted me a long long talk.*
> *He enveloped me with his streams of love.*
> *From this day forth*
> *I am honored forever.*"

Then out of the melee there came running a young girl named Slim Waist. She was weeping. She had slashed her face and arms until they bled.

"Wait! Wait!" Slim Waist cried. She ran up to Flat Warclub and grabbed his leg and hugged it to her bosom. She was a comely maiden, as lovely as any in the band.

Flat Warclub looked down at her with a show of surprise. Where had she been all the while?

"Wait, wait!" Slim Waist continued to wail. "What of me? These other girls you talked to, are they any better than me? Am I not as beautiful? Could I help it that the custom of our tribe confined me to a separation hut the last four days? It is not fair. I could not help it. I prayed to the moon but she turned her face away from me. She would not listen. What am I to do? Can you not stop a moment and talk to me too?" She spoke with a rush of words as she jumped up and down hanging onto his leg. "I also wish to be honored forever from this day forth. That you talked to me. Speak. In the name of all the Dakota gods, grant me this one favor."

Flat Warclub looked down upon her with regret and slowly shook his head. "Maiden."

The people meanwhile, seeing the blood flowing down her cheeks and her arms, backed off a few steps.

"Even if it means that we talk within sight of all my kin, please, kind warrior, talk to me. Make happy the heart of a simple maiden."

Flat Warclub shook his head again, sadly. "There is nothing to be done."

Slim Waist persisted. She clung all the tighter to his leg. She squeezed her breast flat against the calf of his leg. Her brown eyes turned smoky with tears. She had lovely wide lips and they thinned and drew down at the corners. "Grant me this one boon."

Flat Warclub spoke soothingly to her. "Tato heya. It is against the winds now, my daughter."

"But you are not my father. Nor an old one. What is this?"

"Return to your mother. There will be other heroes. Perhaps Bitten Nose, when he returns in glory, will marry you."

"Bitten Nose? Who is he? Is he not the one who kicks dogs and mutters curses at our mother earth because she bruises his feet?" Slim Waist gave Flat Warclub's leg a great jerk. "I do not wish to talk to one who is always consumed with jealousy."

"Calm now, maiden. He yelo. Wakantanka said for me to do this."

"Well, if not talk, can you not at least whisper to me?" She pled beseechingly, arching up her slim waist to show how much she desired him. "At least? So that someday I may brag a little to my grandchildren? I shall always be forlorn if I do not have something to boast about. This is a great day and I wish to be part of it too!"

Flat Warclub looked down at the knot in his warclub. "Helper, what is this? Why was I not told of Slim Waist, that she should come running at this moment and ask me a troublesome question? Where are you? Have you fallen asleep?"

His helper said, "I have been watching."

"Then why was I not told about Slim Waist? It was not I that caused the women to have their turn. It was the Old Ones who started the custom of the separation hut."

"It is all one. Ka. Attend to her. Be gentle with her."

Flat Warclub nodded to himself. "You have said." Many Spots had become very nervous with all the tumult about and began to rear and buck at the end of his lead rope. Flat Warclub had all he could do to hold onto him. "Woman, be careful or my war pony may kick you. Stand back!"

But Slim Waist continued to beseech him, pressing herself against him, catching his leg between her warm breasts. "Well, if not whisper, can you not then at least tickle my palm? I need something to brag about too." She let go of his leg with one hand and held up her palm. "Let me have the tickled promise."

He looked down at her palm as though it were a face to talk to. Slowly he allowed himself a little smile. "But, woman, can you not see that I am busy with two horses? I have but two hands. A hand to a horse."

Slim Waist leaped up and caught an arm over the back of Old Gray. Somehow she managed to hang on, riding on the one arm. She held up her other hand, palm up, for him to tickle.

His helper whispered from his warclub. He could just barely make it out over the hubbub. "Be tender with her. Is it not the custom to show tenderness by rubbing noses with a maiden?"

Flat Warclub's eyes opened, surprised that he'd forgotten. Then he smiled, and with much tenderness leaned down and rubbed his nose in the palm of her hand.

"Eii!" Slim Waist cried, letting herself drop from the horse, and joining the other maidens he had talked to, leaping and frolicking with them. "Perhaps it was not given to me to bear his child, but who else has received Flat Warclub's nose in the palm of her hand? I am the only one. The only one."

Sulk lowered her head and choked back a laugh. "The palm is not the same as the tamni."

But Slim Waist was happy and she helped in praising Flat Warclub and the other mounted warriors.

Many Spots charged ahead, running out to the end of the lead rope. Flat Warclub had all he could do to hold him. He had to wrap the end of the lead rope around his hand several times to make sure of him. Flat Warclub smiled as he manhandled him. Many Spots was ready for the great battle to come. Grazing in the rich meadowlands of The Nation Of The Blue Mounds, Many Spots had become fat and glossy, full of eye-rolling tricks.

The people accompanied the parading warriors almost to the best spring.

The little boys followed them all the way to the north edge of the red cliff.

At last the war party was out of sight of the village.

Flat Warclub put away his princely smiles. His face resolved itself into the hard firm lines of a warrior taken over by a vision. He looked back at Turning Horse. "My helper tells me we must follow The River Of The Red Rock straight south for a day."

"Ae."

"I have never been that far south. But is there not a place to rest below? Where the water foams? So at least my helper has shown me."

"There is."

"Are there trees?"

"There are many."

"That will make a good place to make camp tonight. Yelo. We will gallop and walk by turns so as not to tire the ponies. We want them all fresh tomorrow."

"But will we not also have to travel all day tomorrow before we reach the enemy village? How can our horses be fresh then?"

"I am the leader and I have a plan."

When they came to the river, they turned south. Flat Warclub picked up a route well up on the first bench. They crossed occasional buffalo trails cut into the thick grass. They rode two men abreast, each with his extra horse. The forty men rode in high-eyed silence. The hooves of the eighty horses built up a little passing of clattering noise. They trotted over benches of bare glinting gravel. They breasted through draws lying at right angles to their route full of tall cut-grass. Sometimes for short stretches there were no trees on either side of the river and then the narrow river resembled a little girl still innocent of hair. Twice as the river meandered into some wide flatlands, it broke up into several threads of streams, creating long winding islands. The narrow islands resembled flake scrapers broken off the same core.

They stopped to give their horses drink in a swift creek coming in from the west. A grove of silver maples glittered nearby. All the maples were huge, having attained full spreading growth, and they offered wide circles of cool shade. While the horses cropped grass, the men squatted in the short grass under the maples and chewed a strip of jerky and drank fresh water from the murmurous creek.

Several high brown-bottomed clouds drifted in from the west. But there was no rain in them. The air was very clear. The shadows raced along under the clouds.

Refreshed, Flat Warclub stood up and pulled Old Gray around for mounting. Without a word the other men got to their feet too. In a moment all were mounted and trotting down the bench above the snaking river.

At the end of the trot, when Flat Warclub reined his horses down to a walk, there was a cry, an expostulation about bad luck, behind him. Turning, Flat Warclub saw that Jaw was having his troubles. The mink skin containing the bones of his revered uncle had slipped from Jaw's hands and had fallen to earth, spilling out like the dried seeds and partitions of a broken gourd.

Jaw motioned for them to go on, not to stop. Jaw jumped down off his horse, and holding the reins of both his horses in his teeth, with his hands gathered up the old bones. It took him but a moment to roll them up into the mink skin and get back into the line again.

Face flies came out in the midafternoon. They pestered both horse and man to death. They were the kind that caused the people to wear leather garments all summer long. The horses shook their noses up and down, and jumped up in one spot, and backed up, and tried doubling up on themselves so as to be able to switch their noses with their tails, and eenked and wailed, and popped their tails with great loud reports, in a desperate effort to be rid of the pests. The men too were becking their heads up and down, and waving their hands in front of their faces, and grunting in exasperation.

Finally Flat Warclub rose on his horse and called out, "Let us make a run for it. Perhaps we can leave them behind if we go fast enough for a little ways." He dug his heels into Old Gray. And instantly, popping her tail yet again, because she too was desperate to try anything, Old Gray was off at a full gallop. Many Spots was right at her tail, also snorting and shaking his head up and down, cavorting and rearing.

They licked it across a flat meadowland and then up over an intruding bench of sand, and down into another meadow. All eighty horses galloped at top speed, as hard as they could go, bulging up front with power until they all looked like galloping buffalo.

The nose flies lifted up off man and beast a few feet, and formed a little gray cloud, and followed them surge for surge.

For a moment man and beast were free of the bites.

When at last the horses began to heave under the men, Flat Warclub pulled up. "Hoo-ah. Enough."

The moment the gallopers stopped the flies were at them again, zipping at the noses of the horses and at the faces of the men.

"Aii," Bitten Nose cried with rage, "now they are worse than ever, with the horses all sweaty."

Flat Warclub shook his head. "I did not know a fly could wing it across the country as fast as a horse."

Legbone roiled up on his horse. His riding horse was going wild. She stuck her head between her legs and first wiped the flies off one side of her nose on one leg and then off the other on the second leg. "Perhaps if we rode on the rise to the west the flies would desert us."

"You are a fool of a war leader," Bitten Nose continued to rage, looking across at Flat Warclub. "What does your helper tell you now?" Flat Warclub inclined an ear down at the knot in his club.

His helper was instantly attentive. "Wait. In a moment it will be given you what to do."

"Aye?"

Old Gray made a snaking motion under Flat Warclub. She wried her neck around and pointed her nose toward the river below the shelf.

Flat Warclub looked. It was where the river doubled sharply on itself below a huge cottonwood. A gentle whirlpool was slowly gyrating in the shadow of the cottonwood.

"Look," Flat Warclub cried. "Follow me."

Flat Warclub gave Old Gray her head and in an instant both she and Many Spots were off, galloping for the gentle whirlpool. It appeared the horses knew where the river ran deepest. In another instant all eighty horses were galloping for the deep hole. They pellmelled into the river, jostling up surges of waves, kicking up scarves of water. The men held their weapons and gear high out of the water. The men shouted in high glee at the wonderful shock of being immersed in cool water. The horses groaned with plea-sure. The nose flies didn't let go of their bites right away and many drowned in the water. It wasn't long before soaked flies began to drift down the river. Despite the uproar of the splashing and neigh-ing horses, channel pike spotted the floating flies and emerged from under the roots of the cottonwood. Swiftly they began to lip up the flies. The whirling and jumping pike created a second turmoil in the slowly flowing river.

Presently Old Gray and Many Spots had enough. They turned of their own accord toward the sandy beach, emerging sopping wet, manes as well as fetlocks. The other horses soon followed them out. All the horses flopped their tails about like great wet mops.

"Aaa," the warriors laughed, ducking the flailing tails and the flying drops, glad they were rid of the pesty face flies. "That was a fine thing."

The high clear air soon dried them off. Moccasins shrank tight over insteps. Buckskin clouts drew up snug around the hips.

Flat Warclub led his party onto the first bench again and shortly they were trailed out in a long line heading south.

Many springs fed the river. It widened and deepened with every meander. Kanaranzi Creek came sliding in from the northeast and widened it even more. By the time the river swirled through The Place Of The Rub Rocks In The Middle Of The Ford it was a considerable body of flowing water. Everywhere in it there were strewn great red boulders. The red boulders were much worn as though the gods had used them in gambling games. It was what gave the river its name of The River Of The Red Rocks.

The sun was about to set when they came upon another grove of great maples. A light wind out of the west tossed the notched leaves about, revealing their silver undersides. White foam could be seen on the river through the openings in the maples. There was also a high bank across the river. It was the place of the rapids.

Flat Warclub held up a hand. "Ho. Here we rest for the night."

Bitten Nose didn't like it. He rode up alongside Turning Horse, threw a snarling look at Flat Warclub, then asked, "How can you trust him after that crazy request he made at the Blue Mounds village?" When Bitten Nose snarled sourly at someone, he resembled a horse with its upper lip drawn up in a twitch.

Turning Horse slowly swung his head around and fixed his eyes on Bitten Nose. Turning Horse's single eagle feather dipped once at the back of his head. "What troubles you?"

"Did he not say we would attack the Omaha tomorrow?"

"He said that."

"Well, I know this country. I was once here." A sad look flitted over Bitten Nose's cheeks. "From here to the village of the Omaha it is still almost a day's hard ride."

Turning Horse said, "Our leader says he has a plan."

"If we attack when our horses are puffed out we will all be destroyed. Eii, I know this Flat Warclub and his big talk. I do not trust him."

Turning Horse said, "I trust his helper."

Flat Warclub accepted Bitten Nose's distrust with a soft aloof smile. It was all fated.

Bitten Nose growled, "But I do not trust his plans."

Flat Warclub spoke in a soothing manner. "Tonight, after we have supped under the trees, I will tell all the men of the plan."

They dismounted and each man staked out his pair of horses under the trees. The grass was deep and green. The horses tore at the rich succulent stems as if they hadn't eaten for days. Turning Horse and Bitten Nose and First Standing and Lightfoot went down along the riverbank gathering up pieces of dried flotsam. They built a fire under the largest tree. They were careful to keep it small so that by the time the smoke rose through the tree branches it was completely diffused. Smoke could be made out against the sky a long ways off.

Bitten Nose went down the river the other way to pick up yet another armful of dead sticks. He had just stepped over a tumble of rocks, sending several loose stones in the little avalanche into the river, when a form jumped up out of some tall reeds. It was a rust-tinged buck.

"Eii!" Bitten Nose cried in surprise. Quickly he grabbed for his bow from where he had it slung over his shoulder, at the same time reaching for an arrow from his quiver, and aimed carefully at the fleeing buck. He held the bow level across his chest and drew the bowstring back all the way to the point of the arrow, until his biceps bulged out like great fat cheeks; then let fly. The arrow speared in a straight line, its feather dipping a little as it began to catch up with the bobbing white tail of the buck. The white tail was about to bob out of sight into a patch of cattails, when, on the buck's last hop up, the arrow punched into the soft black skin under its rear thighs.

There was a shrill cry. "Eeee!" The buck stumbled, tail over head, and collapsed out of sight.

"Eii!" the warriors cried. "We eat fresh meat before the battle."

Flat Warclub nodded to himself. Ae, that had been shown him in the vision of his deep faint.

They ate in silence. There was the sound of human teeth gnawing on bones and the sound of horse teeth cropping at the soft rich grasses under the trees.

Water was brought in parfleches to put out the fire at dusk.

Over the still rising steam and smoke from the fire, Flat Warclub spoke. "Attend. Ho-ye. We will depart from the usual custom of the Dakotas to attack at dawn. It is at dawn that the enemy expects the attack. We will fool them. We will attack at midday when the village will be taking its noon nap. Even the dogs sleep soundly then. Thus very early in the morning we will ride across the rise to a thick grove of willows in a draw only a short distance from their village. The place is on The Blood Run. We should get there by midmorning. We will rest our horses until noon. While the horses eat we can put on the warpaint. I have spoken."

The circle of warriors regarded Flat Warclub intently. It could be seen they approved of his stratagem.

Legbone spoke up. "Yes. At last I know you have become a good leader. I would not have thought of that. It is a good thing."

The eighty horses continued to be hungry even after it got dark. They were still in a rush to crop grass. Even as their long white teeth were tearing off one bite, their lips were reaching sideways for the next bite. Flat Warclub let the horses eat their fill, then told the men to water the horses in the still water above the rapids. A horse filled with grass and water was not apt to run off.

Flat Warclub set out four guards, First Standing on the high bank to the east, Raincrow to the north, Lightfoot to the west, and Red Ant to the south.

The men lay spread out on the level ground, their horses tethered to the belts of their clouts. Many of the horses napped with their heads bowed over their master's chests.

The nose of the rapids was murmurous, tumbling, splashing. It sucked at the air as it rushed through the lower stony reaches. Then it curved out in sinewy ropes beyond the turn.

The bruise of the baffled waters whirled in the ears, put pressure on the beat of the heart.

.10.

FLAT WARCLUB

FLAT WARCLUB REMEMBERED SOMETHING JUST AS HE WAS ABOUT to fall asleep. Bitten Nose had not first apologized to the buck before killing it. Bitten Nose had been so full of hate that he had forgotten the usual rites. For a hunter not to make that apology was against the gods.

Flat Warclub got up quietly. He tied his two horses to the tails of Turning Horse's ponies and then stepped carefully around and through the sleeping forms of his men.

Flat Warclub headed for the spot where the spirit of the buck had flown off. He advanced into the cattails until his moccasins sank into soft mud. Then he spoke, reverently. "Buck, listen. One of our men was in a hurry and forgot to thank you. Listen. We are on the warpath to rectify a wrong done our brothers. It must be done. We needed the meat. Ho-ye. It was good to receive your meat. But we forgot to thank you first. We now thank you. Our bellies feel good. We are now full of the good fight and ready for tomorrow. Ka-he Kamon. Therefore I have done this."

Flat Warclub waited.

The rapids above washed and sudsed over and around and down the cataract of red rocks.

"Thank you, buck."

Flat Warclub was about to step out of the cattails, when he heard someone talking to himself a little ways out on the prairie. It was star-dark out and even against the faint line of the horizon forms could scarcely be made out. Flat Warclub opened his eyes very wide, until a touch of higher light entered them. Then he saw who it was. Bitten Nose.

Bitten Nose was sitting on the earth with his legs stretched out in front of him. He was pouring out his heart to the earth itself. Now and then he gave the earth a light slap as though to make sure she was paying close attention to what he was saying. "Listen. I have come out here to talk to you. I don't know what to do. You know how I like to sit on you and meditate. I always learn from you. Listen. I don't know what to do. Tomorrow we go into battle and I find myself under the power of one I despise. What must I do? I hate him. Even my helper hates him. He has talked to many girls. They were girls I desired too. But he had them. Eii, not me."

Flat Warclub was ashamed of what he was hearing. It was wrong for another to hear a good fighter pour his soul out into the night. "Helper," Flat Warclub quickly whispered down to the point hidden in the knot of his club, "what shall I do? I stand here in the cattails and if I move he will hear me."

"Stand still. Do not move. Listen to him," his helper whispered back. "What he will say next will tell you why he is going to do a certain thing."

Flat Warclub stood perfectly still. The brown cattails nodded around him.

Again Bitten Nose slapped the earth in love. "Tell me, ground, what do you say? I listen to you, O ground."

The rapids behind them tumbled and splashed.

"Was it my fault that my brother bit off my nose? Yes, it is true we were fighting over some ponies. But the ponies were mine. I stole them from the Pawnees. Thus they were mine to give. But my brother Always Finds Buffalo wanted to take them from me; not let me give them to him. Thus we fought a savage fight over them. He was my younger brother and I always loved him. Always Finds Buffalo had a great name as a hunter and I rejoiced in that name.

I always praised him to the skies. So why did he take my horses from me without asking? Why did he not wait for me to give them to him?"

Flat Warclub listened closely. Sometimes what Bitten Nose said was almost drowned out by the relentlessly tumbling rapids.

"So we fought. I was almost the victor, when, suddenly, he growled like a bear at me and flashed his teeth. Then he bit off the point of my nose. Always Finds Buffalo hated to lose, so he bit off my nose. He was favored by his mother, and with his father dead he could not forbear and be the bigger man." Bitten Nose wailed to himself in a low tone for several moments. It was as though the loss of his nose was still, even then, too much to bear. "Eii, it was a terrible thing when I saw the blood spouting out of my face directly below my eyes. Eii, blood gouted down my chest. At last I put my hand where the tip of my nose once was and covered my face with my walking robe and hid in my lodge. Eii."

Flat Warclub clapped a hand to his mouth and rolled his eyes from side to side. So that was why the point of Bitten Nose's nose had always looked like a cucumber bitten into, with the teeth marks still showing in the white ridge of the cartilage.

"Well, the next morning I did not know what to do. I could not break the fast with even a crab apple. Finally, covering my face to the eyes with my robe, I sought out my brother. I found him seated beside the open fire in the center of the camp circle. 'Listen,' I said to him, 'listen. You have disfigured me for life. Listen, you know what it means when a husband cuts off the nose of his woman. It means he has caught her in adultery. What will they now say you caught me at? Hrraa! It is too terrible to think upon. You were once my sweet brother . . . hraa!' "

Flat Warclub recalled something from boyhood. Bitten Nose had suddenly appeared in the village of The People Of The Talking Water with his raw-notched nose and asked for asylum. Bitten Nose had come from another branch of the Dakota, the Yanktonais who lived along a big bend in the Great Smoky Water. A home was given him because the people felt sorry for him. They never asked what happened to his nose. When he proved to be a fine hunter they accepted him as one of their own. Finally, when one of the more ugly maidens offered to be his wife, he even married into the band. She alone of all the maidens did not mind his notched nose.

Bitten Nose beat his beloved ground. He cried out as though someone were tearing out his entrails. " 'Listen,' I said to my brother, 'tonight I will try once again to sleep in my lodge. If by the time the sun rises I can forgive you, you are safe. If not, you die.' Well, I went to my lodge and rested all day. My mother bathed my nose with water taken from the Great Smoky Water. She opened her parfleches. She made a medicine with some bear grease and a strong herb and painted my nose with it. All day I was restless in my mother's lodge. I ate sparingly. My stomach would not take any food. At last when darkness came I fell asleep. At that time I did not have a helper and thus I was not awakened in the night by a dream and told what to do. Well, when I awakened in the morning, I found myself still full of mortal hatred for my brother who had done this awful thing to my nose. I did not wait to eat the food my mother prepared for me. I arose and stepped outside. I saw a friend and called him over. I told him to go find my brother and tell him that I had made up my mind that he was to die. 'Tell him,' I said, 'to meet me like a warrior down along the bank of the Great Smoky Water and we will settle the matter.' "

Flat Warclub listened intently. It was as his helper had said. Now he knew him as a man and why he did certain things.

"Well, my brother fled. He ran out onto the endless prairie. I trailed him for months, first east across the Great Smoky Water, then west across the Great Smoky Water. Finally I found him sitting beside a mudhole near The River Of The Bitter White Water. He heard me coming and looked up. When he saw who it was he stood up. He dropped his walking robe to the ground and waited for death. There was little I could do to save him. I had to kill him. He had ruined me for life. I raised my bow and put an arrow through his heart. He was dead even before I pulled on the arrow to remove it. I buried him up on a scaffold. I blackened my face and came home."

Flat Warclub lowered his hand from his mouth.

"O ground, you know what happened next. I sorrowed for months. I mourned his loss for a full year. It also took that long for my bitten nose to heal over. It took many years before I recovered from the deep anguish. I hated my life that my brother had bitten off my nose. I hated my life that I had to kill him. But at last I could eat again. To pick up a new life I went to live with The People Of The Talking Water. O ground, you know all this. But what am I to do now with this Flat Warclub? Does his helper truly tell him all these things about how this war raid will go? Eka. I wonder about all this. I wish to know. Will you tell me? I too wish to sleep in fame someday."

The rapids swirled and splashed.

"How can this Flat Warclub know where to go without having seen it before? If you say, truly, it is his helper, well, such a helper I've never had. My helper has not been of much good to me."

Flat Warclub stood very still in the midst of the nodding cattails. He could feel his feet sinking deeper into the mud. It was not a pleasant thing to see a man weeping. Flat Warclub felt sorry for Bitten Nose. He began to like him a little.

"Well, he is my leader," Bitten Nose went on, "and I must follow where he leads." Bitten Nose beat the ground with the flat of his hand some more. "O ground, talk to me. Will you not be my real helper instead of the weak one I now have? I need a true helper so that I may die in fame someday."

Flat Warclub decided it was time to leave the cattails. He backed through them a ways toward the river. When he reached the bank of the river, he turned and step for slow step headed back to the rest of the men. He managed to get away without having Bitten Nose notice him.

Flat Warclub found his two horses. After some thought he untied his horses from the tails of Turning Horse's two ponies and led them to the southwest edge of the encampment. Then he lay down, tying his horses to the belt of his breechclout, and composed himself for sleep.

It was all coming about as it had been shown him in the vision of his wakan fainting spell.

FLAT WARCLUB

THE BUMP OF ONCOMING THUNDER AWOKE HIM. SOME OF THE after rumbles made the ground quake under him.

Flat Warclub blinked his eyes. Against the dark sky he saw the darker forms of his two horses where they stood with their heads over him. Neither Old Gray nor Many Spots liked what they were smelling on the wind. Flat Warclub sat up. Lightning dazzled across the western sky, coming down in a long stroke. The stroke resembled the peeled branch of a willow. Thunder cracked into the earth almost instantly after, so loud it made the ears pop.

The horses in the war party began to stir and snort. They woke up their masters sleeping under them. In the sharp flickerings of the lightning, men could be made out getting to their knees and securing their horses with both hands.

A gust of wind blew in out of the southwest. With it came the sweet smell of fresh rain falling on curly buffalo grass. There was a nutlike odor of ripening goldenrod in it too. The gods were brewing something for themselves. The men sniffed it and shook their heads.

Some of the horses wried their necks around as if getting ready to run.

The thundercloud drifted in slowly, tagging after the fresh breeze. There were more rumblings in it and then another high flash. The flash revealed its entire outline. The thundercloud resembled a single toadstool, tottering on one side. There were no trailings of rain under it. It was only full of wicked lightning.

Flat Warclub recognized the shape of the cloud. "A thunderbird has come. But yet this was not in the vision."

"Listen," his helper said, "the thunderbird has come to awaken you and tell you it is time to take the war trail. Otherwise you will get to the Blood Run Creek too late to catch the Omaha in their noontime nap."

Ke-tokk! Lightning and thunder thudded as one out of the ground not forty steps off. It was so loud, so bright, so sharp that Flat Warclub thought he had been hit. But after a moment he noticed he could still smell. He was all right.

"Eii. What is this? Was this also preordained?"

"Get up the war party and ride out," his helper said sharply.

"Ae. It is done." Flat Warclub leaped to his feet. He mounted Old Gray and, leading Many Spots, urged her toward where Turning Horse was sitting on the ground holding onto his two horses. Old Gray managed to work her way through the forms on the ground without stepping on them. Flat Warclub made out the face of Turning Horse near the toe of his left foot. "Call the others. It is a great day to die."

"Is it a good thing to ride about in the lightning?"

"There will be no more lightning. Nor will it rain. It is only a thunderbird came to wake us."

Turning Horse nodded. He got up and immediately moved about in the dark to tell the others to mount their horses.

Flat Warclub rode back to the edge of the encampment. Presently all the warriors were up on their horses behind him and ready to go.

The cloud moved on. It made no further sound. Soon the moon slid out from behind it and the grass turned silver underfoot. The men could make out one another distinctly.

With the flat of his right hand Flat Warclub motioned for them to go, raising his fingers to the front and upwards.

The whole line of men started up, following him in single file.

Old Gray had gone but a dozen steps when she shied off to one side. Looking down, Flat Warclub saw a black hole in the ground. It was shallow like a dish, about the size of a buffalo hide, and freshly made. In the moonlight the black dirt here and there gave off shining yellow reflections. There was a sharp acrid smell of ozone about.

Turning Horse rode up beside Flat Warclub. "A lightning hole."

"Ae. Where the thunderbirds struck to awaken us."

"A four-legged will not graze near it for a long time," Turning Horse said. "They consider it wakan."

"Ae. It is a bad thing to anger the thunderbirds."

It was easy to pick out the way in the moonlight. They appeared to be riding across an endless light green robe. The land rose slightly in a wide sweep. Gradually the grass got shorter. The horses reached down to sniff at the grass. The horses craved the short curly grass and some of them managed to swipe off a bite on the run.

After a time Flat Warclub's helper spoke to him. "Do you feel well? Are you read to die? It will come shortly."

Flat Warclub smiled. "I look forward to it eagerly."

"Then sing a little. Some of the braves appear to be dispirited."

"What shall I sing?"

"Ride a little and it will be given to you."

They trotted along. The land began to sink and then to rise in long slopes of silver green.

Flat Warclub raised his voice, keeping time with the jogging of his horse:

> *"Over the ground we come.*
> *Over the ground*
>   *a soldier we come.*
> *Over the earth we ride,*
>   *a ghost."*

It was a familiar war song and soon most of the riders joined in. At first they sang a little like dogs yowling, disparate, but on the second time through they harmonized like wolves howling, as one voice.

Flat Warclub looked back over his shoulder. The thirty-nine dark ovaling mouths behind him were singing a noble song.

"Eii," he thought, "I already know it is a famous thing we are doing. The gods tell me that the Yankton Dakotas will always speak of it. I am content."

The song died away.

They trotted. They walked a ways. They trotted.

The drop-offs at the ends of each slope began to widen into little valleys. Twice in the little valleys they ran into a small herd of antelope. The antelope stared at them until they were almost on them and then broke and scudded over the nearest rise.

Turning Horse rode up alongside Flat Warclub. "I was here once. The Omaha are not too far off."

"Is there a little stream beyond the next hill?"

Turning Horse gave him a look. "Ae. Your vision was surely a good one. Wakan." Turning Horse drifted back with the others.

Gray light opened up behind them. Slowly it turned rosy. Fingers of pink light stroked ahead through the light green grass.

Flat Warclub aimed for a break in the wide hill ahead. He didn't want the enemy to silhouette them against the red dawn. They rode through the break and came out on a ribbed drop-off. Below lay a trickling serpentine stream. In the crimson dawn it appeared to be running with blood.

Turning Horse once more rode up alongside Flat Warclub. "The Blood Run."

Flat Warclub looked down the length of the meandering creek. In places the creek doubled back on itself, severely, almost to the point where it had cut through into itself. Here and there it had cut a gully through the stacked hills. "Is there not a place where the gully becomes very deep with a fringe of willows all about?"

"It lies beyond the fourth bend in the creek."

"There we will take a rest and put on the warpaint."

They were now so close to the Omaha village that Flat Warclub decided to send two scouts ahead, one on either side of the creek. He chose Lightfoot and First Standing. He next turned on his horse and made the motion for everyone to ride as quietly as possible, holding his hands flat out and lowering them slowly.

The sun rose very fast and soon warmed their backs. The grass turned a deeper green, especially along the bottom of the winding gully. The chokecherry leaves glittered a deep green.

They passed under a grove of ash. The horses wanted to stop and drink and eat, but the men urged them on with their knees. The hills to all sides rose to considerable heights. Along some of the tops of the hills grew waving silver sage. Through the break in the hills, farther ahead, hovered a plateau. The plateau was covered with the many mounds of The Old Ones. The mounds resembled bumblebee bites.

They were about to debouch through a last convulsion of tall hills, when the gully cut through the root of a sloping hill. The cut was deep and fringed with willows. The walls of the cut were very steep.

"Ae, here it is." Flat Warclub smiled in satisfaction. His vision was proving itself out at every step. He saw that if he were to place a guard at either end of the sharp cut the horses could never get out. Nor could they be stampeded out of it by lurking horse thieves. The walls were too steep. Even a squirrel would have trouble clambering up its yellow clay walls. Fortunately at the very bottom some moist lush grass grew along both sides of the stream. The running water and the rich grass would refresh the horses and keep them busy for a time.

Flat Warclub assigned the two oldest men in the war party as horse guards, a brave named Wrinkled Belly from his own band and a brave named Jumper from the Blue Mounds band. Within moments all the horses were freed and gently choused down into the natural pen. The men were careful not to stir them up too much. One loud neigh and the Omaha would be alerted.

Presently Lightfoot and First Standing returned from their scouting trip. They had both dismounted and were leading their horses. They had a hand ready over the horses' noses to pinch them shut should the horse decide to neigh.

"What did you see?" Flat Warclub asked.

"The Omaha appear to be at ease. Their bellies are full of our buffalo."

"Did you see any lookouts on the hills?"

"There were none."

"Good. It is all going as my helper has promised. Put your horses in with the others. Then join us as we eat and rest a little."

A dozen good-sized ash trees grew on the south side of the ravine. The grass under them was deep and the air was cool.

The men gnawed at their jerky and drank water from the stream. Tired from the long ride, they soon stretched out on the grass with soft groans of satisfaction.

When the sun was directly overhead Flat Warclub gave the sign that they should prepare themselves for battle. Every man stripped himself down to clout and moccasins. Each man painted his face according to his battle history. Black paint and yellow paint and white paint were put on in the most fearsome manner possible.

Several of the older men, Legbone and Bitten Nose and High Stomach, opened their war bundles and prayed to themselves as they removed the articles in them one by one, a bone whistle, the shell of a baby turtle, a cowrie shell, the dried feathers of what had once been a very wise crow. They told their private fetishes one by one in low singsong voices, noses quivering, eyes darting from side to side in a worshipful manner. Jaw got out his mink skin and counted over the bones of his revered uncle. He began to quiver and shake as the power of his famous warrior uncle emerged from the old yellow bones and entered his own frame.

Flat Warclub fixed his clamshell securely in his long hair. Then he got out his medicine bundle and told over the seven clovers and the one clover.

They were about to call for their war ponies and ride out, when Lightfoot, who had stepped off to one side to relieve himself in the grass, heard the sound of horse hooves pattering toward them from the Omaha village. He came running back even before he had finished, spraying drops to either side. "The Omaha come!" Lightfoot cried low to Flat Warclub.

Instantly every man grabbed for his weapon and shield and dove into the deeper grass.

Turning Horse landed beside Flat Warclub. Both men puffed. A new wrinkle formed across Turning Horse's forehead, gradually becoming a deep crease.

Flat Warclub spoke to his helper. "Listen. What is this? Something is not clear to me. First we are told to catch the Omaha in their nap. Then we see that we are to meet their warriors by accident in a deep gully. Are we to kill these warriors and then proceed to the village and still catch the rest of them in their nap? How is this? Just when will Bitten Nose do his part? Ho yeya. Send a voice and tell me."

The stone from the clouds hidden in the knot of his warclub spoke wearily. His helper was getting tired of making explanations. "Be patient. Listen. You will discover that the fates finally arrange everything exactly as it was always planned. Even the strange interruptions are part of the plan. Continue to hide in the grass and wait. It will be given to you."

They sat like cats in the tall grass.

Presently the bobbed head of the first Omaha appeared around the bend. It was a man and he was riding a fat carefree horse. In a moment more Omaha heads appeared above the edge of the grass. They too rode docile horses.

Flat Warclub whispered, "What is this? They are not riding their war-horses."

Turning Horse whispered, "Nor are they dressed for war. It appears they are going on a neighborly visit somewhere."

Flat Warclub's helper whispered, "Wait until they are almost upon you, and then rise up out of the grass. Then you will see what the gods have in mind."

"I hear you," Flat Warclub whispered. "It is a good day to die."

More Omaha heads appeared, until there was a line of some thirty men. In their midst rode an important man. He was dressed in ceremonial clothes and was carrying something in a long sacred bundle. He had on a headband pricked out with a dozen eagle feathers.

"That is Cloud Without Thunder," Turning Horse whispered. "He belongs to their peace faction. It was he who argued against their taking over our buffalo jump. He wanted the Omaha to share it with us. He said that by working together, their people and our people could round up and drive many more buffalo over it than if we both waited for stray herds to come along."

Flat Warclub looked down at his helper. "How can I kill seven Omaha when they come toward us as a peace party? My medicine bundle of seven clovers and one clover is as nothing."

His helper ignored him.

Turning Horse whispered, "Riding up this gully this way, it appears they might be heading toward our village. Perhaps Cloud Without Thunder and his faction have won out in their last council meeting."

Flat Warclub looked down at his helper some more. "Must I attack men intent on peace?"

"Do not worry." His helper began to speak with the voice of one who was full of the singsong of foretelling. "The gods have decided that you shall be wondered at in times to come. Look about you. Do you not see that everything in this valley and gully of The Blood Run stream is at this very moment bright and blowing? It shall never be like this again. Therefore attend closely. Your comrades, who shall live on to a great age, drowsing out their lives as old soldiers, shall look fondly upon this one morning and see in it something that comes from the rim of an old time."

"I hear you."

They timed their breathing with the ripples of the wind moving through the grass.

Turning Horse saw something. "Not all are men. There are two women with them."

"Where do you see them?"

"They ride behind Cloud Without Thunder. It is his wife and daughter."

"I see them." Flat Warclub saw instantly that the daughter was comely, even as beautiful as Prettyhead. She rode behind her plump mother with all the lazy ease of a young boy. She smiled upon all around her as if it had been specially arranged for her. For a moment Flat Warclub wondered what it would be like to talk to her, then put the thought behind him. It was already fated that he was to be famous as the brave who threw his life away against the Omaha for the good of his people. Thus he could not be bothered with such a little thing as talking to a strange girl.

Turning Horse went on. "The Omaha can be a warm people. Perhaps in appeasement for what they have done, they bring a virgin for our old Seven Sticks to take as wife. Lately he has been complaining that his blood needs warming."

"They are almost upon us. Stand up when I stand up."

"I hear you."

Several of the front Omaha braves were joking with each other. They rode with such nonchalance it was hard to tell who was the lazier, the men or the ponies.

When the Omaha brave on the front horse was not a dozen steps away, Flat Warclub jumped to his feet. "Wana hiyelo!" he cried. "Now is here!"

All the Yankton braves behind Flat Warclub rose out of the grass as one man, shields and weapons ready.

Instantly the front Omaha and then the whole line of Omaha reined in their horses. They stopped as if they were parts of a startled caterpillar.

No one said a word. Both sides stared at each other. The Omaha had such control over their horses that even they stood stock-still.

The wind rippled through the seeded tips of the grass.

The wind carried the scent of the Omaha horses down over the lip of the steep gully. One of the Yankton horses caught the scent and let fly with a loud wondering whinny.

Flat Warclub recognized the gentle neigh.

It was sly Many Spots. Many Spots had always been quick to notice anything new around him.

Flat Warclub quickly whispered down to his helper. "Do we attack now? While the enemy stands gripped with surprise?"

"Wait."

Turning Horse murmured in a low voice. "The brave leading

the party is known as Against The Grain. His grandmother was a Yankton Dakota. He speaks both Omaha and Dakota."   .

The thirty-eight Yankton Dakota and the thirty Omaha stared at each other like prairie cocks, each waiting for the other to make the first move, silent.

Then the venerable chief Cloud Without Thunder lightly kicked the flanks of his spotted pony and rode to the front of his line of men. He carried the sacred bundle very carefully. He guided his spotted pony to within a few feet of Flat Warclub and then reined it in. He held up his right hand. "Houw kola." Then carefully setting the sacred bundle for a moment on the horse's neck in front of him, he gave the sign for peace, clasping both hands in front of his body, with the back of the left hand down.

"Houw," Flat Warclub responded. He was not sure if he should add the word for friend, kola.

Cloud Without Thunder spoke in Omaha. The leader of the party, Against The Grain, interpreted for him. "We ride in peace, friend. May we ask what you do here in our valley?"

Flat Warclub waited for his helper to instruct him. But his helper had nothing to say.

Bitten Nose came striding up. He had an awful scowl under his serrated nose. He did not like what was happening. "Tell them we have come to make war upon them. Without mercy."

Cloud Without Thunder kept his composure. He even managed a soft warm smile. He picked up the sacred bundle lying on the neck of his horse and held it up to the sky. Then he lowered it and slowly unwrapped it. A long peace pipe came to view. It was decorated with quills, blue and yellow, and the red tufts of the red-headed woodpecker. It was a loving pipe. Cloud Without Thunder held the pipe out toward Flat Warclub. "Do you accept the pipe?"

Flat Warclub didn't move.

Bitten Nose snarled. "How can we accept the pipe when you stole our buffalo jump?"

Three times more Cloud Without Thunder presented the pipe to Flat Warclub.

Flat Warclub's helper finally spoke up. "Accept the pipe. No one can deny the pipe. But after you have all smoked the pipe, it will be given to you what to do."

Cloud Without Thunder observed the look of self-reverie on Flat Warclub's face. Cloud Without Thunder waited.

Flat Warclub said slowly. "We accept the pipe. Let us parley under the trees where it is cool."

Cloud Without Thunder nodded. Upon his nod all his braves got down off their horses. Their horses were put in charge of two older men who led them off to one side. The Omaha horses began to crop grass.

The two Omaha women continued to sit on their horses. The Omaha girl watched it all with a quiet eye-rolling wondering air. The mother, however, wouldn't look on but kept glowering at the ground.

Flat Warclub led his men over to where the grass was shorter. They formed a half circle on the north side. Cloud Without Thunder and his braves formed the half circle on the south side. They left an opening to the east. Cloud Without Thunder and Flat Warclub sat at the head opposite the opening. On the Yankton side all the faces were painted for war. On the Omaha side all the faces were composed for peace.

Cloud Without Thunder got out a tobacco pouch and filled the peace pipe. He had a fancy tamper, whittled out of a cherry twig, and used it to tamp down the tobacco firmly. It was apparent he did not believe in touching the tobacco with a tamping forefinger. He went at it in a quiet and reverent manner. He enjoyed every motion of the pipe-lighting ritual. Every brave there, Omaha as well as Yankton, watched him with intent glowing eyes. Even Bitten Nose watched, subdued for the moment.

A clump of sunflowers growing at the edge of the gully was in full bloom. Their yellow flowers shone on the parley like a constellation of small suns.

On a signal from Cloud Without Thunder, one of his braves, the fire bearer, came forward. From a special pouch the fire bearer removed a small flat clay pot containing live punk. The fire bearer held out the flat pot to Cloud Without Thunder, and Cloud Without Thunder with deft forefinger and thumb extracted the decayed root of a cottonwood. One end of the root was slowly being eaten away by creeping ash. Cloud Without Thunder blew on the ash, gently, reverently, and after a moment, like a miracle, the ash disintegrated and a live pink ember emerged. Cloud Without Thunder touched the ember to the tobacco in his red pipe at the same time that he sucked prodigiously.

On one of his deep sucks smoke exploded into his mouth, came out of his nostrils. He sucked until he was sure he had the pipe well started, then relaxed back a second. He looked at the sharp chin of the big red pipestone bowl a long moment; then, after closing his eyes for a second, took seven puffs in honor of the seven directions, east, south, west, north, heaven and earth, and himself sitting in that very place.

Quietly he passed the pipe to his left to Flat Warclub.

Flat Warclub also smoked the pipe, a puff each in honor of the seven directions; passed it on to Turning Horse next to him.

Not a word was spoken as the red pipe moved left down the line. When the last Yankton in line had smoked to the seven directions, the pipe returned along the line, and went all the way around the circle until it reached the last Omaha sitting near the opening facing the east. Then it started to come back, proceeding to the left until it finally reached Cloud Without Thunder.

Cloud Without Thunder set up four stones in a row and placed the pipe on them, the stem facing himself and the chin of the bowl pointing east toward the opening.

The two women continued to sit on their horses. Beside them breathed a patch of wolfberries. The wolfberries were almost ripe, shining like clusters of little pearls. The leather leaves hung limp, with only their wavy edges appearing to waver as though a breeze were moving through them. The mother still was careful not to look at the parleying men, but stared down at the wolfberries.

"Shall we speak?" Cloud Without Thunder said. He looked Flat Warclub full in the eye. His deep wide old brown eyes were full of warm attention. His interpreter sitting next to him translated.

"Wakantonka heyaya," Cloud Without Thunder began. "The gods have advised me that we should go visit the Yankton Dakota living near The Blue Mounds and tell them that we were wrong to take The Blue Mounds from them. The gods have advised me that both the Omaha and the Yankton should together appoint a hunting party whose duty it will be to drive the buffalo toward The Jump On The Blue Mounds. To do this together will give both of our peoples meat continually, every day perhaps, instead of as we now get the meat, whenever the buffalo happen to appear. Together we can spread out our beaters as wide as two good sleeps, and range the land to all sides west of The Blue Mounds Jump, as far even as an eye can reach, and then drive up all the little scattered bunches of buffalo, which otherwise, if left to themselves, would miss The Jump. If we work together we will be rich in dried meat and pemmican all winter long. I have said."

Flat Warclub pondered to himself. He rolled his eyes. He closed his eyes. He whispered within. "Helper? It is a good plan the old Omaha chief has laid out for us. Together we can be rich and fat, as he says. What shall I do? Was I not instructed that I should throw my life away and kill seven Omaha braves?"

"Weep," his helper whispered back.

"What?"

"Weep in the Old Dakota manner. It was the custom of your old ones, when they knew their friends were going to be struck down by a disaster, that they would weep copious tears over their friends."

Flat Warclub nodded. He opened his eyes and looked up and down his half circle of painted warriors. It took but a moment for tears to form in the corners of his eyes. The tears swelled and soon began to trickle down his cheeks. They appeared faster and faster until at last two little yellow streams were running down his cheeks.

When the Yankton warriors spotted his streaming eyes, they jerked back, so that their eagle feathers jiggled. Then, as if rehearsed, they too began to weep copious tears of sympathy for their good friends who were doomed to die no matter what was being said in the parley.

Cloud Without Thunder knew about the Yankton Dakota and their tears. He didn't like seeing them. He raised his hand and made another speech. "Tanyan. All is well. Do not be afraid of making peace with the Omaha. We truly mean to have peace with you this time. We once thought of weeping tears over the Yanktons ourselves but decided against it. The getting of much meat was more important. Tanyan. Tell your men to go down to the stream below and wash off the paint. Then return with us to your home near The Blue Mounds. Listen. Our scouts say there is a great herd drifting out of the northwest in your direction. Listen. We will help you drop them. Listen. In a few days our young women will follow after us. Our horse herders will accompany them with our pack-horses so that we can transport half the meat to our village here. Listen. Do you not already hear the sound of great rejoicing because we have dropped the buffalo? Do you not hear the little children crying out the names of their hunting heroes as you arrive in your camp with all the meat? What is there on all the earth as sweet as the cry of little children as they see the meat coming into camp? The soft bleat of the fawn for its mother's milk is not as beautiful. Listen. Therefore, shall we both weep copious tears upon each other, or shall we sit down and talk soberly about our plan for the surround?"

Flat Warclub's eyes dried up. The eyes of his braves dried up too. Flat Warclub bowed his head and pondered within. "Helper," he whispered in his heart, "what now? It is true the little children are beautiful to see when the hunters come in with the game."

His helper whispered back. "Bitten Nose."

"What?"

"Observe him."

Flat Warclub waited a decent interval and then glanced Bitten Nose's way. What he saw made his nose crack.

Bitten Nose was glowering across at the Omaha girl sitting on her horse. Unlike her mother, who was still staring at the ground in deference to the men holding the parley, the maiden was quite openly watching the proceedings. Her glance had finally fastened on Bitten Nose. The raw serrated edge of his bitten-off nose fascinated her. A little smile played at the corners of her lips as though she thought it very funny that a man should go about smelling and breathing without the tip of his nose. She meant no harm. She had hardly outgrown being a child. But Bitten Nose was enraged.

Cloud Without Thunder had not noticed what was going on between his daughter and Bitten Nose, the one smiling in sweet girlish wonderment and the other scowling in mean bilious obsession. Cloud Without Thunder had more to say. "Are we not near to being brothers of blood? Sometimes I do not require our interpreter to understand your words. A long time ago, somewhere, our mothers were the daughters of the same Old Ones. Many generations ago, somewhere, those daughters separated, the one moving against the stream with her children and the other coming out of the forest toward the stream. Yet the best of what they were was not forgotten. Kola wa yelo, the Dakota is my friend. Let us gather up the mountains of meat that lie out there if we will only work together. Yelo epelo. I have said once more."

Before Flat Warclub could respond, Bitten Nose let go with a loud bawl of hate. He stood up and suddenly made the motion for copulation at the maiden, thrusting the forefinger of one hand into the curled fingers of the other hand.

The maiden's mouth dropped open, she was so startled. After a moment she blushed a blackberry red.

Cloud Without Thunder saw it. "I-ye!" he cried, bouncing where he sat. "What is this?"

Bitten Nose was so incensed he leaped across to where the maiden sat on her pony and grabbed her arm and jerked her to the ground. The maiden let go with a little choked yip when she hit earth. Bitten Nose then dropped to his knees and tried to pry her legs apart; and when she resisted him, screaming, next rolled her on her belly and made the motion to mount her like a buffalo bull. His bow slipped off his shoulder and fell to the ground.

Cloud Without Thunder clawed over his shoulder looking for a weapon. But he had come on a mission of peace and had no weapon. Then he snaked his hand out to grab Flat Warclub's weapon. But Flat Warclub was too quick for him and jerked it out of reach.

Flat Warclub made a motion with his head for his men to grab Bitten Nose.

Turning Horse and Legbone leaped across the bent knees of the seated warriors and pinned back Bitten Nose's arms and hauled him away from the maiden. Bitten Nose raged. He struggled to break free. But the two men managed to subdue him.

Cloud Without Thunder shot a look at Bitten Nose's crotch. When Cloud Without Thunder saw that Bitten Nose was risen, that had no one been there to stop Bitten Nose he might very well have raped his daughter, he jumped to his feet. He almost tottered over in outrage. "What? He will take by force what we intended to give in love to your old chief Seven Sticks? It is one thing for us to offer our daughter as a gift to a great chief, but it is another when one of your wild men seeks to rape her. Listen! Good men do not know of rape. Listen! What kind of warriors do you have in your camp that they go around trying to take their pleasure from virgins against their will in broad daylight? You must be mad bulls. You must have eaten of the loco weed. Tell your man to go mount a boulder, if he must be mounting something all the time. With that bitten-off nose of his."

That last taunt did it. With a roar of wildest rage, Bitten Nose broke free of Turning Horse and Legbone. He jumped forward, landing in a crouch. With a single fluid motion, he picked up his bow, drew an arrow from his quiver, and fitted it to the bowstring. "Ka-he kamon!" Bitten Nose cried. Then he drew and loosed the arrow. In that short distance the flight of the arrow could not be seen. There was a thunking sound. Cloud Without Thunder stumbled back a step at the same time that he began to bow at his waist. The point of the arrow could be seen sticking out of his back a good foot.

Cloud Without Thunder stared at Bitten Nose. Cloud Without Thunder didn't dare take a breath it pained him so much. Then he turned and looked at Flat Warclub with slowly dulling over eyes. His eyes had the look of dwarf cherries, ripe and about to fall. In his bent position he tried to raise a thumb and finger to his lips as though to whistle at someone. Then he fell dead.

"Zuya iya yelo!" Flat Warclub cried, low. "Bitten Nose had gone to war. My helper was right. It is all coming to pass as my helper said. It is all foreordained. Now I throw my life away." Flat Warclub jumped erect from where he had been sitting all the while. In a loud stallion voice, he gave the war yell. "He! He! He! It is a great day to die!" Swinging his warclub, he sallied into the Omaha men still seated on the ground.

Thirty-seven Yanktons piled in behind him.

The whistle that Cloud Without Thunder could not get off was whistled by his interpreter Against The Grain. Against The Grain appeared to know what the other Omaha did not know, that there were armed Omaha warriors not too far off.

Within moments bobbed heads, pricked out with a war feather, showed up over the edge of a hill. The armed Omaha took one look, and then let go with a great roar of outrage. They came on the dead run to save their brothers.

The maiden and her mother didn't bother to take a second look. With a flying leap the maiden boarded her pony, and then both maiden and mother belabored their mounts to get out of the brawl. They got away safely.

The Omaha horses began to squeal from their spot under the trees where the two old Omaha men were holding them. They reared. They bugled. Finally, after a few got away, they all stampeded up the valley toward the Omaha village.

The loudest roars came from Bitten Nose. He went berserk. He emptied his quiver of arrows as though he were a cricket expectorating brown shafts of fluid. Some arrows found flesh; others sailed harmlessly into the grass. Quiver empty, he dropped his bow and grabbed up his club, from where it dangled at his waist, and piled in with the rest of the Yanktons. He didn't bother to unhook his shield from where it hung on his back.

The little flat of grass became a wild melee of furiously wriggling brown maggots attacking one another. Arrows flew across the battleground like maddened dragonflies. There were roars of savage rage; cries of final despair; quavers of high agony as some brave sang his death song.

Flat Warclub mashed in one head after another with his flat warclub. One. Two. Three. The flatness of his club gave it one virtue. It never bounced off an object. It caught things square and solid, though twice he had to give a shuddering skull another whack to still it. Four. Speed and power were given him such as he'd never known before. His helper was right. All things were falling into place.

Braves from both sides began to stumble into each other. Occasionally a friend clubbed down a friend. Braves still on their feet roared. Bodies turned slick with sweat and blood. Dust stived up until it appeared the fighters were demons jumping about in a slowly burning bog. There were many demons. It was as though the fighters were joined by ancient presences from out of the nearby mounds. The smoke of battle rose out of the little valley and drifted off toward the northeast.

Flat Warclub didn't bother to dodge enemy blows or arrows. He would survive until he had his seven. Three more to go. He swung at dodging bodies; missed them. He could smell enemy sweat. He could smell enemy blood. It was like the odor of a saltlick in the midst of a grove of overripe plums. Salty and sticky.

He knocked down his fifth Omaha by accident. The Omaha saw Legbone rush at him with his stone thighbone. The Omaha jumped back and landed directly in the path of Flat Warclub's falling club. Flat Warclub caught the Omaha on the back of his skull an awful blow. The skull broke inward like a goose egg.

The sixth Omaha came hard. He was a big one. For a couple of moments he had the first move on Flat Warclub. But he missed Flat Warclub three times because Flat Warclub didn't make the normal dodging jump. Flat Warclub had the specially chosen one's notion that he should do things differently, even in battle. Flat Warclub saw the look of surprise on the big Omaha's face. A deep sweaty wrinkle creased the fat between the big Omaha's eyes. Flat Warclub cleverly decided that on the Omaha's fourth swing at him he would finally take the usual expected dodging jump. It worked. Once more an Omaha skull hung suspended a moment directly under the fall of Flat Warclub's weapon. Flat Warclub humped all his power into the blow. The skull fell in like a ripe pumpkin.

The Yankton horses down in their pen in the clay gully began to rear and bugle. Some of them tried to scrabble up the steep yellow banks. They got partway up, only to fall back on their tails with a resounding watery whump and a shriek of pain. The two old braves guarding them had all they could do to hold them. Frantically the two old braves waved their shields and shirts, and shouted and roared at them. Dust rose out of the gully and joined the dust high over the battlefield.

A fallen Omaha brave called to one of the Omaha men in the peace party. "Weaseltail?"

"Kola?"

"Bid my wife farewell for me. Take my club and fight."

"I-ye."

Weaseltail picked up his friend's club and shield. He jumped into the battle, snarling and swinging at everything that moved. He was slim and very agile. He managed to dodge all the blows and arrows aimed at him. He was covered with sweat and resembled a very swift-moving bloodsucker as he slipped in and out of the brawl.

Flat Warclub saw Weaseltail club down two Yanktons, Lightfoot and Turning Horse.

Flat Warclub had come to like both Lightfoot and Turning Horse. It enraged him to see his best friends go down. He forgot all about his vision and his mission. He wanted to revenge the death of his two kolas. He took out after Weaseltail.

Weaseltail let out a surprise cry when he saw Flat Warclub after him. Weaseltail had guessed that some kind of magic was protecting Flat Warclub. He knew he didn't have a chance against him. He turned and ducked and ran down the path toward his village. Little yips and shrills of fear escaped him as he ran.

Flat Warclub doubled his speed. He could feel the gods give swiftness to his feet. He flew very fast over the ground. He gained rapidly on Weaseltail.

Right behind Flat Warclub came Bitten Nose. He too had his eye on Weaseltail. The slim slippery kind of fellow had always got on Bitten Nose's nerves. He had never been able to stand it in Flat Warclub and now that he saw it in an enemy he had to crush it and annihilate it. The gods also gave incredible speed to Bitten Nose. He gained on both Flat Warclub and Weaseltail.

Weaseltail looked over his shoulder, eyes wild, mouth ganted. His foot caught on a tree root. He started to stumble, almost recovered with a breakneck stride, then hit a white stone in the path and went down. Flat Warclub was on him like a cat and hit him a fearsome blow over the head. Weaseltail's skull made a sound like an exploding squash. Seven.

Bitten Nose couldn't stop his pellmell berserk rush. He piled on top of Flat Warclub. He too was aiming his blow for the top of Weaseltail's skull. But because Flat Warclub happened to stop directly in the path of Bitten Nose's downward swing . . . crackkk!

Flat Warclub fell. A great lightning had struck him in the brain. Stars scattered.

Flat Warclub rolled over several times, finally fell off the narrow path down a slope. His body flopped into a little glade of grass. His clamshell fell off. His little medicine bundle of the seven clovers and the one clover spilled open.

The end was near. There would be just time to sing his death song:

> *"Yelo, here am I crying my life away,*
> *soon the long long sleep.*
> *Yelo, here all is dark,*
> *the light of my eyes is wiped out.*
> *Yelo, I am very alone,*
> *no father, no uncle, no brothers to help me.*
> *Yelo, I must give my life back,*
> *I am finished using it.*
> *Pity me."*

He sang in a weak tremulous voice. He was almost thrown away:

> *"The juices! The juices!*
> *will they never run again?*
> *Pity me.*
> *What is life without the sweet juices?*
> *He-nala yelo.*
> *It is all over."*

Yet a little light was given him. His eyes rolled in his head and their rolling around parted his eyelids.

He saw Bitten Nose standing over him. For a moment he couldn't understand the look on Bitten Nose's face. Bitten Nose was weeping.

Flat Warclub whispered, "How goes the battle?"

Bitten Nose wept hot yellow drops of salt on him. "The enemy flies. The Buffalo Jump On The Blue Mounds will now be ours forever."

Flat Warclub let his eyes fold shut.

He remembered two last things.

First, he was walking along the sandy shore of Talking Water, His mother Cornmilk was calling him home to come and get mama, it was ready and warm. But he didn't want to come right away. The beach was full of little glowing stones fallen from the clouds and each one was telling him something. The points from the clouds were singing in unison like cicadas in a grove of cottonwoods. The air was very clear. The sky was as blue as the paint of peace. The air smelled of lapped water. His favorite giant cottonwood cliddered its wax-green leaves over him. It was all very clear.

It all had a sweet wonderful dizzy edge to it, dizzier than he remembered it being as a boy.

Suddenly he saw his life coming full circle. In a moment he would start the circle a second time around. The circle always brought the sun, and the sun always brought life and power. It was going to be doubly sweet the second time.

Second, he was sitting in Manly Heart's tepee. He saw her weeping. He saw she'd put away her manly clothes. She wept that he hadn't talked to her to give her a baby. He felt sorry for her. At that moment he liked her better than he'd ever liked any other woman. He wished now that he had talked to her. It would have been a good thing to do. Not even his mother had been as kind to him. Manly Heart had taken him in as a guest when no one else would. Wife Prettyhead wouldn't have invited him in if left to herself. Manly Heart had the big heart. Compared to her, Prettyhead was but an ornament. Manly Heart should have been made the mother, not Prettyhead. Had Manly Heart not provided him with a hearth, he would not have had a place from which to make his offer to throw his life away. Now that he had got to that place where he now lay floating, he knew Manly Heart had perhaps loved him best of all.

Six white spirit lance bearers came with a white buffalo robe. They lifted him onto the white robe and carried him away. He himself was the seventh white spirit.

.12.

MANLY HEART

MANLY HEART SAT ON A HIGH LEDGE ON THE VERY SOUTHEAST corner of the blue mounds escarpment. It was where she'd seen two grass lizards disappear into a slim red crack and where she'd found her spearpoint helper.

She looked south down the valley. She shaded her eyes with a hand.

She spoke to the spearpoint lying between her breasts. "Will they come today?"

Her helper spoke faintly. "Do not ask me. I am dead. I am only an imperfect point made by an old arrowsmith."

"Has Flat Warclub thrown his life away?"

"Did not his helper say he would?"

"Eii, then he is dead."

"Put me back in my old place beside the red crack."

"What? Can a helper cease being a helper?"

175

"Put me back in my old place."

"How can I live without a helper? The head of a house needs a helper."

"Yelo epelo. I have said."

Manly Heart wondered if her helper was tired of life. Her helper probably needed a rest. She decided to ignore the request.

She looked south yet once more. The river meandered below a long line of curving hills. Between scattered groves of trees she could make out the sparkle of trickling waters. She sharpened her eyes to narrow blades as she fixed them on one spot at the farthest curve of the river.

At first she thought it was only the branches of trees waving up and down.

Then she thought it was heat waves at work.

She watched the tiny dancing motions intently.

There were too many of the tiny dancing motions for them to be the branches of trees moving.

It had to be their war party.

She stood up. She shaded her eyes with both her hands, all ten fingers, to give her eyes a long hood.

It was their war party all right. There appeared to be many horses in the long strung-out caravan.

Her heart began to thump.

Perhaps they were all returning alive and victorious. Flat War-club would still be alive then. Eii.

"I wish to see him yet one more time. Then he can talk to me."

The war party beat steadily up the river valley. What looked like a long multicolored centipede gradually broke up into parts and became horses with men riding on them. Soon she could make out each horse. There were five tens of them twice over, one fifty for the left hand and one fifty for the right hand. That meant the war party had captured twenty horses. The war party had left home with eighty.

"Ae, truly, they come home victorious."

She fixed her eyes even more sharply on the line of returning warriors. The center of her vision became as clear as a winter count freshly painted on a new buffalo hide. Even the leaves of the oak near her on the escarpment at the edge of her vision showed up in sharp relief.

She could make out figures on the horses. She counted them. Five and five. Ten and ten. Then another four. Thirty-four. That meant six Yankton warriors had been killed in the battle.

Manly Heart clutched her breasts. She trembled that Flat Warclub might be one of those killed. "May the Dakota gods be pleased with the battle, but let not Flat Warclub be among the killed."

She decided to signal Goodchild, the nearest lookout on Eagle Rock. As she turned, her helper made a jiggling motion between her breasts. It was a snapping motion, and then the spearpoint, having worked itself loose, began to wriggle down past her navel in a tickling manner, and finally fell out of her skirt and landed on the ground. The spearpoint twitched once. Then it quickly wriggled across the pink ledge of rock and, with a flip of its tail, vanished down a red crack. It was the very same crack into which the two grass lizards had vanished.

She clapped a hand to her mouth. It was a sign. Wakan. Again something new was about to happen to her.

Her helper was gone forever. She would have to find some other way to get advice from a good friend.

A deep sigh lifted her. Well, the spearpoint was gone. There was no use looking for it.

She stood a moment longer, pondering on her new fate, hand still to her mouth.

"Yelo. It is." She let her hand fall.

It was important to let the village know what she'd seen.

She ran hopping up the several shiny outcroppings of the rising red rock. She gained the flat top.

Goodchild on Eagle Rock spotted her instantly and jumped to his feet. He held a hand over his eyes and stared at her running toward him.

When she was within hailing distance, running, she cried out, "They come! They come!"

"Eii!"

"They come with many horses." Manly Heart stopped to catch her breath.

"Are there many killed?"

Manly Heart couldn't get herself to tell how many warriors were missing. "It is enough that they return. Tell the camp."

Goodchild climbed to the very top point of Eagle Rock and began signaling toward the camp to the north. He was a good signal maker. He made his gestures slow and clear, with proper pauses in between.

Manly Heart dropped into her run again, heading for the village. She found herself surprisingly light-footed. Her breath, though, burned in her throat. The palms of her hands turned wet.

She ran and ran.

Old chief Seven Sticks stood in the horns of the camp awaiting her. He had seen her coming. He looked at her kindly, head cocked to one side.

Manly Heart came to a stop directly in front of him. "Houw," she gasped. She noticed that the old chief was ringed about by the mothers and sisters of the men who had gone on the warpath. "Waku welo. I return from looking."

"Our lookout Goodchild says you bring good news."

"Hanto yo. Clear the way. They come with many horses."

The camp women let go with a trill of high expectation.

Seven Sticks asked, "Are there many killed?"

"They are still a long ways off. Let them tell the news when they enter the draw of our stream. In a little while."

The whole camp stood waiting. Even the dogs knew something was happening and sat on their haunches looking down the draw for the first sign of the returning warriors.

It took a while. Everyone decided that the warriors had stopped beside some quiet pond to paint their faces and to decorate themselves for the parade through the horns of the camp.

The little children couldn't wait and began to play tag around their mothers and finally around their tepees.

At last the boy Swift Afoot, who had climbed to the very tip of the highest cottonwood, began to shrill like a cicada. He was so excited he couldn't get a word out. All he could do was shrill. It hurt the ears.

"What is it? What is it?" his mother cried up to him testily. "And get down from there. You will break your neck if you are not careful."

"Peace, woman," Seven Sticks said in a calming manner, "it shall be presently given us."

Person In The Moon the old shaman stood beside Seven Sticks. He stood with his head tossed back so that his gray braids hung over his great ears. His eyes were narrowed to slits. There was a look about him as if he had already divined what had happened but in his wisdom had decided not to reveal what he knew.

Then the dogs heard them coming through the ground. They also smelled strange horses on the southeast breeze. They set up a loud and rancorous barking.

Swift Afoot broke off his shrilling. He managed to say something. "Eka. Ho kuwelo. I wonder. They come home howling." He slid down the cottonwood, dropping in little falls and leaps, and landed on the ground on the run. He shot out through the horns of the camp. A dozen other little boys ran after him.

"Here! Here!" the mothers cried. "You can wait inside the camp circle like the rest of us."

Seven Sticks smiled an old indulgent wrinkled smile at the eager boys. He called after them. "Hi-ye! Attend, young ones. It is a brave thing to do to obey the mother."

The dozen boys stopped and, a little crestfallen, came trotting back.

The lookout beyond the arrowsmith on the east rise let out a hoot. "They come into view past the First Rub Rock. They have painted themselves black. Also they have many horses."

Many women began to quiver, holding a hand to their mouths to keep from crying aloud. The little children quit their cavorting about and stood close to their mothers.

The cottonwood leaves rustled above the people. The afternoon air was very clear. Though the wind was in the southeast there were no clouds. It was a high day and shortly a great thing would be known.

A horse's ears appeared around the corner of the best spring. Then behind the ears a single feather on a warrior's head appeared. As the whole horse with the man trotted into view the ears and the feather jiggled in unison.

"It is Legbone," Swift Afoot cried, "and he comes in sorrow."

The right half of Legbone's face and body was painted black. It told that he felt only half alive because of a great loss he had suffered.

A low sad quavering plaint rose from the waiting women.

Immediately behind Legbone came six horses bearing six trussed-up bodies. The six horses were hitched together head to tail.

The plaint became a low wail.

Immediately behind the six bodies came the rest of the war party. All the braves had painted the right halves of their bodies black. At the very end of the caravan rode the two oldest men, Jumper and Wrinkled Belly, chevying up the remaining horses, some sixty of them, all in a bunch.

Legbone put his horse through several tricky maneuvers to signal that they came in sorrow even as they came in victory. Six men had been lost at the same time that The Buffalo Jump was now theirs forever.

The wail became a long cry of lamentation, interrupted occasionally by yips of joy.

The people parted and formed two walls of weepers for the caravan to pass through. Seven Sticks and Person In The Moon stood at the head of one wall. Manly Heart stood at the head of the other wall.

Prettyhead, who had kept herself hidden in the background, couldn't stand it any longer and came running up, weeping. She clutched Manly Heart by the arm. "Oo-eee. Now we shall hear the worst."

Manly Heart couldn't stand to have Prettyhead touch her. She shook her off. With a deep frown she fastened her eyes on the six bodies jouncing on the six horses behind Legbone.

Legbone wept as he rode in through the horns of the camp. He had nothing to say.

Behind him rode the body of Flat Warclub. It hung stiffly, trussed up over the back of his favorite horse Many Spots, legs on one side and head on the other.

All the good women he had talked to, Goodlick, Dress That Swishes, Chattering Leaves, Bad Moccasins, Lastborn, Sulk, Long Tongue, Molest, and finally even Prettyhead sent up a loud shriek of despair.

"Flat Warclub is dead! Oo-eee! Oo-eee! Flat Warclub is dead!

Slim Waist came running up. She walked alongside the stiffly jerking body of Flat Warclub and cried down to its hanging head. "Why did you have to leave before you could talk to me?" She spoke earnestly as if she expected the stiff body to reply.

Manly Heart wanted to club Slim Waist over the head for talking to Flat Warclub in such a ridiculous manner. "Henala yelo. Can you not see it is all over?" Manly Heart was being torn apart herself. She wanted to mutilate herself.

Gusting cries of various women told what bodies came after Flat Warclub's body.

When the head of the parade reached the council lodge, Wide Mouth the camp crier tolled off the names of the dead heroes. He spoke in a high rhythmic voice:

"Flat Warclub! O yeh he tu! He threw his life away and now we shall eat buffalo forever. Great was the thing he did.

"Turning Horse! Hanto yo! Clear the way for a great hunter.

"Raincrow! Ah he! Again a great hunter.

"Red Ant! Mani yelo, kola. You will walk with the gods, friend.

"Lightfoot! Was there ever a greater runner? He was tireless.

"First Standing! Ahh. Ahh. He was always the first to volunteer.

"Le-nake. He-nala yelo. For all these it is all done."

Mothers and sisters and wives of the six men ran about scarifying themselves. Sometimes they clawed at each other to help one another.

The dogs smelled the dead bodies and slunk off and hid in the cattails. One of the dogs howled in grief.

Four times Legbone led the parade around the circle of the camp.

Tears flowed. Blood flowed from the self-mutilations.

A drum beat slowly inside the council lodge. It beat in time with the lift and fall of the horse hooves.

Legbone halted the parade in front of Seven Sticks and Person In The Moon. "I-ye. Now the bodies belong to the relatives."

Immediately the wives and mothers and sisters of the three dead Blue Mounds men came running and untied them and gently lifted them down. Turning Horse. Raincrow. Lightfoot. Their horses were separated from the others and led to one side.

Legbone sat high on his horse. "I-ye. And now we leave with our own dead for our village beside The Talking Water."

A young horse herder ran up to tie the horses of Flat Warclub and First Standing and Red Ant together.

Manly Heart let out a strangled cry. She appealed to Legbone. "No. No. Do not take Flat Warclub with you. He now belongs to our village. Let me be the one to bury his body on a scaffold."

Legbone looked down at her. A kind look appeared in his bull face. "But his mother Cornmilk will weep if we do not bring back the body of her son."

"But he came to manhood in this camp. It was for this camp that he threw his life away and became a great hero, not for his mother and her camp."

Legbone studied her, much troubled.

"Also I was his host," Manly Heart cried with tortured face. "When no one else would put him up, I was the only one in this camp willing to be his host. His new home was my tepee."

Legbone looked around to where Prettyhead was weeping. "What does your wife say?"

Holding her head erect, imperious, Manly Heart ran a finger from her forehead down to her navel. "Separate him from me and you cut me in two."

All the pretty girls drew close. They too pled with Legbone. "Truly, Flat Warclub has made this camp renowned. We shall never forget how he talked to us. He became our hero."

Legbone said, "What shall I tell his mother?"

Manly Heart said, "Tell her I have a home for her if she wishes to come and weep at the foot of his scaffold."

Legbone fell silent, chewing his lips. His horse shifted its weight on its legs. His belly shook as he pondered to himself.

Manly Heart made up her mind. She went over and untied Flat Warclub's horse from the other two Talking Water horses. "He is mine to weep over." Over her shoulder she spoke sadly to all the pretty girls. "I cannot forbid you your tears. No. But mind that you do not weep at the foot of his scaffold. That is reserved for me alone."

Prettyhead was offended. "What, my husband? I cannot weep in the proper manner at the foot of his scaffold? When it was I who prepared the food for him in our tepee?"

Manly Heart snapped herself around, deliberately turning her face away from her wife Prettyhead.

Seven Sticks came stepping across the grass in his old and leisurely manner. After a moment he looked up at Legbone. "Perhaps it might be a good thing for our people if Flat Warclub were buried here on The Blue Mounds. Will your people accept all the captured horses in place of his body?"

Legbone studied it all some more.

Manly Heart couldn't wait for Legbone to make up his mind. She quite deliberately began to lead Flat Warclub's body away.

Prettyhead and all the pretty girls followed at a distance.

Seven Sticks watched the women go with Flat Warclub's body. Then he said to Legbone, "Stay a while. Is there hurry? Tonight we will celebrate the victory and consecrate the dead with a great feast. We will need you to help recite all the glorious things done in your battle on The Blood Run."

Legbone sniffed the air. "This we cannot do. I can already smell the bodies. By the time we reach our camp on Talking Water the vultures will be following us." He looked around at the skies to see if vultures were not already floating above them.

"Well, we thank you."

Legbone's head snapped down. "We go. And we shall take the captured horses and let Cornmilk his mother decide what she wants done with them. Also she can come and get Many Spots, Flat Warclub's warhorse." Legbone grabbed the lead rope to the two horses on which the bodies of First Standing and Red Ant lay trussed and wheeled his horse about and started out of the horns of the camp for home

The rest of the Talking Water braves rounded up the captured Omaha horses and drove them down the draw.

Last to leave was Bitten Nose. He rode his horse in a slouched manner. He no longer held his head in a certain way so people would not notice whether his nose was bitten off or not.

Slowly the caravan passed out of sight toward the river.

Manly Heart led Many Spots with his burden to the door of her tepee. She stepped inside a moment to get a stone axe, a blade knife, and the sleeping robe Flat Warclub had used for his bed while living with her. Then she led Many Spots to a little grove of sapling ash north of the encampment.

The pretty girls continued to follow Manly Heart at a distance. They wept quietly to themselves. They also scarified their arms and legs, drawing blood. In a low voice they wailed the name of Flat Warclub over and over.

Prettyhead walked alone off to one side. The sun shining on her paler skin gave her the look of a newly flowered cattail.

Manly Heart cut a dozen branches the size of her wrist and trimmed them neatly. On four of them she left a well-shaped fork.

Manly Heart selected a spot well up on the rise east of where the arrowsmith sat making his points. It was far enough away from the village so that the smell of the body would not offend anyone.

She built the scaffold alone. She wept as she worked. Sometimes she talked aloud, lamenting that she had not known him better. She recalled the time, vividly, when he lay naked in her tepee talking to Prettyhead. Manly Heart cried, "My fine friend, I miss you very much. You were slim and pliable. You were like a runner. You had the kind of figure I adore. Eii, and you were well knobbed. You were a man."

She lifted his body off the horse and alone hoisted it up onto the scaffold. She had trouble making his stiff body lie flat. It kept wanting to sit up. It had lain trussed up in a bent position for almost two days. She tucked his feet in at one end under the sleeping robe and tied them down.

Before tucking his head in at the other end, holding him down, she had one last look at his face.

His eyes were closed in serene sleep. His arched nose shone where the bone showed. He was smiling. It was as though in a moment he would talk in his sleep.

Even as she held him down his body yet once more tried to sit up.

She pressed him back in place.

She covered his body with her body and wept over him.

Finally, having wept, she tucked the sleeping robe closed over his face and tied his head down. Then she slid to the ground.

Head bent, she started for her lodge, leading Many Spots behind her.

The pretty girls standing off to one side set up a long trilling wail.

Prettyhead kept catching her nether lip and biting it.

Manly Heart led Many Spots to the pasture and released him in the care of the young horse herders.

Carrying axe and knife and the horse's halter, Manly Heart disappeared into her tepee.

After a little time Prettyhead returned to the camp circle. She appeared to be quite worried. Finally she dared to duck inside Manly Heart's tepee.

People watched out of the corner of their eyes to see what might happen next.

Just as the sun set, Prettyhead emerged from Manly Heart's lodge. She was weeping to herself, disconsolate.

The people watched. They wondered.

"My husband has broken a stick at me," Prettyhead wailed. "My husband has divorced me. Now I have lost both."

Prettyhead returned to the lodge of her foster mother Clear Eyes and her foster father Charms The Grizzly.

That night no smoke rose out of the smokehole of Manly Heart's tepee.

Manly Heart wept twice a day at the foot of Flat Warclub's burial scaffold, once in the morning and once in the evening. She always wept alone.

Finally, when at last she was sure his flesh had withered and blown away, she took down his bones, wrapped them in a freshly scraped buffalo hide, and buried them in a secret place at night, no one knew where. She did not want the pretty girls to be weeping over his bones. That privilege she reserved for herself.

After that Manly Heart lived alone. She kept to herself much of the time. The flaps to her tepee were always closed to visitors.

Presently the women in the camp noted a strange thing. Manly Heart took to staying in the separation hut again for the customary five days. Having lost her helper, she had become a full woman again.

She became very thin. She aged rapidly. She went about bent over.

She was known to speak just once after the burial. It was in reply to a question put by Seven Sticks. He had wondered in his mild way why she would no longer talk to the people. She said, "The woman who does not conceal her love has never been in love."

Her neighbors complained that her tepee was not kept very neat. It became the home of many families of field mice.

She heard the complaints. She thought to herself: Suffer the mice to play in my parfleches. They have shown me they can be very happy when I share a few beans with them.

She became known as The Silent Woman. People forgot her old name Manly Heart.

Silent Woman was sometimes seen to hobble out to a pink stone not far from camp. There she would sit bowed over, a hand to one side of her face as though to hide herself from the people.

BLUE MOUND
LUVERNE, MINNESOTA